Brothers,
Boyfriends
& Other
Criminal Minds

Published by Delacorte Press
an imprint of Random House Children's Books
a division of Random House, Inc.
New York

Delacorte Press and colophon are registered trademarks of Random House, Inc.

www.randomhouse.com/teens

Educators and librarians, for a variety of teaching tools,
visit us at www.randomhouse.com/teachers

Library of Congress Cataloging-in-Publication Data is available upon request.
ISBN 978-0-385-73124-9 (trade)
ISBN 978-0-385-90152-9 (glb)

The text of this book is set in 12-point Goudy.

Printed in the United States of America

10 9 8 7 6 5 4 3 2 1

First Edition

For my two beautifully minded brothers,
Mark and Adam,
with love

Brothers,
Boyfriends
& Other
Criminal Minds

ONE

Three murderers live on my block—two on opposite corners like a pair of bookends, and one right across the street from my house. Not the crazed, ax-wielding kind you might see in horror flicks, but genteel killers who go about business in Armani suits and Gucci shoes, their victims disappearing without a trace. This probably sounds creepy, and you might even wonder if I'm afraid for my life, but up until now I've always felt safe. That's because these men are members of *La Cosa Nostra*, This Thing of Ours. Most people call them Mafia.

When I was eight years old my family moved a whopping two and a half miles from our apartment in Bay Ridge, Brooklyn, to a modest house in the pristine section of Dyker Heights, home of the Colombo and Bonanno crime families. While my dad had reservations about rubbing shoulders with the locals, he was drawn to the quiet neighborhood, and my mother, who had a thing about dirt, was thrilled to have her own garden, where she grew tulips and tomatoes.

What I liked most was that I'd finally gotten my own room, complete with purple shag carpeting and a plastic Barbie vanity set. Outside there were lots of kids to play with, and I never thought much about the men who drove around in fancy Cadillacs, flashing gold chains and chest hair. They were just part of the scenery. And if I ever had the good fortune of being invited to one of their kids' birthday parties, there were sure to be pony rides, magicians, live bands, and homemade gelato.

As I got older, I realized that the Mafia presence had other benefits. Because they kept out petty criminals, you didn't have to worry about getting mugged or having your stereo stolen or your ten-speed bike jacked from your garage. However, along with these perks, there were certain rules you had to follow. Such as, never say the word "Mafia" (according to them, the organization does not exist), never ask a rich kid what his father does for a living, and if you're a non-Sicilian teenage boy, never *ever* date a connected guy's daughter.

So when I discovered that Matt, my sixteen-year-old, blond-haired, blue-eyed moron of a brother, was in love with Bettina Bocceli, daughter of Colombo's *capo*, I knew there was going to be trouble. Matt might have been the tormentor of my life, but I didn't exactly want to find him on the bottom of the East River wearing a pair of cement shoes.

It was the last week in August 1977 when I found out about Matt's fatal attraction. School would be starting in ten days, and even though I would technically be a freshman, I'd be spending another sorry year at P.S. 201, the public junior high that went up to ninth grade. The morning was hot and muggy, and since my mother didn't believe in air-conditioning, I'd woken up in a fine layer of sweat. Thankfully, Al Pacino and Cat Stevens were there to greet me. I was still trying to decide which poster to buy for my third wall—a toss-up between the Russian ballet dancer Mikhail Baryshnikov and the Grateful Dead skull-and-crossbones logo, although I figured the latter might cause my parents to call in a priest for my exorcism. And we're not even Catholic.

The house was quiet, which meant my mom had already left for work at the hospital, my dad was putzing in the garage, and my two brothers, Matt and Sammy, were still asleep. After showering, I dressed in my usual—bell-bottom Lee's, T-shirt, and Earth shoes—and tiptoed downstairs for breakfast. My mother was on this new health-food kick, so instead of Cheerios, I chipped a few teeth on a bowl of Grape Nuts, grabbed my book, and headed outside.

I'd been reading a collection of Edgar Allan Poe stories, and right now I was up to "The Masque of the Red Death." After a few pages I decided it was even better than "The Tell-Tale Heart," but just when I was getting to the really gruesome part where little drops of blood begin oozing from the pores of some unsuspecting victim, I heard the steady *bonk, bonk, bonk* of a basketball.

I looked up and saw Matt's friend, Little Joe. With a flick of his wrist he lifted the ball and spun it on one finger. "Hi, April, is Matt home?"

Little Joe wasn't really little; he was just shorter than Matt's other friend, Big Joe. Since just about everyone in our neighborhood was both Italian and Catholic, Joseph was a popular name. Anyway, I liked him because he was different from the rest of Matt's friends—he had manners and always called me April. The others referred to me as Ape, Chimp, Monk, or Monkey—Matt's ingenious nicknames. Little Joe was also the reason why I knew so much inside information about the Mafiosi in our neighborhood. Because the members took the vow of *Omerta*, or silence, not much gossip flew around the streets, but Little Joe had an uncle who was connected, so whenever he whispered to Matt about his uncle's criminal associates, I eavesdropped.

I jabbed my thumb in the direction of our front door, which was slightly ajar. "Yep. If Matt's awake he's probably right there, flexing." Every morning Matt lifted weights in front of the big mirror hanging in our foyer; that way he could fall in love with himself on a daily basis.

Little Joe gave me a knowing look and let the ball drop to his hand. "Hey, Schwarzenegger!" he called. "What are you doing in there, kissing your reflection?" He winked at me, and the two of us laughed. It was one of those rare

4

moments when I felt like I was a part of Matt's world instead of just some pain-in-the-butt sister.

Turned out I was right. Matt flung open the door, and there he stood, bare-chested, breathing heavily, his forearms snaked with veins. "You bozos are just jealous," he said, squeezing his right bicep and making it dance.

Little Joe moaned and threw him the basketball. "Come on, *Arrrrnold*," he said with what I assumed was an Austrian accent. "Enough pumping iron. Give yourself one last smooch and let's play ball. The guys are waitin' for us at the park."

Matt grinned and slipped him the middle finger (a sign of affection among his peers) before going inside to get his shirt. Meanwhile, Little Joe looked at me and cocked his head. "Hey, wait a minute. I knew something was missing. Where's Brandi?"

If you listened very carefully you could hear "Shake Your Booty" by KC and the Sunshine Band piping from my so-called best friend Brandi's basement laundry vent in the house next door. She'd been invited to a dance by some Catholic-school boy named Walter, and for the past week I'd been helping her practice the New York Hustle (a fate worse than death). It was all she could talk about, so yesterday when I'd finally told her that she was seriously getting on my nerves, she'd marched into her house and slammed the door. Fine with me. Besides, who in their right mind would go on a date with a guy named Walter?

I dog-eared the page I was on and rolled my eyes

toward Brandi's house. "She's in her basement, shaking her booty. She's got this big date next Friday. A dance at Xavierian High School."

"Really?" Little Joe stood there with his jaw hanging open. Brandi and I were fourteen, just two years younger than Little Joe and Matt, but they seemed to think of us as being eternally ten and a half. He rubbed his chin. "A date with a guy from Xa-*fairy*-land, huh?"

This was another one of Matt's creative nicknames. Xavierian was a boys' high school, taught by a brotherhood of priests, so Matt assumed that any guy who attended was a fairy. "Yep," I said. "And get this, his name is *Walter*."

For some reason, Little Joe didn't think this was as funny as I did. "So," he said, "how about *you*, aren't you going?"

Little Joe knew very well that high school dances meant disco music, and disco music was against my religion. "Me? No."

He started to laugh. "Oh, that's right, I almost forgot, you don't shake your booty. But you know, pretty soon, guys are gonna be asking you out. Don't tell Matt I said this, but you're getting pretty cute, and you've got that blond hair. . . ."

Immediately my cheeks began to burn. One of the curses of having Scandinavian ancestors was that my skin was so transparent that when I blushed my whole face glowed. If this wasn't bad enough, I also had a mouthful of braces, laced with those darling little rubber bands, so it was hard to feel confident. Usually I was better off with my head in a book.

Before Little Joe could continue this embarrassing conversation, Matt returned, chugging an orange soda. He tossed a can to Little Joe but of course didn't offer me one. I almost said something about sugar being a major cause of pimples, but I held my tongue. Whenever Matt's friends were around, he went from annoying to beastly in two seconds flat. "So, whatcha reading now, Chimp?"

Matt didn't deserve an answer, but since Little Joe was there, I decided to impress him with my fine literary taste. Slowly, I raised the book off my lap, revealing the jacket.

Matt made a face. "Jeez, what's with all the morbid crap lately?"

I sighed. Matt's idea of a good book was the latest issue of *Sports Illustrated* or, if he wanted to take it up a notch, the biography of basketball star Dr. Julius Erving. "It's not morbid," I said. "It's deep . . . mystical . . . symbolic. Things *you* wouldn't understand."

Little Joe whistled. "Oooo, nice one, April."

Matt shot him a look and chugged more soda. When he was finished he let out a huge belch without even saying, "Excuse me." "Yeah, right, Ape, kind of like those Alfred Hitchcock stories you were reading last week. Real deep."

Before I could respond, Matt tossed the basketball back to Little Joe and slid down the banister. Along the way, he said, "Hey, Joe, is she gonna be there today?"

This caught my attention. Since when did Matt know any *shes*?

I lowered my head, pretending to be completely absorbed in the story. Luckily, Matt's right shoelace came undone, and as he sat down to tie it, I listened carefully.

"Come on, Matt," Little Joe said, "I already told you, this is *not* a good idea. You don't get it, they treat those girls like nuns. Lock 'em up and throw away the key."

Matt stood up. There was a strange expression on his face—a mixture of defiance and desperation. It was the way he looked when his basketball team was down by ten points, with only one minute left in the game. "Listen, Joe," he said, "I don't care. I just need to see her."

Little Joe raised his arms in surrender. "All right, all right. I'm pretty sure she'll be there, okay? Happy?"

Matt exhaled loudly. "Thanks Joe, I owe you one."

Little Joe shook his head. "Nah, you don't owe me nothin'. But I'm telling you, Matt, you better be careful."

At that moment Brandi's curtains shifted, and as Matt and Little Joe began walking down the street, I wished I could have been a fly buzzing around their heads. Instead I was the lone chimp in our family, reader of morbid stories, and best friend to the Disco Queen of Dyker Heights.

TWO

The mobsters on our street were about as different as three cold-blooded killers could be. Francesco "Frankie the Crunch" Consiglione, who lived on the corner of Eleventh, was a quiet guy who generally kept to himself. He dressed more modestly than the others, always in black, went to Mass every Friday, and had a big statue of St. Christopher in his yard. His nickname stemmed from his car-crunching business, which, when you think about it, is a good line of work to be in when you're disposing of dead bodies on a regular basis.

Vincent "Gorgeous Vinny" Persico, who lived on the corner of Twelfth, owned a restaurant in Little Italy known for its veal scaloppini and small room in the back where uncooperative wiseguys sometimes got whacked. He also claimed to be in the "entertainment industry" and had recently purchased a discothèque in Bay Ridge. He was friendly, flamboyant, and handsome, I suppose (hence the nickname), and his favorite pastime was admiring himself in the side-view mirror while waxing his Coupe de Ville.

But the most elusive of the three was the man who lived right across the street from us—Salvatore "Soft Sal" Luciano. Little Joe guessed that he was either a hit man, a bodyguard, or possibly *consigliere*—advisor—to the Big Boss, Joe Colombo. However, the thing that set him apart was this: unlike his colleagues who had several gangster-in-training sons, Soft Sal had only one child—an innocent fourteen-year-old boy named Larry.

Now, as I sat on the porch waiting for Brandi to make her grand appearance, Larry barged out his front door wielding a set of drumsticks. He'd cranked up his favorite album, *The Who by Numbers*, and was whacking out a crazy rhythm on the garbage cans lined up in front of his house. Normally I didn't mind, but today it felt like rocks in my head.

Larry was—different, I guess you could say—but he had decent taste in music, and every Tuesday and Friday when the trash went out he became Keith Moon, the drummer for the Who. His father, who spared no expense, had recently bought him this amazing five-piece drum set that he played in the basement, but sometimes Larry liked an audience. Anyway, it was a good thing Matt wasn't around because he would have said something like "Hey,

Ape, why don't you get your kazoo? The two of you retards could jam together." Which tells you a lot about Matt's basic character and warped sense of humor.

As Larry crooned loudly, thumping the big metal cans, Brandi stepped onto her porch, her long brown hair forming a veil around her face. All we needed now was a little violin music to complete the scene. Ignoring me, she sat down, shook a bottle of nail polish, and began stuffing cotton balls between her toes. Meanwhile, Larry took a break from his drum solo. Since Brandi and I were normally inseparable, he glanced back and forth between me and Brandi like something was terribly out of place. "It's okay, Larry!" I called. "Just keep playing!"

Unfortunately, I knew what I had to do. Go over there and apologize. It would calm Larry down, but I also figured having Brandi with me at the park was the only viable way I could spy on Matt. Of course, I could take my five-year-old brother, Sammy, along, but with my luck, Dominick, the guy I'd had a crush on for the past year but who didn't know I was alive, would probably be there, strumming his guitar, surrounded by all his friends. It would be the ultimate sign of lameness to arrive at the park alone, carting around my kid brother. Besides, the thought of watching Sammy run through the sprinklers with his peewee buddies while I had no one to talk to was pretty depressing.

I took a deep breath, set down my book, and walked slowly to Brandi's house. The whole time, Larry was silent, clutching his drumsticks, anxiously waiting for his world to return to order. When I finally sat beside Brandi, Larry let out a huge sigh of relief and smashed a garbage lid with newfound fervor.

As I suspected, Brandi was doing a pathetic job on her toes. Each nail was a mess of lavender clumps and air bubbles. "Here, let me do it," I said. Without arguing, she plunked her foot onto my lap and handed me the brush and bottle. As I salvaged her pedicure, I said, "Listen, I'm sorry for what I said about *Walter*, okay?"

She narrowed her eyes. "Why do you always say his name like that?"

"Like what?" I asked innocently, smoothing out the polish on her pinky toe.

"Like he's the biggest dork on earth. You don't even know him."

"Well, neither do you." Brandi couldn't argue that one. Walter was the nephew of the godson of Brandi's mother's friend, or something ridiculous like that. They'd been introduced at her cousin's First Communion, and two weeks later, he'd called and asked her to the dance.

"Are you jealous, April? Is that it?"

I looked at her and laughed. "No. Why would I be jealous?"

"My mother thinks you are."

I almost dropped the bottle. "Your mother? You actually talked to your mother about this?" That was the thing about Brandi. She believed that her parents, whose favorite pastime was watching reruns of *The Lawrence Welk Show*, were a wellspring of teenage wisdom and knowledge.

"Yes, I did. And she had a very good suggestion. As it turns out, Walter has a friend who doesn't have a date. You could go with him."

"Oh, just like that? I could go with him?"

"Yeah, just like that."

The nail brush snagged a piece of cotton. I pulled out the lavender threads, rolled them into tiny balls, and flicked them onto the sidewalk. "No thanks."

"Come on, April, why not?"

I sighed and squinted down the street. Larry had moved on to the neighbor's trash, but he was watching the two of us from the corner of his eye. His favorite song, "Squeeze Box," was playing now. I cupped one hand around my mouth and called, "Everything's fine, Larry! Keep it up! You sound great!"

Brandi tapped me on the knee. "You're avoiding my question."

"I'm not going on a blind date, okay? Think about it, the guy's probably desperate. Besides, people should have a few meaningful conversations before they go out."

She raised an eyebrow. "Oh, kind of like you and Dominick, huh?"

Brandi was an expert at rubbing salt into a wound. "Shut up."

She poked me in the ribs. "Think about it, you could *get* to know Walter's friend."

I peered at her, wondering why she wouldn't give up, and suddenly her eyes began shifting in all directions. Nervously, she cracked a few knuckles. "Wait a minute," I said. "Don't tell me . . ."

"Um . . . well"—she winced—"you might be getting a phone call tonight."

"What? Are you kidding?"

"My mother talked to Walter's mother. She gave his friend your number."

"Oh, that's just great." With one final stroke, I finished her last toenail and shoved her foot off my lap. "So, what's *this* guy's name? Horace?"

Brandi hesitated a moment. "Actually, Umberto."

My eyes widened. "Umberto? Does he speak English?"

"Yes, of course he speaks English. How else could he *call* you?"

Just when I was contemplating which method I was going to use to strangle Brandi, the garbage truck turned the corner and came roaring up our street. Immediately we craned our necks looking for Larry. We'd been his guardian angels ever since kindergarten and his mother paid us for this service with boxes of cannolis and pinches on the cheek. He was in front of Mr. Crispi's house now, whaling on a rusty old vacuum cleaner. "Aw, shoot," I said, "we're gonna have to go get him." Larry had grown a lot this year—he stood almost six feet tall—and was no lightweight, either. He didn't particularly like it when people asked him to stop drumming.

"Count me out," Brandi said, wiggling her toes. "Don't want to ruin my new pedicure."

"Of course. How convenient."

The garbage truck was getting closer, and Larry was hovering over Mr. Crispi's prehistoric vacuum like a dog guarding a T-bone steak. I was just about to get up and intervene, when Mr. Luciano walked out his front door. He was a homely guy, but from a distance he looked fairly sharp in his three piece suit, his head freshly shaved and gleaming in the sun. He reminded me a little of Kojak, the cop from that TV show, except Mr. Luciano was on the other side of the law. "Larry!" He shook his head, chuckling to himself, and plodded down the stairs. When he saw Brandi and me, he smiled and waved. "Hey, girls, how ya doin'?"

I waved hello, but Brandi didn't. She just snorted and turned the other way. Brandi liked Larry and Mrs. Luciano well enough—helpless victims was what she called them— but not Soft Sal. She said the Mafia gave Italians a bad name, which I supposed was true, but since I didn't have a drop of Sicilian blood running through my Nordic veins, I just thought they were interesting.

We watched as Mr. Luciano gently placed one hand on Larry's shoulder and pried the drumsticks from his fingers with the other. "They have to take the trash now, Larry," we heard him say above the noise. "You can play your drums in the basement."

Larry shook his head violently, but Mr. Luciano calmed him by rubbing his back and whispering something into his ear. After a while Larry surrendered; his shoulders slumped and he let out a huge moan. As they walked home, arm in arm, Larry glanced at us. He never said much, but over the years I'd learned to read his facial expressions, and right now it was as if he was saying, "Jeez, can you believe I had to stop right in the middle of "Squeeze Box"?

"Hey, girls!" Mr. Luciano had stopped in front of his house and was now calling us. Brandi and I looked at each other. "Listen, I, uh, need to talk to you for a minute, okay? Stay there, I'll be right back."

Brandi gulped and started pinching my elbow as he walked Larry up the stairs. "Oh my gosh," she said, "what do you think he wants?"

"I don't know." I had to admit, my heart was beating a little faster than usual. Mr. Luciano had always been friendly—he waved hello, occasionally asked how my mom was doing, and sometimes he'd even tease me by singing a few bars of that old Frank Sinatra song, "April in Paris"—but he'd never asked to "talk" to me or Brandi before.

Brandi was still pinching my elbow when Mr. Luciano returned. This time he was carrying Princess, his teacup poodle. After crossing the street, he set her down and she trotted to the fire hydrant. "So . . ." Mr. Luciano flashed us a quick grin and rubbed his palms together. Strangely, he seemed a little nervous. "How've you girls been?"

He'd already asked us that question, but I wasn't about to remind him of it. Brandi didn't answer; she just turned to me wide-eyed. "Um, pretty well, thanks," I said.

He nodded. "Good, good. And how's your mom?"

"She's . . . fine." My mother and Mr. Luciano both had vegetable gardens, and sometimes they'd compare notes on stuff like peat moss and fertilizers.

He cleared his throat and narrowed his eyes. "How about your brother?"

"Sammy? He's okay."

Mr. Luciano shook his head. "No, I meant the other one."

"Matt?" My voice sounded shrill, and just like the poor guy under the floorboards in "The Tell-Tale Heart," I was sure Mr. Luciano could hear the loud thumping in my chest. I wondered if he'd heard about Matt's retard jokes. If so, this was not going to be pretty.

"Yeah, that's the one. Matt. Sunshine Boy." He laughed a little at his own joke.

"Um . . . Matt's . . . fine." I tried to swallow, but my mouth had gone dry.

"Good, good, I'm glad to hear it."

Brandi reached behind me and pressed her thumb into my back.

"Well, listen," he said, "I need to ask you girls a favor. It's about Larry."

"Oh? Larry?" I said, relieved to be off the subject of Matt.

"Yeah, you see, I got a little problem. As you know, Larry's always gone to Catholic school, but now the priests, well, they're saying he's too disruptive, so this year we're gonna send him to P.S. 201. They've got a special program for kids like him, supposed to be real good, and I was hoping you girls could walk him back and forth to school, keep an eye on him, let me know if there's any . . . trouble."

Brandi blinked a few times and began to stammer. "Um . . . wouldn't it be better if . . . I don't know, someone *else* walked him to school? I mean . . ." She trailed off, realizing it was a mistake arguing with Soft Sal.

Mr. Luciano didn't take offense. He sighed deeply. "Larry don't want me or his mother taking him to school. He's getting real independent. Typical teenager, you know."

Larry was the furthest thing from a typical teenager, but I wasn't exactly going to bring that up. Instead I nodded in agreement.

"And," Mr. Luciano continued, "Larry asked specifically if he could walk with you girls. He likes you a lot."

"Oh, well." I looked at Brandi, shrugged, and smiled weakly. "We like him, too."

"Great." Mr. Luciano gave us a firm nod. "Then it's settled. We'll, uh, work out the details another time." He turned his gaze toward the fire hydrant and made what I can only describe as kissing sounds. Obediently, Princess came trotting back, and he scooped her up in one hand. "We'll talk again," he said. "Real soon." And with that, he winked at me and crossed the street singing, " 'April in Paris, chestnuts in blossom . . .' "

THREE

"Oh my gosh," Brandi said, nervously cracking the rest of her knuckles. "I don't believe this."

Inside, Larry had lowered the stereo and was now poking his head out the window and waving to us. I waved back. "What? It's no big deal," I said, trying to convince myself this was true. "Mr. Luciano just needs us to look after Larry."

"Well, I don't like it," Brandi said. "You know what they say, once you get in with the Mob, you can never get out."

"Oh, please, that's ridiculous. We're not *in* with the Mob. He's just a father asking us to do a favor for his son. It's totally normal."

Brandi looked at me like I was crazy. "Normal? Believe me, April, there's nothing normal about that guy. He's a creep. Probably broke a few kneecaps last night, maybe even killed someone."

"Well, I guess that's a reason to stay on his good side." I laughed a little, but Brandi didn't think it was funny. "Listen, I don't think he murdered anyone recently. You only have to kill once to be a made man."

"What? What are you talking about?"

I shrugged. "It's something I heard Little Joe tell Matt. Mobsters only have to kill one time to prove their loyalty. Then they can get made. It's like an initiation or something."

"Oh, so the rest of the time it's just for fun, huh?" Brandi shook her head. "And another thing, why was he asking about Matt? What did he call him again?"

"Sunshine Boy," I muttered. I'd been wondering the same thing but was afraid to say it out loud. Right then I decided not to tell Brandi about Matt and Little Joe's conversation, the one involving the mysterious girl Matt was supposed to meet at the park today. Knowing Brandi, she'd blow it completely out of proportion. "Hey," I said, "why don't we forget about this? Let's go play some tennis."

She shrugged. "All right. Promise not to keep score?"

I rolled my eyes. "Fine." Brandi and I were both pretty good tennis players, but I was better, and she had a strong aversion to losing.

She leaned over and blew on her toes. "Is Sammy coming with us?"

Brandi loved toting Sammy wherever we went; for some reason it made her feel important. But before I had a chance to decide whether or not I wanted Sammy along, I heard him flying down our driveway wheeling his dilapidated stroller. He took a quick left and came to a halt in front of us. "Okay, guys, I'm ready!" He climbed in and sat down with a huge *plop*. The seams of the stroller were splitting, and the bottom sagged just a few inches above the ground. He looked like a giant Goldilocks sitting in Baby Bear's teeny-tiny chair. As he reached into his pocket and pulled out Luke Skywalker and Darth Vader, he said, "So where are we going today?"

Sammy believed that my one and only purpose in life was to be his personal chauffeur and travel guide. I pulled Chewbacca out from under his behind and handed it to him. "The park," I said. "Brandi and I are going to play tennis. You can be the ball boy." Before he could protest, I walked a few paces and called to my dad in the garage. "Hey, Dad! I've got Sammy! I'm taking him to the park, okay?"

My father stepped into the daylight squinting like a mole, a streak of white paint decorating his left cheek. He was a history teacher at Fort Hamilton High School and usually spent summers working on his doctoral dissertation, but this year my mom had other plans. She'd dressed him in a cap and overalls, handed him a toolbox and a can of paint, and said, "Stephen, this house needs help."

Now he smiled. "Thanks, April. And listen, next

week, I don't care *what* Mom says, I'm taking you guys to the beach. One last hurrah before school starts, okay?"

I bit my lip. The last time my dad took me and Sammy to the beach, we'd gone to Riis Park out on Rockaway. We didn't know it, but bays four and five were nude. When Sammy saw this ninety-year-old man's saggy rear end and unmentionables, I think he was damaged for life. I know I was. After that we hightailed it to bay thirteen. "Okay, Dad," I said. "But how about next time we go to Sandy Hook?" I figured the Jersey Shore might have a few less sickos than the sands of New York.

He nodded knowingly. "Sounds good. Now go on, have fun today." He waved goodbye and disappeared into the garage.

When I returned, Brandi was already kneeling beside Sammy, running her fingers through his curls. I opened the pouch that hung on the stroller where Sammy's diapers and bottles used to go; now it held our tennis gear. "Look's like everything's still here," I said, "Racquets, balls, sneakers . . ."

Sammy dug in his pocket again and pulled out a handful of change. "Look, April! Dad gave me money for candy. I'm gonna get a lollipop with bubble gum inside."

It was amazing how spoiled that kid was. "That's a Blow Pop, Sammy."

"Right." He smiled. "A Blow Pop."

The candy store was on the way to the park, so I figured we'd pacify Sammy before playing tennis and spying

23

on Matt. As we strolled down the street *The Who by Numbers* faded into the distance and was replaced by Italian opera music and the smell of homemade tomato sauce. I closed my eyes, breathing in the sautéed onions, garlic, tomatoes, and sweet basil. The ladies in our neighborhood made their sauce in the morning, letting it simmer for hours in big iron pots. Later they'd use it to make lasagna, ziti, manicotti, or veal Parmesan. Unfortunately, the only time any of these delicacies touched my lips was when Brandi's mom invited me over for dinner. My mother worked full-time and her latest pièce de résistance was tofu burgers with a side of bulgur wheat.

As we approached the corner, Gorgeous Vinny drove up in his Coupe de Ville. "Hi, dolls," he said, unlatching the door and catching a glimpse of himself in the rearview mirror. "Nice day for a stroll, huh?"

Brandi rolled her eyes.

"Yes, Mr. Persico," I said. He looked a little different today, younger for some reason. "So what's the latest news on John?" *John* meant John Travolta. For months now Gorgeous Vinny had been telling us how the star from *Welcome Back, Kotter* was coming to his disco to promote his new movie, *Saturday Night Fever*. Brandi thought he was full of crap—that he'd never get the *real* gorgeous Vinny Barbarino to come to his sleazy club, but for some reason I gave him the benefit of the doubt.

"Oh, we're still working on it," he said. "John's agent is

supposed to give us a call soon. Don't worry, I'll keep you dolls posted."

As we crossed the street, Brandi took a quick peek over her shoulder and elbowed me. "I knew there was something different about him. He's wearing a toupee."

"No way!" But when I turned around, Gorgeous Vinny was adjusting his new hairpiece in the side-view mirror.

Thirteenth Avenue was the dividing line between Dyker Heights and Bensonhurst, and as we turned the corner, the landscape changed. Colorful vegetable stands dotted the sidewalks with every variety of pepper, tomato, eggplant, and squash you could imagine. Tony's Pizzeria was already swarming with customers who ate standing at the counter, folding their slices in half and chugging down Cokes. Huge salamis and blocks of cheese hung in deli windows, and the sweet smells of amaretto and anisette wafted from the bakeries. Up ahead, a big crowd dressed in black stood outside Lozano's Funeral Parlor, and as the pallbearers hoisted the casket into a limo, Brandi leaned over and whispered, "Probably Mr. Luciano's most recent victim."

Since it was Friday, we slowed down as we approached St. Bernadette's Catholic Church. I parked the stroller, Sammy climbed out, and Brandi pushed open the ornately carved wooden doors. She was a devout Catholic and every Friday dropped fifty cents into the offering box and lit a votive candle for her twin sister, who'd died at birth.

As I gazed at the vaulted ceilings and stained-glass windows, Sammy tugged on my T-shirt. "April, can I light a candle for Uncle Jimmy? Please?"

Uncle Jimmy was my dad's younger brother, who'd died in Viet Nam before Sammy was born. Every year, on Jimmy's birthday, my dad would take out pictures and tell us about how brave he'd been. I shrugged, pulled two quarters from my pocket, and handed them to Sammy. "Sure, why not? But be quiet and don't make a fuss."

Sammy dropped his coins into the box and joined Brandi at the marble basin filled with holy water. Together they dipped their fingers in and made the sign of the cross. I had to admit, for a Lutheran, Sammy made a pretty convincing Catholic.

After that Brandi took his hand and led him to a statue of the Virgin Mary, where they each lit a candle and bowed their heads. While I waited near the entrance, the doors opened and, like a big ominous shadow, Frankie the Crunch walked in. I hoped he wouldn't notice me standing there, but as he passed by, heading toward the confessional, he took off his hat and said, "Oh, hi, babe."

"Hi, Mr. Consiglione." He looked tired, like he hadn't slept all night, and seemed to be favoring his right leg.

He scratched his five o'clock shadow and with a wry smile said, "Jeez, you got such an innocent face. Say a prayer for me, okay, babe? God knows I need one."

"Oh, right, sure thing."

But today Frankie the Crunch was not the only one

who needed a prayer. I did too. Our final stop before the park was Moe's Candy Store, and as we drew near I got a bad case of butterflies. Dominick lived in the apartment right above Moe's, and sometimes we'd see him sitting outside on a rusty lawn chair strumming his guitar.

I'd had a crush on Dominick ever since he won third place in the eighth-grade fall talent show for performing "Wish You Were Here" by Pink Floyd. At the same time, our English class had been reading *The Outsiders* by S. E. Hinton, and even though I'd never actually spoken to Dominick, I imagined him to be just like Ponyboy—the sensitive, artistic, brooding type, whose parents had probably been killed in a car wreck. I figured this would explain why he cut school, got into fistfights, occasionally smoked pot in the boys' bathroom, and wrote explicit, yet poetic, lyrics on the cafeteria tables. Anyway, besides being misunderstood, Dominick was also pretty cute, which didn't hurt.

Sadly, today there was no trace of him in front of Moe's, so I took a deep breath and opened the candy store door. "Hello, ladies, hello, Sammy." Moe stood behind the counter, a cigarette dangling from his lips. "What can I do for you today?"

Sammy hopped out of the stroller and showed Moe his fistful of change. "Hi, Moe! Guess what? Dad gave me money for a Blow Pop."

Moe took a long drag on his cigarette and chuckled as he blew out the smoke. "Well, well, what do you know?

Lucky you." He pointed to the candy display. "Blow Pops are on the bottom shelf. We've got five different flavors."

As Sammy ran eagerly to the display, I picked out a pack of Black Jack gum on the counter and handed Moe a quarter. He was grinning at me in a very strange way. "You just missed him," he said.

I blinked a few times. "Missed who?"

He arched an eyebrow. "You know, the kid who lives upstairs."

My jaw fell open and Brandi elbowed me in the ribs.

"I know, I know," Moe said with a wave of his hand, "you thought it was a big secret. But hey, I've got loads of experience with this sort of thing. Been watching kids for years."

My cheeks flamed and I had no idea what to say.

"But if you want my opinion," Moe continued, "you could do way better than him. A nice girl like you." He flicked a cigarette ash to the floor.

What I wanted to do was tell Moe that he should mind his own business if he planned on keeping his regular customers, but instead I just stood there like an idiot. Finally Sammy came back and placed his change on the counter.

"Ah, yes," Moe said. "Watermelon. Good choice."

Sammy smiled, peeled off the wrapper, and popped the candy into his mouth.

I couldn't wait to get out of there. "All right, let's go," I said, shoving Sammy toward the stroller. He hopped in and I quickly headed for the door. Brandi trailed after us.

"But listen! Remember what I said," Moe called. "People aren't always who you think they are."

Outside, Brandi busted up laughing.

"Har-de-har-har," I said, glaring at her.

She grinned devilishly. It was hard to believe she'd just been in church. "How do you think Moe knew?"

"I have no idea," I said. "And I don't want to know."

"I bet it's the way you trip over your feet and turn beet red whenever Dominick walks into the store."

"Shut up."

Thankfully Sammy was oblivious to everything except his lollipop. I folded a stick of Black Jack into my mouth and handed Brandi a piece, wondering why it was always my quarter buying the gum. She chewed thoughtfully as we continued past the A&P, the florist, and the hardware store. "Moe's right, you know," she said. "You and Dominick are in, like, two different worlds."

"Oh, please, let's not start this again." Brandi's idea of the perfect boyfriend was a guy with hair above the ears, straight As, and cuff links. She thought Dominick was way too dangerous, and I told her that was exactly why I liked him. After all, I needed someone to rescue me from my boring life.

"I bet Umberto's a lot nicer."

"Ugh," I said. "Did you have to remind me?"

"I bet you'd have a great time with him at the dance."

"Oh, yeah, maybe I should brush up on my Italian.

That way he can tell me about his boat trip across the Atlantic."

"I told you, April, he's American. He speaks English."

Sammy craned his neck. "Who's Dom-nick? Who's Ummm-berto?"

I sighed. "No one, Sammy. Just . . . turn around and mind your own business."

I didn't usually speak to Sammy this way, and it made me feel bad. He frowned and popped the candy into his mouth. An ambulance flew by, which got his attention.

"Now," I said to Brandi, "can we drop this, please?"

Brandi wasn't listening; she was busy molding the piece of Black Jack around her two front teeth. She turned to me and smiled, showing off her goofy gap-toothed grin.

It was amazing, the things I had to put up with.

After crossing the avenue, we walked along the outskirts of the golf course and finally arrived at the park. The place was really hopping today. On one end the paddleball courts were filled with sweaty, shirtless guys smacking black rubber balls, and on the other, little kids ran barefoot through the sprinklers. Roller skaters whooshed by, and Frisbees sailed through the air. We took the shaded cobblestone path that cut through the center. On the right were the softball fields, and on the left, the tennis courts. Up ahead, Matt and his friends were playing basketball, and as far as I could see there were no mysterious girls hanging around.

While Brandi searched for an empty court, my eyes

roamed to the bathroom wall—the one spray-painted with the words DISCO SUCKS in big orange letters. Just beyond it was a group of picnic tables where chess players and musicians sometimes gathered. I strained my ears and heard the faint plucking of guitar strings. It was the intro to Led Zeppelin's "Stairway to Heaven."

Dominick was here.

FOUR

"Look," Brandi said, "it's Björn Borg and Jimmy Connors battling it out at Wimbledon."

She was pointing to two guys in the middle of a heated singles match. They were about our age, maybe a little older. Bjorn had a blond shag with a bandana wrapped around his forehead, and Jimmy sported a short, dark, feathered cut with an Izod T-shirt and tight white shorts. Both were sunburned, sweating, and whacking the ball with gusto.

I grinned, knowing we could kill them. "Well," I said to Brandi, "looks like there are no other courts open. Shall we?"

She nodded. "Yes. Definitely."

Last summer, in a rare moment of generosity, Matt had taught Brandi and me to play tennis. We'd practiced a lot over the year, even in the winter when it was freezing cold.

Matt and Little Joe could still destroy us in doubles, but we'd gotten pretty good and could beat a lot of guys our age.

While Brandi and I exchanged our Earth shoes for sneakers, Sammy hopped out of his stroller, knelt down, and began searching through a patch of clover growing from a crack in the pavement. I tossed Brandi a racquet and she held it in one hand like a semiautomatic weapon. "Come on, Sammy," I said. "Let's go. Brandi and I are gonna kick some butt."

"Wait! Look at this!" He plucked a clover and held it up for me to inspect.

To my surprise, the thing actually had four leaves. "Wow, I can't believe it! You found one!"

Sammy beamed. He had a whole collection of lucky charms hidden inside a cigar box under his bed—a smelly rabbit's foot, a moldy acorn, a miniature plastic horseshoe, and an old penny he'd found heads up in the gutter. It was amazing how that kid could get such a kick out of little pieces of junk. "Bring it along, Sammy," Brandi said, nudging me. "Now we're sure to win."

We waited outside the gate until Bjorn and Jimmy were finished with their set. As they guzzled water from a cooler, Brandi and I strolled onto the court with Sammy trailing behind, clutching the clover to his chest. Our strategy was to act like two airheads who didn't know the first thing about tennis. After letting them win a few games, we'd go in for the kill. "Um, excuse me," Brandi said, "there are no other courts open, so would you guys like to play a game of doubles?"

They looked at us in disbelief, rolled their eyes, and groaned. "Aw, come on," Jimmy Connors said, "can't you find some, I don't know, *girls* to play with?"

I gritted my teeth, trying to ignore his sexist remark. One thing was certain: these guys definitely needed their all-star tennis butts royally kicked. "Well, actually," I said, attempting a flirtatious smile, which probably looked more like a smirk considering my braces and rubber band problem, "we're trying to improve our game, and we thought you guys could give us a few pointers."

Bjorn Borg wiped his face with a towel while Jimmy surreptitiously picked a wedgie from his shorts. "I don't know," Björn said skeptically. "I mean, I *guess* we could."

Jimmy was looking at the sky, frowning. "Fine," he said with a wave of his hand. "Let's get this over with."

While Brandi and I took our places opposite them, Sammy set his clover in the shade and got ready on the sidelines. "Hey, wait a minute," Jimmy said. "What's the kid doing?"

Sammy scowled and placed his hands on his hips. "What do you think I'm doing, stupid? I'm the ball boy."

Brandi and I laughed while Jimmy gave him a hard, cold stare. "Whatever. Just don't get in the way, all right?"

We let them win the first two games, but as Bjorn got ready to serve for the third, Brandi said innocently, "Oh, by the way, you know we're playing for the court, right?"

This was my cue.

They looked at each other and started to laugh. "Oh, okay," Jimmy said, "for the court. Sure thing."

This time when Björn served I was ready. I whacked the ball low and clean, and it blew right past Jimmy. At first he just stood there with his jaw hanging open, but then he shook his head and muttered, "Lucky shot."

After that Brandi played the net like a pro while I hit lobs with extra topspin. Soon we were tied two games apiece. Sammy was having the time of his life chasing balls and keeping score. "Forty, love!" he called.

We won the next three games, which meant we only needed one more for the set. But just when Brandi was about to serve, I saw Dominick appear from behind the bathroom wall. His dark, wavy hair was tied back in a ponytail, and he wore a pair of overalls, but the bib and straps were unhooked and dangling around his knees. In one hand he held a guitar case covered with rock band stickers, and in the other, a bat. A group of his friends followed behind, and they seemed to be headed for the softball field opposite us.

Brandi saw him too, and after I missed an easy back-hand, she stared me down. "Concentrate, April. Forget *him*. We're winning now, don't blow it."

"Okay, okay." I swallowed and tried to focus, but between points I stole glances at the field. Dominick and his friends had chosen up sides and begun to play. To Brandi's dismay, our tennis game went to deuce about fifteen times, but in the end she hit a winning serve and the set was finally ours.

Björn and Jimmy were completely rattled. "All right," Jimmy said, "enough of this crap. Take the kid and get off the court."

"You forgot something," Brandi said. "The court's ours now, so you'll either have to leave or try to win it back."

Bjorn narrowed his eyes and bounced the ball a few times. "Oh, yeah? Says who?"

"Says *everyone*," Brandi snapped. "Those are the rules."

Björn shrugged. "I don't know about any rules." He looked at Jimmy. "You know about any rules?"

Jimmy shook his head. "Nah."

"Hey!" Sammy yelled indignantly. "You can't do that!"

"We can do whatever we want, kid," Bjorn said, "and right now we're telling you to get outta here."

Sammy blocked the sun from his eyes and squinted toward the basketball courts. "That's what you think! I'm gonna get my brother!"

Björn and Jimmy laughed, but underneath you could tell they were a little nervous. "Fine, kid, go get your brother," Jimmy said.

Sammy snatched his clover from the bench and barged out of the gate. He bounded up the path calling, "Matt! Hey, Matt!"

Brandi made a face at the two of them. "We'll be back in a few minutes. Come on, April, let's get a drink." She looped her arm into mine and as we strolled to the water fountain I saw Dominick winding up on the pitcher's mound. Instead of tossing the ball straight to the batter, he lifted one leg and pitched it from underneath. Brandi shook her head. "What exactly do you see in that moron?"

I shrugged. "I don't know, a sense of humor?"

Brandi slurped water noisily, and I squinted ahead, looking for Sammy. That was when I noticed that Matt wasn't playing basketball anymore. He was leaning against the fence nearby, talking to a girl. When Sammy reached them and began explaining our situation, Matt's eyebrows joined together in an angry line. He whistled to his friends, who immediately stopped their game and gathered around. While he passed along Sammy's message to Big Joe, Little Joe, Fritz, and Tony, the mysterious girl dropped to one knee, seemingly enraptured with Sammy and his lucky clover. I noticed that she had a nice smile.

Matt hoisted Sammy onto one shoulder and whispered something to the girl, and then he and his buddies marched ahead. By now, Brandi the Camel had sucked down about a gallon of water. She wiped her mouth with the hem of her shirt. "That's weird," she said. "That girl, the one Matt was just talking to, she looks familiar."

"Oh? Really?"

"Yeah. Do you know her?"

I pressed the metal button, leaned over, and took a drink. The water was warm and tasted like rust. When I raised my head, I saw that the girl had taken a seat on the

37

ground. She'd drawn her knees up to her chest and looked as if she was trying to disappear. Her smile had vanished. "No," I said, "I've never seen her before."

We met Matt and his friends back at the tennis courts. Sammy smiled at me from his perch, and Matt gave me a reassuring nod as he pushed open the gate. "Hey," he said, strolling up to Bjorn and Jimmy, who at this point were looking a little worried. "I heard my sister and her friend just won a set against you guys." Tony stepped forward and crossed his arms over his chest, while Fritz sneered and Big Joe made his baddest, ugliest face. I almost started to laugh.

Bjorn and Jimmy stood there gaping. "Um . . . yeah . . . well . . ."

Little Joe winked at me and twirled the basketball on one finger.

Matt continued. "Look, I don't know where you guys are from, but around here, if you win a set, you get the court. Understand?"

They nodded in unison.

"Good," Matt said, "I had a feeling you guys were reasonable. Now, you can play them again if you want, maybe even win it back, but you can't kick anyone off. Got it?"

They nodded again.

"Great," Matt said. "Now that that's settled . . ." He set Sammy on his feet and glanced toward the fence where he'd left the girl. Only, now she wasn't alone. A well-dressed twenty-something-year-old guy, smoking a cigarette and looking like he had no business being in a public park, was helping her to her feet. They seemed to be having words, and after she stood up, she pulled her arm back and stamped her foot. Matt lunged toward the gate, but Little Joe caught him just in time. "*Don't,* Matt," he whispered fiercely. "Just let her go."

I watched as the guy took a long drag on his cigarette and led the girl to a black Jaguar convertible that was parked by a fire hydrant just outside the basketball courts. Little Joe kept his eye on Matt as they all walked out of the gate and up the path. The girl, I noticed, never lifted her eyes. I wasn't sure why, but I got a terrible feeling in the pit of my stomach. "Matt!" I called.

He turned around.

"Hey, I just wanted to say thanks."

He nodded. "Sure, Ape, no problem."

He and his friends continued on while the girl folded herself into the passenger seat of the car and drove off. I watched until it became a speck in the distance, and then suddenly I heard Sammy laughing. "April, look! Over there!" He was pointing to the softball field.

My mouth fell open.

"Oh . . . my . . . God," Brandi said.

Dominick was on home plate. Apparently he'd scored a run and was now mooning the guys out in the field. Not to mention everyone else who happened to be passing by.

"Yep," Brandi said. "I guess he certainly does have a sense of humor."

FIVE

That night I had one of the worst dreams of my life. I was sitting on the hood of the black Jaguar convertible we'd seen at the park, wearing a not-so-clean bra along with Sammy's Batman Underoos. A full moon lit up the evening sky, but, strangely, there was a big crack running through its center. The young, well-dressed gangster sat beside me humming "Stairway To Heaven," and planting kisses up and down my neck. He whispered in my ear, "See that, April? Dominick's in heaven, mooning the entire world."

I should have realized that the dream was an omen of how the rest of the week was going to turn out. Over the next few days, Matt was in one of his "hormonally charged" moods, as my mother liked to call them. Aside from the usual brooding, slamming doors, and blasting of Jethro Tull's "Aqualung," he woke up each morning with a new crop of whiteheads and spent hours hogging the bathroom, squeezing the heck out of his face. What little sympathy I'd felt for him at the park was completely lost after he'd plucked me off the sofa and tossed me halfway across the basement one night while we were watching TV. My crime? Switching the channel from the Muhammad Ali fight to what I thought was our favorite show, *Saturday Night Live*. I guess Matt didn't feel like laughing.

So I think it's fair to say that when my parents left me and Sammy alone with him one evening while they went to a PTA meeting, dinner, and a movie, the act could be classified as child abuse.

However, before leaving, they bribed us with a pizza from Gino's and even got Matt's favorite, a cheese and pepperoni calzone, which was a huge sacrifice for my mom considering all the bleached flour, sodium, and animal fat. "Well," Mom said, placing the steaming pie on the kitchen table, "looks like you guys are all set."

Sammy plucked a slice from the box and took a bite and as he was chewing reached up and put a stranglehold around my mother's waist. "*Pleeease*, Mom, *pleeeease* don't go!"

I looked at my dad and stuck a finger down my throat like I was about to puke. He couldn't help laughing. Sammy could be overly dramatic, but the thing that bugged me the most was that he never acted like he was going to keel over and die when I left the house. And if you tallied up the hours, I spent half my life with the kid.

41

"Oh, Sammy," Mom said, patting his head. "I told you, Dad and I want to meet your teacher before school starts. Kindergarten's a very important year. After that we're just going to have dinner and see a movie. You'll have a great time with April and . . ." She paused for a moment. "Wait a minute. Where's Matt?"

I'd taken a few bites of pizza by now and felt a buzz going. Poor Mom, little did she know, her daughter was a junk-food junkie. "Where else would he be?" I said. "In his room. I think he's on the phone again."

My mother sighed deeply. "The worst thing we ever did was install that phone jack in his room. Seriously, Stephen, what were we thinking?"

My dad shrugged. "Maybe he's talking to a girl. That wouldn't be so bad, would it?"

I almost choked. If they only knew. It hadn't taken long for Brandi to figure out that the girl at the park was Bettina Bocceli. They'd both gone to St. Steven's Elementary School, and it was common knowledge that Bettina's father was a ranking Mafioso. Once, Brandi had seen Bettina's father pull up to school in a Rolls-Royce, break out a wad of hundred-dollar bills, and stuff one into the front pocket of the gardener's shirt. It made me wonder if he paid off the priests and nuns, too. Maybe even God himself.

"Still, he doesn't have to be so secretive," Mom said, crumpling one side of her mouth. "Oh, well, it's getting late, we better go." She turned to me. "April, please have Sammy in bed by nine. School's starting next week and we have to get him on a decent schedule. Oh, and please read to him."

"I know, Mom, I know." I swear, if someone held a gun to my head and told me to recite Sammy's favorite book, I wouldn't even break a sweat.

"Thanks, honey," she said, planting a kiss on my cheek. It felt nice, but I rolled my eyes anyway.

"Hey! What about me?" Sammy spread his arms; his face was smeared with tomato sauce. My mom and dad started to laugh.

"Okay, okay," Dad said, "how about a group hug?" They walked over to Sammy and all three of them hugged in a little circle. It was pretty nauseating. "You be good for your sister now." He tousled Sammy's hair, and my mom gave Sammy one last kiss before they exited through the back door.

I'd already scarfed two slices of pizza, and now I was eyeing the brown paper bag that held Matt's calzone. "You know, Sammy," I said, unfolding the top and peeking inside, "you can't do stuff like that in front of your friends at school. Kisses, group hugs. If you do, I guarantee a bully's gonna beat you up."

He stopped chewing and looked at me like I'd grown Vulcan ears. "I know *that*. Jeez, April, I'm not an idiot."

"All right, Sammy, just making sure." The calzone was

wrapped in foil, so I pulled it out of the bag and peeled open one side. "Hey, Matt!" I called. "Your calzone's getting cold!"

I waited about five seconds, and when there was no answer, I peeled off the rest of the foil, cut the calzone in half, and watched the pepperoni oil drip, forming a thick orange puddle on the plate. Matt's face was going to look like a land mine in the morning. "Hey, Sam, what do you say we do Matt a favor and eat some of his dinner?"

He grinned. "I don't know. Are you sure?"

"Yeah, why not?"

He shrugged. "Okay. But if he gets mad I'm telling him it was your idea."

Sammy was getting a little too smart for his own good. I cut two pieces, gave one to him, and took a bite of the other. "Hey, Matt!" I called. "Your calzone is *really, really* good!"

Sammy and I started cracking up. Still no answer from Matt. "Okay, wait here," I said to Sammy. "I'll go get him."

I padded quietly up the stairs, tiptoed to Matt's room, and pressed one ear against his door. He was tossing a basketball against the wall, a no-no in the Lundquist household, and I made a mental note of this in case I needed to blackmail him later. His voice was muffled, but I was able to make out the name "Joe" a few times. Since Big Joe was a Neanderthal whose vocabulary consisted of phrases like "You talkin' to me?" and "Forget about it," I figured it had to be Joe of the smaller variety.

Quickly, I ran to my parents' bedroom and grabbed a stethoscope from my mother's drawer. Outside Matt's room, I stuck the earpieces in my ears and pressed the drum to the door. Now everything was clear. "All right," Matt said. "I'll lay low for a while, but I need to talk to her for just a few minutes. Can you ask her to call me from Marcella's house?" Brandi had also informed me that Marcella was Little Joe's cousin (daughter of his connected uncle) and Bettina's best friend. There was a period of silence, followed by the basketball rhythmically hitting the wall. "Great," Matt said. "Thanks, Joe, really, thanks a lot. I'll see you tomorrow."

Next thing I knew, SLAM! The basketball hit the door. All I can say is, imagine an M-80 exploding two inches from your head. "Get outta here, Monk!" Matt screamed. "Mind your own freaking business!"

I yanked off the stethoscope and was about to run downstairs, but suddenly the phone rang, and curiosity got the better of me. I tiptoed back and, with my ears still ringing, pressed the stethoscope to the door.

"Hello?" At first, Matt's voice was pleasant, but a second later he sounded like his old rotten self. "Yeah, hold on a minute." It's a good thing I'd stepped away and hidden the stethoscope behind my back before he pushed open the door. He handed me the phone and said, "Make it quick, Chimp, I'm expecting an important call."

Matt brushed past me and headed downstairs while I put the phone to my ear. I figured it was Brandi wanting to give me an update on how cute Vinny Barbarino looked on *Welcome Back, Kotter.* "Hey, what's up?" I said.

"Um . . . hi." To my surprise, it was a guy's voice. "Is this . . . April? April Lundquist?" For a split second I actually thought it might be Dominick on the line. My heart started thumping.

"Yes, this is April."

"Hi." Silence and a little heavy breathing. "This is kind of embarrassing since I don't know you and you don't know me. But anyway, my name is Bert."

"Bert?" Immediately I formed a mental picture: the yellow pinheaded Muppet with the unibrow.

"Yeah. Walt's friend, from Xavierian."

Oh my gosh. With all the wacky stuff going on, I'd forgotten about the phone call I was supposed to be getting from Walter's desperate friend. And now to complete my mental picture, Walter was the guy in the bathtub with the rubber duckie. "I . . . guess I was confused because Brandi told me your name was—"

"I know, Umberto," he said, "which is the amazingly *guido* name my mother likes to use, but everyone else just calls me Bert. It's less ethnic, if you know what I mean."

"Oh, okay."

"Anyway," he went on, "do you know why I'm calling?"

"Actually . . ." I paused, wondering how I was going to get out of this. "Brandi mentioned something about a dance, but, you see, I'm kinda—"

"Great, I was hoping someone gave you the heads-up. To be honest I didn't want to do this because I think it's pretty lame to call a girl you've never met, but Walt's parents are *really* strict, and they'll only let him double-date. Can you believe it? Poor guy."

He was talking so fast I could hardly process the information. "Yeah, that is a little weird," I said, wondering if Brandi knew that Walter was not only a fairy, but a mama's boy as well.

"Exactly," he agreed. "So, if you don't mind going with me, Walt and I can pick you and Brandi up next Friday at seven-thirty. His brother's going to drive. He's seventeen."

This was getting complicated. "Well, you see, I'm not exactly—"

"And like I said," he interrupted, "I'm sorry to do this to you and all, but I couldn't let Walt down." He laughed a little. "I swear, after this night, he seriously owes me one."

I sat there blinking, wondering if I'd heard correctly.

"Oh . . . sorry," he said. "I guess that didn't come out right. That's not what I meant. Jeez, what a jackass."

Bert seemed honestly pained, but I let him suffer a few more moments before saying, "That's okay. It's the same for me. I'm only doing this for Brandi."

"Oh, right." There was a long period of silence, and during this time I realized that I'd actually *agreed* to go to the dance with him. "Well," he continued, "I should probably mention that I'm not going to dress up or anything. And when it comes to dancing, I'm not exactly into disco."

I thought about telling him that we had something in common, but instead I said, "Gee, that's too bad since I was planning to wear my spandex pants and platform shoes." I could hardly believe this came out of my mouth.

Bert didn't laugh. "Um . . . just curious," he said. "How tall are you?"

The conversation was getting stranger by the minute. And this was not the right question to ask me, even on a good day. Another curse of having Scandinavian ancestors was that I seemed to be growing into one of those strikingly tall Viking women with the blond braids and horned helmets. "Five eight," I said, "maybe five nine. It's been a while since I've measured myself."

"Really? Wow." Bert seemed stunned. "You, uh, might want to pass on those platform shoes. I'm not exactly the tallest guy."

Great. Now Bert was a *short*, yellow, pinheaded Muppet with a unibrow. "I was joking," I said. "I don't like disco either, and I don't own any platforms. Or spandex pants."

"Oh." He laughed awkwardly. "Sorry. You may not believe this, but I'm really not such an idiot in person."

That was yet to be seen.

"So," he said apprehensively, "I guess I'll see you next Friday?"

Next Friday. That would give me nine days to plot Brandi's murder. "Yeah, okay. Did you say seven?"

"Seven-thirty. Walt knows where you live, so we'll just ring the bell. And thanks, you know, for saying yes."

I closed my eyes. "Sure, no problem."

"Bye, April. Oh, and by the way, I really like your name."

I supposed he was trying to redeem himself, and I had to admit, after being called Chimp for so many years, it almost worked. "Thanks," I said. "I'll see you next Friday."

I hung up, trying to figure out how in the world I'd gotten suckered into this. But a second later, the phone rang, jolting me. This time I really hoped it was Brandi; I wanted to chew her out while the memory of Bert's call was still fresh in my mind.

"Hello?" I sounded a little dazed.

"Hi. May I speak to Matt, please?"

Just then I remembered that Matt was expecting a call from Bettina. However, the girl on the other end seemed to have, of all things, a British accent. Not what you'd expect from a mobster's daughter. "Oh, yeah, just a minute, I'll get him."

Matt's phone had a long extension cord, so I picked up the base and walked to the top of the stairs. "Hey, Matt! Phone's for you!"

There was mad scuffle in the kitchen. "All right," he called. "I'm gonna pick up in the basement. Hang up when I tell you to."

"Okay!" I yelled back, gripping the receiver and grinning. Sure thing, Matt. In your dreams.

49

There was a loud click. "All right, Ape, I've got it. Hang up. *Now.*"

I pressed down the receiver button, covered the mouthpiece with my hand, and ever so gently let the button rise. Barely breathing, I sat on the top step and listened.

"Really?" Matt said, sounding dejected. "Two whole weeks? Are you *sure* we have to wait that long?"

Now the girl's British accent was even more pronounced. "I'm sorry, Matt. It's just that in two weeks my father will be in Florida"—she paused for a moment— "on what he calls business. Anyway, I'm hoping everything will blow over by the time he comes back. But even then, we'll have to be careful."

"But," Matt said, "what about play practice? Will you be there? I mean, we can't lose Juliet."

She sighed. "I hope so. I'm just not sure at this point. He . . . my father . . . knows about us meeting at the performing arts center."

"Oh?"

Suddenly, just like with one of those Looney Tunes characters, a lightbulb clicked on in my head. A couple of months ago, Matt had tried out for a part in *Romeo and Juliet* at the Brooklyn Performing Arts Center and had landed the role of Romeo's best friend, Mercutio. The director of the play, who was originally from London, had a fit when he heard everyone reciting Shakespeare in Brooklynese, so he insisted they all use British accents. I guessed Bettina/Juliet was taking her role very seriously, both on- and offstage.

"I'm sorry, Matt," she said. "The whole thing *bloody* stinks." I think she was trying to make him laugh, but it wasn't working.

"No," he said, sighing deeply. "The whole thing's bloody *hell*."

Neither of them spoke for a while, and I felt a sharp pang of guilt listening in. Still, I didn't hang up.

"Matt, I . . . I really have to go. They're watching me, even here at Marcella's house. I swear, I hate this. I hate *them*."

Matt exhaled. "No, Bettina. Even if you tried, you couldn't hate anybody. But listen, hopefully I'll see you at play practice. I just wish I'd gotten the part of Romeo."

She laughed. "Me too. That way I could kiss you in front of everyone and they'd never even know how much I was enjoying it."

Oh, brother, this was getting embarrassing.

"I . . . love you," Matt said.

Oh, God.

I heard her swallow. "I love you too, Matt," and with a shaky voice she began to recite her lines. "*What's in a name? That which we call a rose by any other name would smell as sweet.*"

Matt continued, "*Call me but love, and I'll be new baptized; Henceforth I never will be Romeo.*"

I was seriously beginning to feel ill.

"*Good night, good night,*" Bettina went on. "*Parting is such sweet sorrow, That I shall say goodnight till it be morrow.*"

As soon as the star-crossed lovers hung up, I raced back, tossed the phone onto Matt's bed, and fled to the sanctuary of my room. I did this for two reasons: one, if Matt had seen the expression on my face, he'd have known immediately that I'd been eavesdropping, and two, I needed to think.

I lay on my bed for a while, searching Al Pacino's face for words of wisdom, but he just stared coolly ahead. Cat Stevens, poetic and aloof, was no help either, so I gazed at my blank wall, the one that would soon be home to either Mikhail or the Grateful Dead.

It was strange, I thought, this part of Matt that I barely knew. Underneath all his athletic bravado, he actually had a sensitive side. Last year I'd caught a glimpse of it when my parents, Sammy, and I went to see him perform in *Jesus Christ Superstar*. He'd actually gotten the role of Jesus, and in the end when the bad guys strung him up on that chain-link fence, I'd cried. Matt had moved me to tears. It was almost incomprehensible.

Matt stayed in the basement the rest of the night, and after I put Sammy to bed, I tiptoed down there, thinking maybe I could cheer him up. As I did, I heard Rod Serling's voice on the TV: *There is a fifth dimension beyond that which is known to man . . . the middle ground between light and shadow . . . It is an area we call the Twilight Zone. And*

52

literally, that's exactly what I'd stepped into. The Twilight Zone. Halfway down, I saw that Matt wasn't watching TV; he was sitting cross-legged on the cold, bare floor, tears streaming down his face. We locked eyes for just a moment, and then he grimaced, picked up one of Sammy's Garfield slippers, and threw it, aiming right for my head. "Get outta here, Monk!"

I'd ducked just in time, but as I ran back up the stairs, he pegged me in the butt with Sammy's battery-operated Fat Albert Doll. As it tumbled down the steps it said, "Hey, hey, hey. It's Fat Albert."

SIX

Obviously Matt wanted to be alone, so I left him wallowing in his misery and planted myself on the living room sofa with my latest gruesome tale, *Heart of Darkness*, by Joseph Conrad. I needed something extra dark and depressing to distract me from my current troubles and this was definitely doing it. The storyline went like this: a psycho named Kurtz living in the jungles of Africa was into killing the natives and decorating his fence posts with their shrunken heads. Move over, Edgar Allan Poe.

But after a while, my eyes got heavy and even the gory details couldn't keep me alert. I lay down with the book propped against my chest, falling into that dream state somewhere between sleep and wakefulness. Next thing I knew, I heard a loud clattering sound, and *Heart of Darkness* tumbled onto the rug. Slowly, I peeked over the side of the couch and saw my dad picking up ice cubes he'd dropped on the kitchen floor. My mom was at the table, pouring two glasses of that nasty Red Zinger iced tea. The television, I noticed, was still droning in the basement.

"I guess you're right, Stephen," she said, setting down the pitcher and taking a seat. "Mrs. Flannery may not be the most nurturing kindergarten teacher, but Sammy's pretty tough, so I'm sure he'll do fine."

I heard the water running, so I assumed my dad was at the sink, rinsing off the ice cubes. He came back to the table, plopped several into their glasses, winced, and took a swig. "Oh, sure," he said, clearing his throat and trying not to gag, "Sammy will do fine."

My mother sighed and began rubbing the space between her eyes like she was about to have a migraine. "Actually," she said, "it's not Sammy I'm worried about."

My dad frowned and nodded like he knew exactly what she was referring to. He took a seat, patted her hand reassuringly, and spooned a massive amount of sugar into his tea. "We'll just wait and see," he said, stirring slowly. "I don't believe we're in the danger zone yet."

Danger zone? I froze. Uh-oh. Could they possibly know about Matt and Bettina?

My mother craned her neck toward the basement door, then stood up and gently closed it. I guess she figured Matt and I were down there, happily watching *Dragnet* together. She sat down and stared into her glass. "I don't know, Stephen, I'm really worried about her. I mean, remember last year's parent-teacher conference?"

Suddenly I realized they were not talking about Matt. They were talking about *me*. And just those three words strung together—"parent-teacher-conference"—said it all. Last year, my English teacher caught me hiding a copy of *The Exorcist* inside our assigned text, *A Tale of Two Cities*, and after she lectured me about how rude and grossly inappropriate that was, she called my parents in for a meeting. Needless to say, they were horrified.

But unfortunately, it didn't end there. A few weeks later, I got nailed for drawing caricatures of my Spanish teacher, Señor Bloomberg, in women's underwear and passing them to my friend Olympia. Olympia, in turn, passed them to the rest of the class. Because I was a quiet kid who normally didn't get into trouble, I got off with a couple of warnings, but my parents had already decided that this was highly deviant behavior.

Right then, I could have crept upstairs to my room and spared myself the rest of this embarrassing conversation, but a sick part of me wanted to keep listening.

"It's the same thing every year," my mom continued. "And it only seems to be getting worse. She daydreams in class, doodles, does *weird* things, and never wants to get involved in extracurricular activities."

At this point I wanted to interrupt and say, "Excuse me, just because I don't belong to any teams, leagues, or do-gooder clubs doesn't mean I'm a menace to society."

"Hmmm," my dad said, "I know what you mean." If anyone would, I thought my father would come to my defense, but he just sat there taking sips of my mother's stupid tea.

"And all the creepy books she's been reading lately," she went on. "Oh, and how about that . . . that *candle* in her room?"

My dad sighed. "Yes, the candle is a bit odd."

What they were referring to was the extremely cool purchase I'd recently made at Spencer's Gifts—a skull candle that dripped blood (actually red wax) when you burned it. My parents didn't know, but I had two more stashed in my closet, and I wasn't planning on saving them for Halloween.

"I mean, she has so much potential, but . . ." My mom's voice trailed off. "Gosh, remember when Matt was in ninth grade? Not only was he captain of his basketball team, he organized the chess club *and* got the role of Hamlet in the school play."

"I know, I know," my dad said, "but we shouldn't compare. They're two different kids. And besides, April's always been a late bloomer."

Late bloomer? What exactly was *that* supposed to mean?

My mom sighed again. "It must be hard for her, having Matt for an older brother. He's a tough act to follow."

"And it doesn't help that Sammy's so charming and lovable," my dad added.

I rolled my eyes. This was *un*believable.

After a long period of silence, my mom said, "Well, it's

getting late, we'd better get to bed." She drained her glass of tea, stuck the pitcher back in the fridge, and turned off the lights. "Let's just hope this year will be better than last."

As the two of them padded quietly up the stairs, my dad reached over and goosed my mom. Playfully, she swatted his hand and giggled. Great, I thought, just what I needed to see. A perfect ending to a perfect night.

I lay there for a long while, and as my eyes adjusted to the darkness, the first thing that came into view was Matt's monster-sized trophy case sitting in one corner of the living room, filled with trophies that read things like HIGH SCORER and MOST VALUABLE PLAYER. Next was Sammy's bulletin board on the far wall, jauntily displaying his artwork from nursery school. I wasn't sure why, but I began feverishly searching the room for something of mine. What I found, sitting atop the piano (the one my mother wished I still played), collecting dust, was the lopsided psychedelic ashtray I'd made in fourth grade.

And then it hit me. I was the oddball, the enigma, the embarrassing question mark in our family. I guess I'd known it all along, but it was strange to have it spelled out so clearly. Funny what an ashtray can do.

Very slowly, I picked up my book and tiptoed up the stairs, making sure not to step on any creaky spots. In the darkness of my room, I undressed, pulled on a pajama top, and crawled into bed. Hugging my pillow, I replayed my parents' conversation in my mind while little tears slid down my face. Quickly, I wiped them away.

Oh, well, on the bright side, at least I knew which poster I'd buy for my third wall. Hands down, it would be the skull-and-crossbones logo of the Grateful Dead. I hadn't realized it before, but it matched my candle perfectly.

SEVEN

Over the next few days I avoided my parents as much as possible, but before long my dad was insisting on a trip to the Jersey shore. One last hurrah before school started. Yippee.

Surprisingly, Matt had decided to stop brooding over his two-week loss of Bettina and grace us with his presence. He'd invited Little Joe, and as usual, Brandi would be coming too. Sammy had wanted to ask a friend, but there was no room left in the car, which was a good thing, because one five-year-old collecting crab shells and dead jellyfish while begging every five minutes to be buried in the sand was about all I could handle.

"Hey, April?" Brandi said, rummaging through my dresser. It was ten in the morning and we were getting ready to leave. From the tone of her voice I could tell she was about to ask a favor. "May I . . ." She pulled out my lemon yellow bikini—the one I was planning to wear. "Borrow this?"

I chewed my lip while Brandi made pleading eyes and pointed sadly to what she had on—a blue and white striped sailor top with a bow. Beneath her cutoffs was the matching bottom, complete with lace ruffle on the butt. For some reason Navy attire had been in style last summer, but this season it was the epitome of dorkdom. "Oh, all right," I said, figuring I could wear my suit from last year—a classic red polka-dot bikini. Unlike Brandi, I was not a trendsetter.

"Oh, thanks, April, you're the best!" Quickly, she pulled off her sailor suit and slipped on the yellow bikini. I had to admit, with her dark hair and olive skin, it looked better on her than on me.

"Not bad," I said as Brandi admired herself in the mirror. Meanwhile I fished out my old suit, buried under a pile of socks. When I put it on, I discovered that the bottom fit okay but the top, the kind with those sliding polyester triangles, was a little skimpy. I turned around and Brandi tied the strings for me. "So, what do you think?" I said, facing her.

She shrugged. "Well, your boobs got bigger."

Suddenly my bedroom door was flung open, and there stood Matt and Little Joe. I screamed, "What are you doing? We were getting dressed! God, can we at least have some privacy around here?" Little Joe looked embarrassed, but I noticed that his eyes landed on my red polka-dot top.

When Matt saw Little Joe's expression, he reached over and put him in a headlock. "Get a shirt on, Chimp!" he said to me. "And come on downstairs. Dad needs help. Now!"

By the time Brandi and I reached the kitchen, I'd surmised that my dad had actually asked Matt for help, but since Matt was in the middle of a very important football game with Little Joe, Larry, and Sammy, he'd raced upstairs and gotten Brandi and me instead. Brandi followed behind as I marched to the front door. Outside, Larry was running up the street for a pass. "Look at those bums," I said.

Brandi spied over my shoulder. "Yeah, really."

Matt threw the ball. "That's it, Larry!" he called. "You got it, man, you got it!"

Larry was a decent football player, but he didn't always go by the rules. After he caught the ball, he hugged it greedily to his chest.

"Okay, Larry!" Sammy called. "Now pass it to me!" Sammy held out both arms, but Larry shook his head and squeezed the ball tighter. Eventually Little Joe had to go and pry it from his hands.

I figured arguing with Matt wasn't worth the effort, but I made a mental note to pay him back later.

"So, what do you need, Dad?" I asked as Brandi and I returned to the kitchen. He was filling a cooler with piles of mystery food wrapped in aluminum foil. My mother had already left for work, but I had a sneaking suspicion that she'd had something to do with the contents of our lunch.

"Let's see," he said, looking a bit frazzled. "We need suntan lotion, beach chairs, umbrellas, oh, and Sammy's blow-up alligator tube. Everything should be in the storage closet in the basement."

Brandi and I padded downstairs. When we opened the storage closet we found that a bunch of spiders had been busily spinning webs and laying eggs all over our beach supplies. So, after cleaning up the mess with a pair of Matt's underwear (payback number one), we hauled the stuff outside and began loading up my dad's blue Monte Carlo.

Little Joe ran over to help us, but the rest of them continued their game. Up the street I noticed that Frankie the Crunch was watering his little flower garden and paying tribute to St. Christopher while he kept an eye on the guys playing football. Gorgeous Vinny was on the other end polishing his Coupe de Ville. Now Larry was winding up, ready to throw the ball. "All right, Larry!" Matt called. "Not too high now, remember what I told you!" But, like always, Larry zinged it into the trees. He had a very strong arm. "Whoa!" Matt exclaimed when the ball finally crashed to the ground. "Man, Larry, that was some pass!"

Both Frankie the Crunch and Gorgeous Vinny started clapping. "Way to go, Larry!" Gorgeous Vinny called. "Show those turkeys what you're made of!"

Frankie the Crunch didn't say anything. He just set down his hose and bowed reverently toward Larry like he was some kind of football god.

Larry grinned proudly, and when he saw Brandi and me, he ran over to us. Gallantly, he picked up Sammy's alligator tube and stuffed it into the trunk. "Hey, thanks, Larry," I said. "You know, I saw that catch you made earlier. Not bad."

He nodded enthusiastically. Not only was Larry excited about the football game, he was eagerly anticipating our walk to school in just a few days. As promised, Soft Sal had "worked out the details" with Brandi and me, and come Monday morning, we'd be ringing Larry's doorbell, 8:45 sharp.

Little Joe slapped Larry on the back. "I'm telling you, April, this guy is something else. Watch out, O.J." I wasn't sure but I thought Little Joe glanced again at my chest, which was now covered with my Rolling Stones T-shirt— the one with the gigantic tongue sticking out from a pair of lips. I wanted Matt to get the hint.

Sammy ran over. "Hey, what about me?" he said to Little Joe indignantly. "Aren't I a good football player?"

Little Joe laughed, picked up Sammy, and swung him around a few times. "*You*, mister, are ready for peewee league!"

When Matt finally joined us, I gave him a frosty look. I was still annoyed about having to do his dirty work, but what *really* irked me was how one minute he acted like

Larry's best friend and the next he was cracking retard jokes behind his back. "What's your problem, Monkey?" he said, aiming the football at my head.

I didn't flinch. "Nothing. I just don't like lazy bums, or"—I cast a quick glance at Larry, who was drumming his fingers against the hood of the car—"hypocrites."

Matt made a face and started poking around in the trunk. "Hey, Ape, did you pack my suntan lotion?"

I narrowed my eyes. "Yes, I did, *Sunshine Boy.*"

Brandi gulped and elbowed me in the ribs. "What are you doing?" she whispered.

I wasn't quite sure, but from the look on Matt's face, it appeared to be payback number two.

Matt glanced up and down the street, then peered at me suspiciously. Little Joe's jaw, I noticed, had gone slack. But before either of them could say anything, Mrs. Luciano called from her front window, "Larry! Come on! Time to eat!" She waved at us. "Thank you, boys! Thanks for playing football with Larry!"

Dazed, Matt waved back. "Oh, sure, Mrs. Luciano, no problem." While Larry plodded across the street, Matt slammed the trunk shut. "Listen, Monk, I want to know right now, where did you hear that?"

I blinked innocently. "What do you mean? Hear what?"

He hesitated for a moment. "You know what."

I shrugged. "I have no idea what you're talking about."

He peered at me awhile longer, and Little Joe just stood

there rubbing his chin. A second later my dad came lumbering down the driveway, cooler in hand, a load of beach towels draped around his neck. "Okay, everybody, pile in! Jersey Shore, here we come!"

I gave Matt and Little Joe my most angelic smile, and as we got into the car I overheard Little Joe say, "Forget it, Matt. It's just a coincidence. Don't be paranoid."

Our trip to New Jersey turned out to be a fiasco. We sat in traffic most of the way, breathing in sulfuric fumes from the turnpike, and had to cross three toll bridges before we even hit the coast. Every five minutes, Sammy looked up from his Rubik's Cube and whined, "Dad, are we there yet?" Halfway, I was about ready to clobber him. When we finally arrived at Sandy Hook Beach we were all starving, so after taking a quick dip, we spread out our towels while my dad divvied up the food.

"Ugh," Matt said, biting into his sandwich. "I should have known. Mom's health crap. I swear, Dad, I can't take it anymore."

Slowly, I lifted one corner of my multigrain bread and saw that my mom had made us all peanut butter, honey, and banana sandwiches. To top it off, the peanut butter was the natural kind—clumpy with a slimy layer of oil at the top. Little Joe had taken a bite of his and was having trouble swallowing, so my dad quickly poured him a drink. What came out of the pitcher looked like cherry

Kool-Aid, but from the expression on Little Joe's face I realized what it was. Red Zinger.

My dad sighed, reached into his pocket, and pulled out his wallet. He handed us each a five-dollar bill. "Go ahead, guys, get whatever you want. Just . . . don't tell Mom, all right?"

While my dad fed our lunch to a flock of crazed seagulls, the rest of us ran to the concession stand and bought trays of junk food—hot dogs, French fries, knishes, and Cokes. As we ate greedily on our towels, I saw my dad pluck a note from the cooler. I smiled, thinking of the letters my mom used to leave in my lunch box when I was a kid. Every day it was something different—*I love you, sweetie,* or *I miss you, honey,* or *I've got a special surprise waiting for you at home!* After my dad read the message, he cleared his throat and surreptitiously slipped the paper into his back pocket.

I set a knish and a Coke in front of him. "So, looks like Mom wrote you one of her famous lunch notes, huh?" I wondered if it was something romantic. After seeing my dad goose her on the stairs that night, I figured anything was possible.

"Oh, yeah," he said with a wave, "you know how she is." He squeezed a packet of mustard onto his knish and spread it with one finger. For some reason he seemed a little uptight. "So," he said, glancing at Brandi and me, "what do you girls have planned this fall? Anything special?" He took a bite of the knish.

I stopped chewing. "Um . . . we're going to school, if that's what you mean."

He swallowed. "Well, yes, I know that. But what about after school?"

I glanced at Brandi, who didn't seem to think this was a strange question. She set down her bag of fries and wiped the grease from her hands. "I'll probably try out for the Boosters again," she said.

I rolled my eyes. The Boosters were P.S. 201's sorry excuse for a cheerleading squad. Last year Brandi and our mutual boy-crazy friend, Olympia, had begged me to try out with them, but like disco music, anything that had to do with miniskirts, pom-poms, or cheering for a bunch of egomaniacs like Matt was against my religion.

"And I might join choir," she added. "Olympia told me they're going to do songs from *Hair* this year."

My dad nodded. "Sounds nice." He looked at me. "How about you, April? Anything special planned?"

And then it dawned on me. My mother's little note must have said something like this: *Stephen, please talk to April. Find out if she's planning to be normal this year.*

Unfortunately, Matt had been listening in on our conversation. He stuffed a bunch of fries into his mouth and said, "Yeah, Ape, maybe you should join the Stoop-Sitting Club. I hear they need a new president."

I made a face. "Har-de-har-har."

Little Joe elbowed Matt and gave me a sympathetic smile.

My dad continued. "Well, Mom mentioned you might be interested in joining a tennis league. She knows some of the coaches at Poly Prep. And who knows, maybe you should think about piano lessons again."

Matt pointed his knish at me. "Yeah, really. I mean, why did I have to take three years of piano lessons with the Amazing Thunderbutt, and Ape gets off after, what? Two months?"

"Matt," my dad warned.

Sammy started cracking up, and when some Coke shot out his nose he laughed harder. The Amazing Thunderbutt was our old piano teacher, Gladys Higgenbottom. Her breath smelled like cat food, and her enormous rear end took up half the piano bench.

"Hey, Sam," Matt said, "I wouldn't be laughing if I were you. You're her next victim." Matt hummed a few bars of "Twinkle, Twinkle, Little Star," stuck out his butt, and pretended he was going to smother Sammy with it.

We all laughed, but my dad just sighed and shook his head.

"Listen, Dad," I said, "I don't want piano lessons. And Brandi and I just like to play tennis at the park. You know, for fun."

Little Joe chimed in. "April's *very* good at tennis."

I gave Little Joe an appreciative smile and took a sip of my Coke. "Besides, I'm gonna be pretty busy this year."

My dad raised an eyebrow. "Oh? How's that?"

I shrugged. "Well, I'll be in the library a lot, reading,

and someone's got to take care of Sammy, right? Oh, and Brandi and I have a job, sort of."

Everyone looked at me, including Brandi. "A job?" my dad said.

"Yeah. Mr. Luciano asked us to walk Larry back and forth to school. Keep an eye on him, let Mr. Luciano know if there's any trouble."

Brandi nodded in agreement. "We start Monday."

Matt and Little Joe had gone back to stuffing their faces, but now they stopped chewing and exchanged glances.

My dad seemed concerned. "Mr. Luciano's not paying you, is he?"

"Oh, no," I said. "We're just doing it as a favor. You know, for Larry."

"Well," my dad said, "that's fine, I guess, but be careful. Larry can be difficult sometimes. And April?"

"Yeah?"

"Please keep that tennis league in mind. Mom and I appreciate your helping with Sammy, but we can always work out some other babysitting arrangements."

Sammy piped up. "No way! I want April to take care of me. Not some stupid babysitter."

"All right, Sammy," my dad said. "I'm talking to April now."

I winked at Sammy. He could be a pain in the neck, but when it came right down to it, I liked having him around. At this point my dad seemed desperate to hear something positive, but how could I tell him there was no way I was going to join some lame tennis league at Poly Prep, not when Brandi and I could still annihilate the likes of Björn Borg and Jimmy Connors while possibly running into Dominick at the park. I mean, it was like killing two birds with one stone. "I don't know, Dad, I'll think about it, okay?"

He sighed. "Okay." Poor Dad. Mom must have been putting him under a lot of pressure.

Matt, I noticed, had been watching me from the corner of his eye the whole time. I figured the Sunshine Boy comment, along with my newfound employment with Mr. Luciano, had him guessing. I liked the feeling of power it gave me.

After Matt finished his lunch, he smeared Coppertone over his entire body, flipped on the radio, and lay back in the sun. Little Joe began a crossword puzzle, and Sammy had somehow conned Brandi and my dad into helping him build a sand castle.

By now my Nordic skin was starting to burn, so after dabbing on some of Matt's extra-strength lotion, I adjusted my red polka-dot triangles (the right one, especially, was giving me trouble) and opened my latest hair-raising novel, *Carrie*, by Stephen King. It was a little cheesy but a good beach read. Meanwhile "Bennie And The Jets" began playing on the radio, and Matt, to my dismay, started singing along. Eyes shut, he bobbed his head around to the beat. *B-b-b-Benny and the Jets-ssss . . .*

Little Joe and I looked at each other and laughed. "You know, Matt," I said, poking the sole of his foot with my big toe. "I'm surprised you, of all people, still like Elton John."

Little Joe set down his pencil and nudged him. "Yeah, man, I mean, what's the deal?"

Matt opened one eye. "What are you fools talking about? Elton John is solid."

I raised one eyebrow at Little Joe and tossed a French fry at Matt. "News flash, Matt," I announced. "Elton John is queer."

"What?" He sat up, stunned, and turned to Little Joe.

Little Joe nodded. "It's true, man. Everyone knows it."

My dad had apparently overheard our conversation. Being a history teacher, he was obsessed with getting the facts right. "Actually," he said, "Elton John is bisexual. I read an article about it in *Newsweek*."

Matt's eyes covered half his face. The radio wailed on, *Oh but they're weird and they're wonderful, Oh Benny she's really keen. . . .*

Sammy scooped sand into his bucket. "What's bisexual?"

No one answered right away. Finally my dad said, "Well, Sammy, it just means that he likes both girls *and* boys."

Sammy shrugged. "So what? I like girls and boys. Well, boys are better."

Everyone laughed except Matt. He sighed deeply and

lay back down. Meanwhile, Elton went into the grand finale, *Benny, Benny, Benny and the Jets-ssss* . . .

Turned out the third and final payback was the best one yet.

Matt's extra-strength Coppertone was definitely *not* doing its job, and after only two chapters of *Carrie*, I was beginning to look like a lobster. "Hey," I said, "how about we go in the water and have a chicken fight?" Last summer, Little Joe and I had teamed up against Matt and Brandi at Manhattan Beach. Normally Brandi and I didn't like to be on opposite sides, but chicken fights were the exception.

Brandi, who was knee deep in the moat of Sammy's sand castle, looked up, blew a wisp of hair from her face, and said, "Sounds good to me."

Little Joe tugged on the fringes of Matt's cutoffs. "Come on, Macho Man. Your sister and I challenge you and Brandi to a chicken fight."

Matt, who was still mourning Elton John's bisexuality, sat up and shrugged. "Oh, all right." He waved. "Come on, Brandi, you and I are gonna cream Joe and the Monk."

The water was rough, and it took a while for us to get past the breakers. Sammy ran to the shore to watch, and I heard my dad call, "Be careful, guys! The tide's moving out."

Finally we entered a patch of calm water. "Okay, hop on," Little Joe said. He ducked under and I climbed onto his shoulders. Last summer I hadn't thought twice about doing this, but now it felt strange. After all, my crotch was straddling his neck.

"Okay! I'm ready!" Brandi called from atop Matt's shoulders. I wondered if she was having the same problem.

As Brandi and I went at it, Matt spit water from his mouth and announced in his best Howard Cosell voice, "Okay, sports fans, we've got the mad Viking, Helga the Horrible, battling it out with her Sicilian enemy, the amazing Italian Stallion!"

Brandi and I were swatting at each other and laughing hysterically when, out of nowhere, a gigantic wave came and knocked me right off Little Joe's shoulders. Water surged up my nose, and as I tried to swim to the surface, another wave hit. I willed myself not to panic, but when my head hit bottom and scraped along the hard, rough sand, I wondered if this was it: I, April Lundquist, was about to die in a chicken fight.

I was under for a long time, but just as my lungs were about to burst, I felt the water release around me. Like a beached whale, I'd been washed up on shore. Relieved, I filled my lungs with air, pushed back my sand-caked hair, and saw Matt, Brandi, and Little Joe running toward me. "April, oh my gosh, are you okay?" Brandi called.

"Yeah, yeah," I said, a little dazed. "I'm all right." I noticed a look of surprise on Little Joe's face. When the wind blew, I suddenly knew why. My right polka-dot triangle was no longer where it was supposed to be. Horrified, I yanked it into place.

When Matt saw Little Joe grinning, he tackled him, and the two of them began wrestling in the sand. "That's my sister, you moron!" Matt said. It sounded like he was joking, but I wasn't quite sure.

Meanwhile, Brandi helped me to my feet. She glanced at my lemon yellow bikini, looking guilty for having borrowed it. A minute later my dad and Sammy came running over. I hoped to God they hadn't seen anything. Sammy, bucket in hand, flung his arms around my waist. "April, are you all right? I was so scared." The poor kid was practically crying.

Besides being completely humiliated, I was a little scraped up, but I was alive and all my body parts were intact. "Yeah, Sam, I'm okay, I guess."

A few yards away, Matt had pinned Little Joe to the shore. As a wave crashed over him, he sputtered, "Come on, Matt, get off me! Do you know how heavy you are?"

My dad put his arm around my shoulder; he seemed a bit shaken up. "We better get you back on dry land," he said.

As my dad and I walked toward the beach chairs, Brandi and Sammy joined Matt and began pouring buckets of water over Little Joe. My dad chuckled and patted my head. "So, looks like we could have joined the nudists at Riis Park after all, huh?"

EIGHT

"Well, well, look who's here, right on time." Mr. Luciano greeted Brandi and me at his front door wearing a red velvet smoking jacket with matching slippers. It was Monday morning, the first day of school, and as promised, we'd arrived for Larry at 8:45 sharp. "Come on in, Larry's just about ready."

Brandi and I exchanged eyebrow messages as we followed Soft Sal into the living room. Entering the Luciano house was like stepping into a sixteenth-century Italian gallery in the Metropolitan Museum of Art, complete with marble columns, cherubic statues, and paintings of plump, half-naked women. Mr. Luciano sat down in a chair that looked like the papal throne, stuck an unlit cigar in his mouth, and motioned for us to make ourselves comfortable on the plastic-covered sofa.

In the kitchen Larry was moaning, "No, Ma, no, please,

not my hair, *please!*" A second later he raced into the living room, curls sticking up in all directions, his mother trailing behind. When he saw Brandi and me he smiled.

"Hi, Larry," I said, wincing a little. Mrs. Luciano had no idea how cruel kids in P.S. 201 could be if you didn't dress right. Larry didn't stand a chance in his crisp blue khakis, button-down shirt, and polished loafers.

I had to say something. "Um, Mrs. Luciano?" She stood there, comb in hand, shaking her head at Larry. "You probably don't know this, but most of the kids in school, they just wear jeans, T-shirts, and sneakers. It's pretty casual."

"Oh?" Mrs. Luciano didn't look too good. There were bags under her eyes, and her perfectly coiffed Barbra Streisand hairdo was flattened on one side.

Larry, who didn't normally speak much, blurted out, "See, Ma! See! I told you!" Pleadingly, he looked at his father.

Mr. Luciano chuckled. "Well, Larry, looks like you need to go upstairs and change your clothes. But hurry, we can't keep these lovely young ladies waiting."

Larry let out a happy groan, hugged his father, and ran upstairs while Mrs. Luciano walked over to the sofa and gently pinched Brandi's and my cheeks. "You girls are angels, you know that? Looking after my Larry. Angels." Then she patted her husband's shoulder and shuffled back into the kitchen.

Next came a period of awkward silence while Mr.

Luciano sat there chewing his cigar. Finally he said, "So, sweetheart, how's your mother?"

The "sweetheart" he was addressing was me, of course. I swallowed hard and felt the backs of my legs sticking to the plastic-covered sofa. "She's fine. You know, working hard."

He smiled. "Yeah, she's a real career woman, isn't she? And it's nice, you know, the way she helps other people, being a nurse and all." He tapped his fingers on the arms of the chair. Soft Sal wasn't exactly what you'd call skilled in small talk. "How about your brother?"

Discreetly, Brandi pinched my leg. "Oh," I said, my heart beginning to pound, "Sammy's starting kindergarten today. He's pretty excited." I shot a little prayer toward the crucifix hanging on the wall. I didn't want this conversation to veer toward you-know-who.

Mr. Luciano nodded. "Nice, nice. How about the other one?"

I blinked. "Other one?"

"Yeah, you know. Romeo."

Brandi coughed and pinched me harder.

"Oh, do you mean . . . Matt?"

"Yeah, Matt. Is he staying out of trouble, keeping his nose clean?"

Brandi gulped.

"Um . . . yes, I think so."

He nodded again. "Good, good. Your brother's a nice kid. A very nice kid. But sometimes *nice* isn't enough. You gotta be smart, too, if you know what I mean." He tapped one finger against his forehead a few times and winked at me.

I wasn't about to break the news to Mr. Luciano, but on a scale from one to ten, I'd give Matt an eight and a half for brains and a minus two for nice. And that was being generous.

Brandi reached behind me and dug her thumb into my back while Mr. Luciano plucked a lighter from the table and ignited his cigar. As he blew a smoke ring, Larry came barreling down the stairs. Now he had on a pair of faded jeans, a Pink Floyd T-shirt, and black Pumas. He spread out his arms in a *ta-da*.

Mr. Luciano shook his head. "Oh, boy, better not let your mother see you now."

After our little conversation with Soft Sal, I was feeling a bit shaky. I peeled myself off the sofa and helped Brandi to her feet. "Well, goodbye, Mr. Luciano," I said. "We'd better get going."

He puffed on his cigar. "Goodbye, girls. Take good care of Larry."

"We will," I said. Brandi and I quickly gathered our books from the table, and when the kitchen door swung open and Mrs. Luciano appeared, Larry took off like a shot.

Mr. Luciano stood up and called from his chair, "Remember what we talked about, Larry! Listen to your teachers, and no monkey business!"

*   *   *

When we finally caught up with Larry, he was halfway up the block and panting heavily. I patted his shoulder. "Congratulations, you escaped!"

Nervously he glanced down the street, and when he saw that his mother was nowhere in sight, he let out a huge sigh of relief. He kept up the rapid pace, but when we turned the corner onto Eleventh Avenue he slowed down and began picking clusters of honeysuckle from Mrs. Falcone's garden trellis. Brandi, who had been thoughtfully quiet until now, piped up. "Hey, uh, Larry, what *exactly* did your father mean when he said, 'No monkey business?' "

Larry pulled a stamen from one of the flowers and sipped the nectar. "Larry?" Brandi leaned over his shoulder. "Did you hear what I said?"

Larry might have been retarded, but he wasn't deaf, and he certainly wasn't stupid. He purposely ignored Brandi's question and plowed ahead to a patch of dandelions growing near the curb. After pulling a few, he closed his eyes like he was making a wish and blew the fluff into the air. "Leave him alone," I said. "It's his first day of public school. You don't want to get him all riled up."

Brandi eyed him suspiciously. "I'm telling you, April, he's got something up his sleeve. I can tell."

This worried me, but I decided to give Larry the benefit of the doubt. We watched him carefully, and for the next few blocks he innocently plodded along, collecting a variety of leaves, twigs, and pebbles. But when we turned the corner onto Eighty-first Street and P.S. 201 came into view, he stopped dead in his tracks. "Larry?" I said. "Larry, what's wrong?"

He gazed at the chain-link fence surrounding the schoolyard. Next thing I knew, he reached inside the waist of his pants and whipped out his drumsticks. Turned out Brandi was right, only instead of something up his sleeve, it was something down his pants. He raced toward the fence.

"Larry! Oh my gosh, what are you doing?" I called. Up ahead crowds of students were filing through the gates on either side of the yard.

I turned to Brandi. "This isn't good."

"Yeah, no kidding."

We raced toward Larry, and I started tugging on his arm. "Larry, you can't do this. Remember what your father said?" At the mention of Soft Sal, Larry seemed to come out of his trance. "Larry? Put the drumsticks away, okay? They don't let you do stuff like this at school."

But this was the wrong thing to say. Immediately, Larry's eyebrows shot together and he pounded the fence defiantly. I guessed no one was going to tell Larry Luciano what he could or could not do at school. Especially when it came to drumming. Meanwhile, the first bell rang, and now the students began streaming into the building. We had exactly seven minutes to get to class.

"Listen, Larry," I said, figuring I had to try another tactic since this one obviously wasn't working, "I guess, well, you can drum the fence if you want, but you've got to keep moving. We can't be late." He thought about this a moment, nodded, and began walking and drumming at the same time.

Brandi whispered in my ear, "How are we going to explain him?"

I stared at the mob ahead. "I have no idea." We continued along, and pretty soon kids were squinting up the block, wondering what was going on. At one point, Larry had to lift his sticks to avoid a group of eighth graders leaning against the fence. A few of them chuckled as he reached up and batted the air above their heads, but I gave them the evil eye and they quickly stopped.

Finally we reached the gate. I thought Larry might settle down at this point, but no such luck. When we passed a bunch of ninth graders taking last drags on their cigarettes, one of them, a disco lover wearing gold chains and a Farrah Fawcett T-shirt, said, "Who's the retard with the sticks?" The rest of them laughed. Larry kept drumming.

"Shut up and mind your own business," I said.

"Whoa, whoa, wait a minute." Mr. Disco took a step toward me and lifted his chin. "You're telling *me* to shut up?"

I felt Brandi's hand on my shoulder. "April, what are you doing?" I shrugged it off.

"Yes," I said to him, "I'm telling *you* to shut up." I walked over to Larry and took his arm, but he pulled away and started to moan.

This set the morons off laughing again. Mr. Disco narrowed his eyes. "Who *is* this guy?" he said. "Your demented boyfriend?"

Brandi leaned over and whispered in my ear. "Ignore him, April. He's not worth it."

But there was something Brandi didn't realize. If I didn't say something now, Larry would become a target for the rest of the year. I marched up to Mr. Disco. "Let me get this straight. You want to know"—I pointed to Larry—"*who* that is?"

He nodded. "Yeah, I do."

I gave him a cold, hard stare. "That, my friend, is Larry Luciano. Son of *Salvatore* Luciano. Aka Soft Sal. Got it?"

The "aka" did it. Now there was fear in his eyes. He glanced at his friends, flicked his cigarette butt to the ground, and said, "Yeah, right, whatever."

I stood my ground until the group disappeared into the crowd. I figured the news about Larry's ranking Mafioso father would travel quickly, and now that that was settled I had to persuade Larry to put away his sticks and come with us to class. But when I turned around, Dominick was standing beside Larry, watching him in fascination. "This guy's amazing," he said, to no one in particular. "A natural."

Slowly, I walked over to Brandi, who was eyeing Dominick with disgust. Ever since the mooning incident at the park, she'd decided Dominick was not only dangerous, but vulgar and obscene as well.

"Hey," Dominick said, tapping Larry's shoulder, trying to get his attention. "What's your name, man? I've never seen you before."

Larry turned to Dominick, but before answering he craned his neck and studied the guitar case that was strapped to Dominick's back. "Larry," he said, in that slow, drawn-out way of his. "My name's Larry."

Dominick smiled and stuck out his hand. "Nice to meet you, Larry." The two of them shook. "So, you're a Floyd fan, huh?" he asked, pointing to Larry's T-shirt.

Larry touched his chest and nodded slowly.

"Me too. Listen, we definitely need to jam together. Maybe I'll see you at lunch, what do you say?"

Larry nodded again, and that was when the final bell rang. As the latecomers scrambled toward the door, Dominick leaned over and said something into Larry's ear. In response, Larry handed him the sticks and then pointed to me and Brandi. "Uh-oh," Brandi said, "look who's coming."

Dominick walked directly up to me. "You're April, right?"

I swallowed. "Yeah."

He held out the sticks. "I'm Dom. Larry says you should hold on to these for him."

We locked eyes for a moment, and all I could manage to say was "Oh, okay, thanks." I took the sticks, and his thumb brushed against mine.

"Bring them with you to lunch, all right?" he said. "Larry and I are gonna jam."

I wondered how they were going to "jam" without a set of drums, but I decided not to ask. Instead, I nodded like the whole thing made perfect sense. "Oh, sure."

He smiled, and I noticed that his right eyetooth stuck out just a little. For some reason, it made him look even cuter. I figured this might be my only chance to make an impression, and now that I'd put Mr. Disco in his place I decided I could do this. "Um, Dom, I . . . really like your music."

His eyebrows shot up. "Yeah? You've heard me play?"

"Uh-huh, last year at the talent show. And sometimes I hear you at the park, or in front of Moe's. You may not know this, but we like a lot of the same bands."

He stood there for a moment watching me; my face began to grow warm, but I didn't look away. It was like he was seeing me for the first time, like I wasn't just some brainy girl with braces, but maybe a person he'd like to get to know. Possibly even more. "Thanks," he said, "for telling me. So, I'll definitely see you later, right?"

"Oh, yeah. I'll be there."

"Great."

As Dominick walked away, I felt a sharp pain radiating from my big toe. I looked down and saw that Brandi was stepping on my foot. "April, *what* are you thinking?"

I grinned. "I'm thinking he might like me."

"Well, yeah, what do you expect after telling him how wonderful he is? The guy's an egomaniac."

I ignored Brandi's comment and watched while Dominick joined his friends at the door. Before stepping inside he turned around, raised one fist, and called out, "Yo, Larry! Pink Floyd rules!"

Larry grinned, raised his fist in return, and echoed, "Yeah, man! Floyd rules!"

By the time we got Larry settled into his class, which was called the Alternative Learning Program, Brandi and I were both ten minutes late to our homerooms. This year I was in 9-SP-1 and Brandi, 9-SP-2. The SP stood for "Special Progress," classifying us as the brainy dorks of the school, but if you looked closely at the general population of P.S. 201 you'd realize it wasn't saying much.

Anyway, Brandi's teacher was pretty cool about her being late, especially when she explained how we were helping a "poor retarded boy" find his class, but my homeroom teacher, a scary-looking guy with horn-rimmed glasses and a Count Dracula widow's peak, marked a red "X" beside my name in his little black book, and happily informed me that if I got three "X"s this marking period I would be serving Saturday detention.

However, none of this seemed to matter at the moment because today marked a major turning point in my life. Dominick DeMao actually knew that I, April Lundquist, was alive.

"Um, Miss Lundquist, are you planning to play the drums for us this morning?"

"Huh?" I slid into my seat and realized I was still holding Larry's sticks. "Oh . . . no. They belong to a friend of mine."

"Really?" Count Dracula strolled to my desk and stuck out one hand. Patches of coarse, dark hair sprouted from his knuckles. "Maybe I'd better hold on to those for your *friend*. We wouldn't want any accidental impalings today, now would we?"

I panicked and gripped the sticks tighter. "No, you see, I can't do that. My friend, the drummer, he's supposed to jam with this other guy at lunch today. He plays guitar. They're counting on me to bring the sticks." I thought this made perfect sense, but he didn't seem to be buying it.

"Oh? Really?"

"Yes. They're both very good musicians."

"I see. Well, if that's the case, I'll hold on to them for you, or should I say, for your *friend*. You can stop by and pick them up before lunch. I'll be here."

I looked at his outstretched hand and sighed. Considering all the trouble I'd been in last year, all I needed now was for Count Dracula to call my parents about a set of lethal drumsticks I'd refused to hand over. Reluctantly, I placed them in his palm.

By now, peals of laughter were rising from the class. Angie, Bernadette, and Grace, my so-called friends from eighth grade, were sitting together looking confused. I imagined they were deciding whether or not it would be a good idea to hang out with me this year. I smiled weakly and waved. Next thing I knew, a hairy knuckle tapped the cover of my book. "So, Miss Lundquist, besides being a music aficionado, I see you also enjoy learning about the dark side of human nature."

On my desk sat *The Lottery and Other Stories*, by Shirley Jackson—my latest library loan. "The Lottery" was the last story in the collection, but I'd cheated and read it first. It was about a group of villagers who would gather together in the town square, draw names from a box, and stone to death the person who'd received the black mark. I wasn't sure if I liked the story, but it certainly had me thinking. I swallowed. "Um, yes, I guess I do."

While he stood there examining the jacket, I glanced at the board and saw that Dracula's real name was Mr. Cornelius. Not only was he was our homeroom teacher, but we'd be having him for English, too. Lucky, lucky me. "Well, then, Miss Lundquist," he said, "looks like you and I have something in common." And with that, he turned on one heel and waved a drumstick in the air like he was conducting an orchestra. "Okay, class, we have fifteen minutes left of homeroom, and I've got work to do. Please, if you do not have a book to read, you may choose one from the shelves. Anyone caught talking"—he glanced in my direction; there was a definite smirk on his face— "will be taken into the hallway and stoned to death."

A laugh escaped my throat, and the whole class looked at me like I'd completely lost my mind.

"So," Mr. Cornelius said, glancing around at the puzzled faces, "it appears that Miss Lundquist is the only one who caught my joke."

Every eye in the room was on me now. I shrugged, picked up my book, and buried my face, wishing I could disappear. But Mr. Cornelius was the least of my problems. Staring up at me from the center of page twenty-three was a crisp, clean hundred-dollar bill.

NINE

At noon, Brandi pushed her way through the lunch line. "April! Oh my gosh! Did you get one too?" Her eyes were wild and had the look of someone who'd just escaped Bellevue.

"Hey!" a short, pimply kid shouted from the back of the line. "What do you think, you're something special? Line's back here!"

I yanked Brandi in front of me and said to the lunch lady, "Can my friend get a tray, please? It's her first day here, and she's a little confused."

The lady was a new employee, complete with hairnet, smiley face button, and an amazingly noncynical attitude toward lying teenagers. "Oh, sure, honey," she said, plopping a clump of cheese ravioli onto a tray and handing it to Brandi. "Here you go, dear. Millie's got the green beans up ahead. Oh, and there's chocolate pudding for dessert. You don't want to miss that."

"Thank you." I shoved Brandi along and said, "Will you calm down? You're making a scene."

"I told you we never should have agreed to take Larry to school. Now look! We're taking money from a"—she paused and glanced around—"*hit man*. Do you realize what that means?"

Of course I was totally freaked out by the money that had mysteriously appeared on page twenty-three of my book, but what I really wanted to know was the size of Brandi's bill. It had to be smaller than mine since *I* was the one always sticking my neck out for Larry. "How much did you get?" I said.

She leaned in close and mouthed, "One-oh-oh."

I couldn't believe it. And I thought Mafia men understood about loyalty and devotion.

"How about you?" Brandi said.

I shrugged. "The same."

"Green beans, ladies?" It was Millie, with the shimmery pink lipstick and unfortunate chin stubble. The green beans were pale and limp, but I figured Millie had had her share of rejection in life, so I held out my tray and let her pile them high.

"Thanks, Millie." She gave me a big smile. "Listen," I said to Brandi, "just because he gave us money doesn't mean we have to accept it. We can just . . . give it back."

"What? Have you totally lost your mind?"

Right then, Tessie dumped a spoonful of watery chocolate pudding onto Brandi's tray and said, "Move along, girls, you're holding up the line."

The brown puddle on Brandi's tray reminded me of the night Sammy had crawled into my bed with a nasty case of diarrhea. "Oh, no thank you." I yanked my tray away, but it was too late. A big blob of pudding hit the floor. Tessie stood there in horror, staring at her splattered stockings. "Oh, shoot," I said. "I'm sorry, really, it was an accident." But when she looked up, her eyes were darting daggers at the two of us.

"Let's get outta here," Brandi said, giving me a quick shove. Once we were safely out of the lunch line, she added, "Listen, April, I thought you understood the rules of *La Cosa Nostra*. If a mobster gives you money, you don't say *anything*. And giving it back would be a major insult. I swear, you never know what he might do. It's all part of that"—she waved her hand around—"*Omerta* thing."

"Really? Are you sure?"

"Yes, I'm sure. Come on, picture it. 'Oh, uh, Mr. Luciano, we can't take your money, because, well, you earned it through extortion and murder, and it wouldn't be right. Besides, we're afraid you might kill us one day.' "

I looked at my plate of ravioli, wondering why I hadn't just taken the tomato, tofu, and bean sprout sandwich my mother had offered to make this morning. At least it wouldn't have reminded me of vomit.

"April! Brandi!" Olympia, all tan and breezy after spending her entire summer in Greece, was running toward us.

"Uh-oh. Brace yourself," Brandi said. "Olympia had a boyfriend this summer, her second cousin or something disgusting like that, and she's carrying pictures. She showed them to me in homeroom."

Oh, Lord.

Olympia grabbed the sides of my face and kissed both my cheeks with European flair. "Come on, you guys, I'm sitting over here," she said, pointing to a table. On it sat a half-empty Dannon yogurt cup and three stuffed grape leaves. Olympia was always on some diet that involved starvation, since her main goal in life was to fit into size twenty-six Levi's.

"So, how was Greece?" I said, setting down my tray and quickly scanning the cafeteria. Larry, I noticed, was sitting with his class, nibbling on a piece of bread, looking totally bored. Dominick was in his usual corner with his motley crew of pothead and wannabe musician friends, scarfing down what looked like the remains of a baloney sandwich. As I took my seat, I patted the drumsticks, which were neatly tucked away in my left sock. As promised, Mr. Cornelius had given them to me right before lunch.

"Greece was *fabulous*," Olympia said, handing Brandi and me each a stuffed grape leaf. "Try one. I made them myself. It's my grandmother's recipe."

I stared at the thick green wrinkly ball. Even my

mother wouldn't subject me to this. "Thanks," I said, unhooking the rubber bands from my braces. Brandi, I noticed, had set hers aside. I held my breath, popped the thing into my mouth, and chewed. It tasted like dirt. "So," I said, taking a swig of milk, "why was Greece so *fabulous*?"

Olympia smiled and stirred her yogurt. "Well . . . I met a guy."

"Oh, yeah?" I swallowed the remains of the grape leaf, doing my best not to choke.

She nodded. "His name's Alexei."

"Oooo, Alexei," I said. "Sounds . . . sexy."

"Oh, please." Brandi snorted. "Must we rhyme?"

I chased the grape leaf with a bite of ravioli and made a mental note to pack a lunch for tomorrow. "Yes," I said, "we must. Olympia, tell me more."

"Well, okay." She took a dainty spoonful of yogurt. "He's eighteen, which, I know, sounds a little weird, but in Greece it's totally normal for girls to date guys who are much older."

Brandi nodded. "Yeah, I hear they marry their cousins, too."

Olympia glared at her. "I told you, Alexei is *not* my cousin. He's a distant relative. *Very* distant."

Brandi shrugged. "Whatever. Same thing."

"Anyway," Olympia went on, "I have pictures. Want to see them?"

"Oh, yeah, definitely."

While Olympia dug into her bag, Brandi leaned over

and whispered, "Doesn't she know that incest is a serious crime in the United States?"

I stifled a laugh, stuffed a few more pieces of ravioli into my mouth out of sheer hunger, washed it down with another swig of milk, and suddenly noticed that Dominick's seat at the far end of the cafeteria was empty. I looked around, but he was nowhere to be seen.

"Here you go," Olympia said, handing me a monstrous stack of photos. "Tell me what you think."

I pushed aside my tray and began shuffling through the pile. At first there were the usual pictures of Olympia's ancient, leathery-faced relatives, but before long I came to a shot of a dark, curly-haired, extremely good-looking guy in a fishing boat. There was a huge smile on his face, and in his hand was a slimy purple sea creature. "Olympia?" I said. "Is this Alexei holding an octopus?"

She laughed. "Yep. That's how we met. I went swimming in the Aegean Sea one morning, and that octopus attacked me, suction cups and all." She shuddered. "It was *soooo* disgusting. Anyway, Alexei heard me screaming, so he dove in from his boat and pulled it off my neck."

I looked at her. "You've got to be kidding."

"No, I swear," she said, crossing her heart. "That's exactly what happened. Later that day we found out that our grandparents knew each other."

Brandi nudged me. "Yeah, April. Didn't you hear? It was in all the newspapers: Greek God Rescues American Beauty from Neck-Sucking Octopus."

"Very funny," Olympia said.

I studied the picture. "Well, he's gorgeous."

She smiled. "Thanks. He's really nice, too. He'll be at university this fall, but we're going to write. Hopefully we'll see each other next year."

Brandi swiped the photo from my hand. "I don't know, Alexei's all right, I guess, but I kind of like the octopus."

I balled up my napkin and threw it at her. "Jealous."

"Oh, all right," she finally conceded. "Alexei is gorgeous, and *sexy*, and I'm sure he's got this fabulous personality. But what I want to know, Olympia, is when are you going to tell us all the juicy details?"

Olympia licked the last dab of yogurt off her spoon. "Never."

"Hah, some friend." Brandi picked up her grape leaf, popped it into her mouth, and gagged. "Jeez, Olympia, this thing tastes like crap!" She spit it onto her tray. "Are you trying to poison us, or what?"

While the two of them argued about the grape leaf, I continued flipping through the stack of photos. There were several more of Alexei on his boat, and plenty of Olympia and Alexei together—holding hands in Athens, arm in arm at the Pantheon, kissing beside a fountain in Corinth—but soon I came to a picture that Olympia might have wanted to censor for her own personal viewing. It showed Alexei, posing against the side of a cliff in a skimpy orange Speedo, legs slightly apart. It was practically obscene.

"So," Olympia said, tapping my toe with her foot. "Enough about the stupid grape leaf. Brandi tells me you have a date Friday night."

I looked up from the photo. "I do?"

"Yes. Did you forget about Umberto?"

I rolled my eyes. "Oh, please. Did you have to remind me?"

Suddenly, both Olympia and Brandi fixed their gazes on something behind me. Brandi's eyes widened.

"What?" I said, spinning around. And there stood Dominick, grinning at the photo of Alexei. "So," he said, plucking it from my hand, "this is what you SP girls do at lunch. Pass around pictures of naked men. Interesting." He looked at me. "Do you have the sticks?"

Mortified, I practically flung the photos at Olympia. "That's her cousin, I mean, her boyfriend. I mean, it's not my picture."

"Uh-huh, right. And I guess you don't have a date Friday night with Umberto, either." His eyes bored into mine.

"No, actually, I don't. I'm doing that as a favor for her." I pointed to Brandi.

"I see."

Brandi glared at me. "Why, may I ask, are you explaining this to him?"

I shrugged and Dominick tapped my shoulder. "What about the sticks?"

"Oh, right. They're in my sock."

"Well, come on, then. Let's get Larry."

Without thinking, I stood up and was about to follow Dominick through the maze of tables. "Oh, wait a minute," I said, turning to face Brandi and Olympia. "I'll meet you guys out in the schoolyard, okay?"

Brandi wouldn't even look at me. Olympia blinked a few times and said, "Yeah, sure, April. We'll see you outside."

As soon as Larry saw Dominick and me heading for his table, he sprang from his seat and began running toward us. Dominick leaned over to me. "I hear Larry's father is Soft Sal Luciano."

"How did you . . . ?"

He shrugged. "News travels fast. You live dangerously, don't you?"

The truth was, about the most dangerous thing I'd ever done in my life was take a flying leap over a johnny pump when I was ten years old, but instead of confessing this to Dominick, I said, "Yeah, I guess I do."

After Larry joined us, we walked out of the lunchroom, through the schoolyard, and past the handball courts, and hopped the fence into the neighborhood playground. The whole time, people stared, and I had to admit we looked like a comical version of the Mod Squad: gawky, blond SP girl; musical rebel; and retarded drummer boy on a secret mission in kiddieland. Dominick's friends were gathered near the see saws, and as they stepped aside, I saw what they'd been looking at—a drum set. I thought it resembled the one from Mr. Ruffalo's band room, and in the back of my mind I knew this probably wasn't a good thing, but I decided not to dwell on it. After all, I was the girl who worked for Soft Sal Luciano. I lived dangerously.

When Larry saw the drums up ahead, he got real excited and quickened his pace. Dominick waved to his friends. Pee-Wee, king of the burnouts, held up a guitar and called, "Come on, man, let's play some music!"

Ronnie, the bass player, laughed. "Wicked! Far out!"

A crowd of fans had begun to form, and one of them, I noticed, was Roxanne DeBenedetto—Dominick's ex-girlfriend. She sat atop a stone chess table with a group of friends, flashing that cute little gap between her two front teeth. She and Dominick had gone out for nearly six months last year—January through mid-June (I kept track)—until she dumped him for Chris Capelli, whose family owned a beach cabana on the Jersey shore. I guessed Roxanne was a real heartbreaker, because rumor was, now that she'd had her Malibu tan, she'd given Chris the ax too. Lucky, lucky me.

"Hey, Dom!" she called. "Brought some friends along, huh?" Her posse eyed Larry and me and broke into laughter.

Dominick glared at them. "Yeah, maybe I did. What's so funny?"

"Oh, nothing," Roxanne said with a wave. "We were just wondering, that's all." She lit a cigarette, took a long drag, and watched me with an amused expression.

Dominick leaned over and whispered in my ear, "Ignore her."

Easier said than done.

Larry had no clue that they were laughing at the two of us; in fact, he even joined in. As I stood there feeling like a complete idiot, Dominick cleared his throat and announced, "All right, everybody, listen up! We've got a new member of our band. In fact, he's the best damn drummer I've heard in a long, long time." He took Larry's hand and raised it over his head. "This, my friends, is Larry Luciano!" All the potheads and wannabe musicians started to cheer. Larry grinned a mile wide. "And," Dominick went on "last but not least . . ." He stooped over, rolled up my jeans, and pulled out Larry's drumsticks. "This is April! Keeper of the Sticks!"

Everyone went wild. It was like something out of a dream or even a movie. I could hardly believe it was happening to *me*. I didn't even care anymore about Roxanne and her stupid friends, and when the cheering died down I met her gaze while she flicked a cigarette ash in my direction.

Dominick handed the sticks to Larry and said, "Do you know any songs from *Quadrophenia?*"

Little did Dominick know, the Who was Larry's favorite band, and Keith Moon was his absolute hero. Larry nodded enthusiastically, and after Dominick led me to one of the swings for a front-row seat, the two of them took their places and began to play.

They started with "Love Reign O'er Me," and after that went into "Behind Blue Eyes." Dominick played lead guitar and sang, Pee Wee accompanied on rhythm guitar, and Ronnie did backup vocals and bass. It all sounded really good, but what amazed me the most was the way Larry and Dominick fed off each other. Dominick would play this amazing riff, and then Larry would join in with this awesome beat, and soon they'd transition into something else that blew everyone away. The whole thing was magical. I could tell they felt it too, because while they were playing they kept nodding and grinning at each other. It was as if they were saying, Yeah, we're good together, *really* good.

For a while I kept my eyes peeled for Brandi and Olympia, but since I knew they'd never break the rules and hop the fence into the playground, I gave up and just listened to the music, swinging gently in my swing. I thought Dominick and Larry would have gone on like that forever, but before long the fifth-period bell rang. Sadly, Dominick set down his guitar and clapped Larry on the back a few times, and as the band gathered their stuff and the crowd disappeared, he walked over to me. "So, what'd you think?" His eyes were black and sparkling in the sun.

I glanced toward the chess tables, glad to see that Roxanne and her friends had already hopped the fence and were making their way back to school. "I think you guys were awesome," I said.

"Yeah? Really?"

"Uh-huh."

Dominick sat in the swing next to mine and scooted

up beside me. He gazed into my face and smiled. "You've got such pretty eyes, and . . . I like your hair. It's so, well, blond."

I laughed a little, twirling the ends. "Yeah, I guess it is." And then he did something that totally shocked me. He leaned even closer and brought his lips to mine. As we began to kiss I panicked for a second, thinking my braces were going to get in the way, but I soon realized that teeth were not involved in kissing. Once I relaxed, it was perfect—soft, lingering, dreamy—better than I had imagined. When we were done, I just sat there looking at him.

"Wow," he said, "I think you're pretty awesome, too."

It could have been my imagination but as Dominick went to get his guitar, I thought I saw Roxanne peering at us from behind the handball courts. When I turned to get a better look, she was gone.

TEN

I decided not to tell Brandi and Olympia about kissing Dominick in the playground. Instead, I went home that afternoon, tucked the hundred-dollar bill under my mattress, lay on my bed, and replayed the moment over and over in my mind.

It's embarrassing to admit, but I'd never kissed a guy before. I mean *really* kissed. There had been that incident with Thomas Hildebrand in sixth grade when I'd made the mistake of letting him give me a light peck at Olympia's Halloween party. The next day he rode his bike to my house and wrote THOMAS & APRIL in huge letters in the middle of the street with a white crayon. It took days to wear off, and during that time I had to endure endless agony from Matt and his idiot friends. Needless to say, I never spoke to Thomas again.

Anyway, kissing Dominick was a completely different

experience, and just like the hundred-dollar bill, I decided to tuck it away for a while until I knew exactly what to do. So the following morning when I scanned the schoolyard, unable to locate Dominick, and overheard some kids saying that he and Pee Wee had been suspended for the rest of the week on account of taking Mr. Ruffalo's drums, I was sort of relieved. I mean, I did feel sorry for him, for Pee Wee, too, but in the end, everything worked to their benefit.

Here's what happened: When news got out about their suspension, students began protesting. Even Mr. Ruffalo pled for a lesser charge, claiming that all they'd done was *borrow* the drums for one measly lunch period. However, Mrs. Brennan, our vice principal, didn't see it that way. She explained that, according to the New York City School Penal Code, taking a drum set off school property without permission was considered theft. This only fueled the fire, and by Friday, Dominick and Pee Wee were considered heroes of P. S. 201, sort of like a modern-day Robin Hood and Little John—in this case, stealing instruments from the rich and giving music to the poor.

I thought it was pretty funny, but of course Brandi didn't find any of it amusing. In fact, she was horrified that I'd been, in her words, "an accomplice to a crime." "Whatever you do," she said as the two of us were getting ready in my room for our big double date, "do *not* mention any of this to Walter and Umberto. I don't want them getting the wrong idea about us, if you know what I mean."

"Oh, please," I said, buttoning the back of her shirt. Actually, it was *my* shirt, but what else was new? "Are these two guys such amazing dorks that they can't even laugh at a funny story?"

"It's not funny," Brandi said. "That . . . that creep, whose name I refuse to mention—"

"You mean Dominick?"

"Whatever. He put you in serious danger. You could have gotten into a lot of trouble, April. Don't you realize that?"

Before I could respond, the doorbell rang. I looked at the clock—7:30 on the dot. "Oh, well, I guess that's them."

Brandi thought it would be more appropriate for me to answer the door alone while she waited on the sofa. "I don't want to seem too anxious," she said, taking a seat. "Besides, it's your house." She licked her lips a few times and crossed and uncrossed her legs.

I sighed, rolled my eyes, and headed for the door. When I opened it, two guys stood in front of me, each holding a single red rose. I suddenly realized I didn't know which one was Walter and which one was Umberto. In a moment of sheer selfishness, I prayed the one on the right was Umberto, since he was much better-looking. But of course, the one on the left held out the rose. "Hi," he said, "I'm Bert."

"Oh . . . hi."

"This is for you."

"Right, sorry." I took the rose from his hand, and one of the thorns stabbed my thumb. "You really didn't have to get me anything."

He shrugged. "It's just a flower."

Suddenly, out of nowhere came a burst of cheers, whistles, and applause. I peered over Umberto's shoulder and saw that Matt and his stupid friends were gathered at the bottom of our stoop. Apparently, they'd witnessed the entire thing. "Whoa-ho," Big Joe said, "what do you know? The Monk's got a date." He grinned. "Maybe two."

"Kinky," Fritz said.

Matt, decked out in Shakespearean costume for his dress rehearsal—frilly shirt, velvet tunic, feathered cap, and ballet tights—gave Big Joe a shove and whacked Fritz on the back of the head. After that he stood there gaping.

Tony piped up. "Hey, Ape, ain't you gonna introduce us?"

Little Joe, I noticed, had taken a seat on the curb and was peeling bark off the trunk of our tree. He turned around, and when our eyes met, he frowned and quickly looked away.

At this point Walter's face was beet red, but Umberto didn't seem to mind the teasing. "It's okay," he said, "my sister and her friends put me through this already. I'm immune." He spun around and gave them a friendly wave. "Hey, guys. I'm Bert, and this is Walt. We're taking April and Brandi to the dance at Xavierian."

"Oooo, Xavierian," Tony said while the rest of them

cracked up. But before he could make one of his stupid "fairyland" jokes, I cleared my throat and gave him a frigid stare. He knew darn well that if he said one more word, I might just tell Fritz that Tony'd been making out with Fritz's girlfriend last week. *That* would go over big.

"Ignore the imbeciles and come in," I said, practically shoving them into the foyer. I stuck out my tongue at the fools before slamming the door. Brandi was still sitting on the sofa.

Slowly, Walter walked over and handed her the rose. "Thank you," she said. "Is your brother waiting outside in the car for us?"

I sure hoped so. I wanted to hightail it out of there before my parents and Sammy came upstairs for an inspection. Right now they were in the basement watching *Mutual of Omaha's Wild Kingdom.*

"Um, no, actually, he's . . ." Walter paused, glancing toward the door. The poor guy was incredibly nervous. He could hardly speak.

"Well, you see," Bert said, helping him out, "Walt's brother figured we might be a while, so he went to get a slice of pizza. We've already stopped by Brandi's house and met her parents." He grinned at me. "Now it's your turn."

"April? Was that the doorbell?" My mother was climbing the stairs now, and from the sound of it, Sammy and my dad were trailing behind. When she reached the top and saw Brandi and me each holding a rose, she took in a breath and said, "Oh, how nice! Let me get the camera!"

Meanwhile, my dad and Sammy entered the living room. "Soooo," my dad said, scratching the back of his head, "you guys must be . . . ?" I guess I had failed to mention their names during dinner.

Umberto held out his hand. "Hi, Mr. Lundquist. I'm Bert, and this is Walt."

As they shook hands, Sammy ran to my side and wrapped his arms around my waist. "April, don't leave," he whined. "You promised to read to me before bed, remember?"

I didn't recall any such promise, and when I saw Sammy give Umberto a dirty look, I realized what was going on. The little fibber was jealous.

By now, my mother had returned with the camera and had already taken a few "natural" shots. "Oh, Sammy," she said, "don't be silly, I can read to you tonight."

Sammy wrinkled his nose and pressed his face against my stomach. "Please stay," he moaned.

"Hey, sorry about that, bud," Umberto said, walking over and patting him on the head. "I mean, I understand how you feel. There's nothing like a good book. Alfred Hitchcock's *Stories to Be Read With the Lights On* is my favorite one right now."

I looked at him, stunned.

My mother laughed. "That's funny. April just read the entire Alfred Hitchcock series this summer."

Did she really *have* to mention that?

"Wow," Umberto said, as if we had something in common.

"Yeah, well, we'd better get going," I said, pulling Sammy off me. I gave him a shove toward my father.

"No, no, not yet," my mom said, holding up the camera. "I need to finish this roll. It'll only take a minute."

After posing in various groupings by the fireplace, mantel, and stairway, the four of us said our goodbyes and escaped through the back door. Out front I could hear the tinkling melody of the Mister Softee truck. I hoped to God the ignoramuses would be too busy stuffing their faces to bother with us. No such luck. They'd already purchased their frozen confections and were waiting with bated breath.

"So," Matt said as we drew near. He pointed his chocolate-dipped cone at the two boys. "Which one of you is taking out my sister?"

"That would be me," Bert said, not skipping a beat. I had to give him credit. Any ordinary person would have busted out laughing, being interrogated by a guy in tights.

"Uh-huh, I see." Matt looked Bert up and down, finally fixing his gaze on his shoes. They weren't exactly platforms, but the heels were a good three inches high. Matt arched an eyebrow and smirked.

Big Joe took a step closer. There was a dollop of vanilla custard with rainbow sprinkles on the tip of his nose. "Listen up," he said, "you two better treat these girls right, you understand?"

Umberto nodded slowly, and Walter leaned against the fence like he was about to keel over and die.

Tony and Fritz joined in. "That's right," Tony said, taking a bite of his pink strawberry shortcake, "because if you don't, you'll have to deal with *us*."

Fritz pointed his Bomb Pop at poor Walter. "Listen, kid, I'll be talkin' to Brandi tomorrow. So if I were you, I'd be a perfect gentleman. Get my drift?"

Little Joe was the only one not participating in the interrogation. He sat alone on the curb, eating a blue Italian ice with a wooden spoon. He wouldn't look at me.

"Will you guys cut it out?" Brandi said. "I mean really, what's your problem?"

She took Walter by the arm, marched toward the street, and peered up and down for any sign of Walter's brother. Nothing. That was when Larry came barreling out of his house. "Wait! Wait!" he yelled, flying down the stoop. "Mister Softee, don't leave yet!"

Mr. Luciano was trailing behind, clutching his wallet. When Little Joe saw him, he stopped digging a crater into his Italian ice and locked eyes with Matt.

Umberto leaned over to me. "Do we have to meet these guys too?"

"Oh, no," I said. "They're just our neighbors."

He laughed. "I was joking."

"Oh. Sorry."

Mr. Luciano crossed the street, and when he saw me standing in front of our house, he waved and called out,

"April! Sweetheart! Wait there a minute, okay? I need to talk to you."

Brandi turned to me with frightened eyes, and my stomach flipped. Slowly, I lifted one hand and waved back. "Sure thing, Mr. Luciano."

He waited patiently at the back of the Mister Softee truck while Larry placed his order. Meanwhile, Matt inched over to me. "Since when does he call you sweetheart?"

I shrugged. "I'm . . . not really sure."

Little Joe got up from the curb; his mouth was a deep shade of blue from the ice. He joined Matt, who stood there adjusting his tights and tugging at the collar of his ruffled shirt. The two of them looked completely ridiculous. Little Joe turned to me. "What do you think he wants?" I realized it was the first time he'd spoken to me since the bikini incident at the Jersey shore.

"I don't know," I said, "probably something about Larry."

He nodded and stared at Umberto's shoes. "Um, April, did you notice the guy's wearing platforms? Without them he's about five inches shorter than you."

"They're not platforms, they're heels," I said, wondering why I was sticking up for Umberto.

By now, Mr. Luciano had paid for Larry's double-dip cone and was strolling toward us. As usual he was decked out, this time in a gray pinstriped suit with a maroon shirt and white tie. Perched on his head was a fedora. He stopped for a moment and slid his wallet into his back pocket, which allowed me to notice a handgun tucked into his belt. Matt must have seen it too, because at that moment all the color drained from his face.

"Sweetheart," Mr. Luciano said with an affectionate smile. "Listen, I really want to thank you." He paused and tipped his hat at Brandi. "Actually, I want to thank *both* of you for taking such good care of Larry. That music teacher, what's his name, Mr. . . ." He snapped his fingers a few times. "Ruffalo. Yeah, that's it. He called today. Wants Larry to play drums at the Christmas concert this year."

Larry stood by his father's side taking messy bites of his cone. He lifted his eyes and grinned.

"Wow, Larry," I said, "that's great. Really, I'm proud of you."

"Yeah," Brandi said. "Congratulations, Larry."

Mr. Luciano patted him on the back. Then he turned to Matt, eyeballing his tunic and tights. "So, Matt, looks like you've got a dress rehearsal tonight, huh?" His voice was friendly.

Matt blinked, and I saw his Adam's apple move up and down. "You . . . know about the play?"

For some reason Mr. Luciano thought this was funny. He laughed out loud. "Of course I know about the play. In fact, one of my business associates has a daughter who's got the part of Juliet. Small world, don't you think?"

Matt nodded. "Yes, I guess it is."

Big Joe, Fritz, and Tony continued chomping their

Mister Softee treats like nothing was wrong with this picture while Brandi, Little Joe, and I exchanged knowing glances.

By now, Larry's ice cream cone was melting quickly, and as Mr. Luciano whipped out a handkerchief to wipe Larry's hands, I got an even better view of his gun. "Well," he said, "it's getting late, and I've got to get Larry home. But listen, Matt, good luck with the play. What's that expression again? Oh, yeah, break a leg."

Brandi gulped and Little Joe's mouth fell open.

"And you," Mr. Luciano said, chuckling and pointing the soggy handkerchief at Little Joe, "take care of your buddy, all right? You never know what might happen to a guy wearing a dress. Especially in this neighborhood, if you know what I mean."

He winked and Little Joe smiled weakly. "Yeah, sure, Mr. Luciano. I'll take good care of him."

At that moment, Walter's brother pulled up in an old station wagon. He popped the last bite of a slice of pizza into his mouth and rolled down the window. "Bohemian Rhapsody" poured into the street. "Hey, are you guys ready?" he called.

By now, Mr. Luciano and Larry were halfway home. Quickly, I pulled Matt aside. "Listen, Matt, I'm not stupid. I know what's going on. I know about Bettina, and I know about her father. You're in trouble, and whatever you're doing, you need to stop. You can't see her anymore."

Matt didn't say anything for a while; he just stood

there staring into space. Finally, he took a deep breath. "Listen, Ape, don't worry about me. Just go ahead. Have a good time at the dance."

"But how can I have a good time when—"

"Go on," he said, sounding more like his rotten old self. "Get outta here. I mean it."

I turned to Little Joe, but he just shrugged like Matt was the most stubborn person in the whole world and there was nothing either of us could do about it. Reluctantly, I joined the others and climbed into the backseat of the car. As we drove off, Matt cupped one hand around his mouth and called out, "You punks better have my sister home by eleven! I'll be waiting up!"

ELEVEN

The dance turned out to be a disaster. Not so much for Bert, Walt, or even me, as for Brandi. In the car she sat on a slice of pepperoni that had fallen off Walt's brother's pizza and wound up with a big grease spot on her butt. If this wasn't bad enough, a few minutes into the dance Walt spilled red punch all over her blouse—actually, *my* blouse—then tried to mop it up with a wet napkin, leaving her with a big pink see-through stain. Let's just say it was a mistake for Brandi to wear a lace bra that night.

Anyway, after drying herself off with the hand dryer in the girls' bathroom, she seemed to shake it off, but when Walt refused to dance, claiming he had two left feet (he actually used that expression), this sent her over the edge, and for the rest of the night, she and I did the New York Hustle while Bert and Walt ate miniature tuna fish sandwiches and watched.

Needless to say, we got home way before eleven, and to my surprise, Sammy and my parents were already asleep. I hated to admit it, but I was a little disappointed. For some reason I'd imagined that my first date would be like one of those corny sitcoms where the parents pace the floor chewing their fingernails until the girl comes home and they barrage her with questions. But I guess after meeting Bert and Walt they were just glad I was out "having fun" with a couple of "nice boys" instead of sitting in my room playing Grateful Dead albums and burning my skull candle.

Matt, however, kept his promise and was waiting up. "Hey, Monk, is that you?" he called from the basement. When I heard his voice, a flood of relief swept over me. Not only was he alive after his dress rehearsal, but it sounded like he was still in one piece.

"Yeah, it's me."

I plodded down the stairs and stared in disbelief. Matt, still in costume, now with Sammy's plastic toy sword in hand, was fencing with an imaginary opponent while playing my favorite Doors album on Sammy's Fisher-Price record player. As Jim Morrison belted out *Love me two times, ba-by, Love me twice today . . . ,*" he jumped on top of the coffee table, tossed the sword into the air like a baton, and caught it. There was a huge grin on his face. "So, how'd your date go with those two clowns?"

I lowered the music and studied his legs. I hadn't noticed

it before but you could see swirls of hair beneath his tights. Disgusting. "Um, o-*kay*, I guess."

"That shrimp in the platforms didn't try anything on you, did he?"

I rolled my eyes. "No, the shrimp in the platforms didn't try anything on me. Now, *what*, may I ask, are you doing?"

Matt leaped off the table and landed right in front of me. I could smell his Musk for Men aftershave. "I'm celebrating, Ape!"

I looked at him like he was crazy. "Celebrating? What, the fact that you're not dead?"

Matt chuckled and shook his head. "Oh, ye Chimp of little faith. Don't you realize the gods are in my favor? From now on, Mercutio is no longer. I, dear sister, have been given the part of Romeo." He took a bow.

My eyes widened. "You're kidding. What happened to . . . what's his name?"

"Oh, you mean Brandon Ritchie?" He shrugged. "Chicken pox. Poor guy."

He started to snicker and I gave him a shove. "Oh, yeah, right. You sound *soooo* sorry for poor Brandon." I couldn't believe I'd spent half the night worrying about Matt, and here he was celebrating Brandon Ritchie's chicken pox.

"Hey, is it my fault the guy's got bad timing? Now, watch this." He set down the sword and picked up two other props—Sammy's Fred Flintstone cup and my old life-sized Barbie. In his best British accent, he began to recite Romeo's famous last words. *"Here's to my love!"* He paused and took a sip of imaginary poison from the top of Fred Flintstone's head. *"O true apothecary! Thy drugs are quick. Thus with a kiss I die!"* He clutched Barbie to his chest, kissed her faded pink lips, convulsed a little, then keeled over. A moment later he stood up. "So, what do you think?"

"I think you're mental."

"Hey, come on, Ape. Can't you be happy for me? I mean, this is *big*. I've got the lead role. My career as an actor is about to take off."

"Right," I said, "and on opening night, you'll be kissing Bettina in front of like a thousand mobsters. Doesn't that worry you? Just a little?"

He tossed Barbie and Fred onto the sofa. "Monk, you're exaggerating."

"No, I'm not! Listen, Matt, you need to be careful. Every time I talk to Mr. Luciano, he asks these questions about you. It's seriously freaking me out."

He blinked a few times. "He does? Like what?"

"Well, like *this*." I cleared my throat and tried to make my voice sound raspy, like Marlon Brando's. "So, sweetheart, how's your brother? You know the one, Sunshine Boy? Is he keeping his nose clean? He's a nice kid and all, but sometimes nice ain't enough. You gotta be smart, too, if you know what I mean."

Matt's face twitched a little. "You know what, Ape? I think you've been watching too many *Godfather* movies."

"Matt!" I wanted to strangle him. "Come on! Don't you get it? We *live* in a *Godfather* movie. They're dangerous people. You can't mess around with them *or* their daughters. Brandi told me that Bettina's father is one of Colombo's *capos*. That's *huge*."

He rolled his eyes. "Yeah, yeah, I know."

"And what about that guy in the black Jaguar convertible—the one who picked Bettina up at the park? I'm telling you, Matt, he looked armed and dangerous."

"Him?" He waved this away. "Nah, that's just Bettina's overly protective cousin Nicky. He's harmless."

"Well, he sure didn't look harmless to me."

Matt sighed. "Listen, Ape, I know what I'm doing. Besides, except for play practice, I haven't seen Bettina or talked to her on the phone for two whole weeks."

Suddenly I remembered that little phone conversation I'd listened in on. "Okay," I said. "But what about when Bettina's father goes away on his little *business* trip? What are you gonna do then?"

Matt narrowed his eyes. "How did you know about that? Has Little Joe been talking to you?"

I shook my head. "It doesn't matter how I know. Matt, these guys have thugs working for them all over the place. I mean, is Bettina really *that* important to you?"

Matt didn't say anything for a while. He just stood there staring at me. Finally, he took a deep breath and flopped onto the sofa. "Yeah, she is. Totally worth it. You don't understand, Ape. You're too young."

I didn't appreciate this comment, but I was not about to bring up the fact that I, too, knew what it was like to be in love. Well, sort of. Ever since Dominick kissed me in the playground it was all I could think about. But now I had to try a different angle since Matt was being such a mule. "Okay," I said. "Think about this. What if Mom and Dad find out? I mean, they'll kill you before Colombo's hit man gets a chance to pour the cement."

Matt didn't think this was funny, and at the mention of our parents, his face darkened. He stood up and grabbed my arm. "You haven't said anything to them, have you?"

"No!" His fingers were digging into me. I tried shaking him off, but he grabbed me tighter. "Cut it out, Matt! That hurts."

"Listen, Monk." He was trying to sound tough, but I could see fear in his eyes. "*Swear* to me that you will *not* tell Mom and Dad about Bettina and me."

"Matt, stop!" He was scaring me now.

"I mean it!" he said. "*Swear.*" He looked like he was possessed.

"All right, fine. I *swear*. But only if you promise not to do anything idiotic. And if something happens, you need to promise that you won't see her anymore."

Matt shook me. "I already told you, Monk. I know what I'm doing."

"Do we have a deal, or don't we?" I said.

He gave me a lethal stare, but I didn't back down. Finally, he let go and waved me away. "Fine, whatever. Deal. Now, get outta here and leave me alone. And from now on, stay out of my freaking business!"

My arm throbbed and I felt a sob rising in my chest. I didn't want Matt to hear me cry, so I ran upstairs as fast as I could. In my bedroom, I punched my pillow over and over. At that moment I hated Matt more than I ever had in my entire life. But for some reason I knew I'd keep my stupid promise. I only hoped he'd keep his.

Brandi moped for most of the weekend, but on Monday morning, she greeted me with an enormous smile. "Guess what?" she said. "Walt called last night."

We were crossing the street, heading over to Larry's house. "Oh?" I said. "And you're happy about that?"

"Well . . ." She shrugged. "Yeah. I mean, I know he acted pretty lame at the dance, but after talking to him on the phone I realized that he's just shy. Anyway, he asked if you and I would like to play tennis with him and Bert next weekend. I said yes. I hope that's okay."

"What?" I was just about to ring Larry's doorbell; I stopped with my hand in midair. "Wait a minute. Walt asked if you and I wanted to play tennis with him and Bert, and you said *yes*?"

She nodded guiltily.

I threw up my hands. "Come on, Brandi, didn't the guy ever hear of *singles*? You know, two people, one ball?"

"Please?" she begged. "I already told him we would."

The consolation prize for going to the dance with Bert had been that I'd never have to see him or Walt again. But as usual, Brandi hadn't kept her end of the bargain. She looked at me with pleading eyes.

"Fine," I said. "Whatever. But I'm telling you right now, this is the last time. No more favors. A few games of tennis, and after that, you and Walt are on your own."

Part of me wanted to bring up the fact that I already had a boyfriend, well, sort of if you counted the kiss, and because of this I really shouldn't be giving Bert the wrong idea. But since I wasn't exactly in the mood for one of Brandi's lectures about what a creep Dominick was, I kept my mouth shut and pressed Larry's doorbell.

A moment later, Mrs. Luciano appeared. This morning she was all dolled up with fake eyelashes, teased hair, and bright red lipstick. "Hi, girls," she said with a big smile. "Come on in. Larry's almost ready. Oh, and I have a little surprise for you in the kitchen."

Brandi and I looked at each other. Surprises in the Luciano house could be just about anything—from pinches on the cheek to maybe a dead guy hanging in the freezer.

We followed her in, and as we passed a marble bench in the hallway, she patted it a few times and said, "Just leave your books here. You can get them on the way out."

We hesitated, and from the look on Brandi's face I could tell we were thinking the same thing. If we set down our books, Soft Sal would probably crawl out of the wood-work with a wad of bills and slip a couple more hundreds between the pages. However, Mrs. Luciano was eagerly waving us on, and wonderful smells were wafting from the kitchen, so we went.

Inside, on a red and white checkered tablecloth, sat two steaming cups of espresso and an assortment of Italian breakfast pastries. Mrs. Luciano smiled and said, "*Mangia, mangia*. Sweets for the sweet." It reminded me of the scene in *The Lion, the Witch and the Wardrobe*, where the beautiful White Witch gives Edmund the enchanted hot cocoa and Turkish delight. After that, he was in her service. Forever.

"Wow, thank you, Mrs. Luciano," I said.

Brandi was eyeing the pastries. "Thank you, but . . . we don't want Larry to be late for school."

Mrs. Luciano laughed. "Don't be silly! There's always time to eat! Now, enjoy. I'll check on Larry."

Already my mouth was watering, and as soon as she left, Brandi and I sat down and began stuffing our faces. We each ate two cannolis and two chocolate-covered biscotti, and let me tell you, after eating Grape-Nuts for breakfast for the past few months, it was heaven. We licked our fingers, drained our espresso, and with full bellies joined Larry and his mother in the living room. She was busy combing his hair, and now Soft Sal was perched on his papal throne. Our books, I noticed, were no longer sitting on the marble bench, but lay on the coffee table directly in front of him. Talk about obvious. Brandi nudged me.

"So, girls," he said, reaching over and handing us our books. He even knew whose were whose. "Did you enjoy the pastries?"

"Oh . . . yes," I said. "Thank you, they were delicious." I elbowed Brandi, who, at the moment, seemed to have forgotten her manners.

"Oh, yeah," she said, "they were great. Thanks."

He nodded. "Wonderful, wonderful. We just wanted to do something nice, you know, since you girls have been so good to Larry."

I glanced at *A Clockwork Orange*—the book Mr. Cornelius had recently loaned me. I figured that if I'd had X-ray vision, Benjamin Franklin would have been staring up at me with some kindly words of advice like *He that lieth down with dogs, shall rise up with fleas.* "Um, Mr. Luciano," I said, "it's really not necessary to give us anything. I mean, we like helping out with Larry."

Mrs. Luciano was trying to make a part in Larry's hair. He pushed the comb away and gave me a big smile.

"Yeah," Brandi chimed in. "We don't need anything. Really."

Mr. Luciano laughed. "Nonsense," he said. "Everyone needs a little something every now and then. Besides, we've got plenty to spare." He looked at his wife. "Isn't that right, Marianne?" I noticed that no one was mentioning

124

the word "money," so it was hard to know if they were talking about cash or cannolis.

Mrs. Luciano reached over and pinched our cheeks. "That's right," she said, "not to worry, girls, we have *plenty*. Now, Larry, come here and let me fix your hair." She licked her thumb and was about to tame his cowlick when he dodged her and ran out the front door. "Oh, Larry!" she called, shaking her head. "Well, I guess you girls better run along."

Quickly, we said our goodbyes, and as we chased Larry up the street it finally hit me. Not only was my idiot brother dating a made man's daughter, but Brandi had been right. Whether we liked it or not, we were officially doing business with the Mob.

For some reason, Larry was in a very good mood this morning. He walked along the avenue singing "Pinball Wizard" and jingling change in his pocket. Brandi and I watched him closely as we turned the corner onto Eighty-fourth Street and P.S. 201 came into view. The chain-link fence was still a temptation for Larry, but we'd made a deal that he was not allowed to take out his drumsticks until *after* school, and even then, the fence was off-limits. Fair game was trash cans, stop signs, johnny pumps, and lampposts. "Larry," Brandi said, "you remember what we talked about, right?"

He'd been walking a few paces ahead of us, so he turned around, rolled his eyes like we were total morons, and sighed deeply. After one week of public school, Larry had acquired quite the attitude. "Yeah, yeah, I remember," he said. "But it doesn't matter 'cause Dominick's coming back to school today. We're gonna play music at lunch. I'm in his band."

"Whoa!" Brandi said. "Wait a minute, Larry." But he ignored her and plowed ahead. "See that, April," she whispered to me. "It's what you get for hanging out with that lowlife. You've created a monster."

When we caught up with Larry, he started singing "Pinball Wizard" really loud, hoping to drown out Brandi, but it didn't work. "Larry," she said, tugging on his sleeve. "Dominick and Pee Wee got suspended last week for stealing those drums. You can't play music with them at lunch anymore. You'll get in big trouble."

He stopped singing. "Uh-huh. We can *too* play. Dominick told me."

This got my attention. "Larry, what do you mean Dominick told you?"

He groaned and threw up his hands like he couldn't tolerate our stupidity any longer. "Dominick *called* me, okay?" he shouted. "Yesterday, on the *phone*. He said we could play in Mr. Ruffalo's room. I'm in the band."

This totally shocked me. How could Dominick call Larry instead of me? Especially since I was probably the only Lundquist in Dyker Heights and there must have been at least fifty Lucianos. It didn't make any sense.

But I didn't have much time to think about this,

because as we approached the schoolyard, there stood Dominick and Pee Wee surrounded by a pack of screaming fans. I swear, you would have thought Mick Jagger and Keith Richards had come to town. Anyway, all of this would have been all right, except for the fact that Roxanne DeBenedetto was there too. And from the look of things, *she* was Bianca, and Mick didn't seem to mind.

"Larry, my man!" Dominick called. He waved Larry over, completely ignoring me, and I got a sick feeling inside. As Larry ran to join the members of his band, Brandi shrugged and said, "Well, I guess it's no surprise that Larry and the juvenile delinquent wound up together. They're both destined for a life of crime."

TWELVE

All week Dominick was surrounded by his groupies, so we were back to square one in the barely-noticing-I-was-alive department. Occasionally, he'd offer me a smile in the cafeteria, or a two-finger wave from the water fountain, or flash me a peace sign in the hallway. I thought about giving him the full-blown silent treatment, the kind where you don't even make eye contact, but I figured that would be too obvious, like I was mad or something. Which of course I *was*, but I couldn't let *him* know that.

Anyway, Tuesday afternoon when I was at the orthodontist's office waiting to have my braces tightened (a bimonthly torture), I read this article in *Redbook* about body language and how it can tell you a lot about how a person feels. So, for the rest of the week, this is what I did: whenever I saw Dominick, I struck a cool, blasé pose, flicked my hair around, and chatted with my friends, even if I had nothing important to say. I wanted him to know that I was just fine, and that he was the last person on my mind.

But the truth was that all I could think about was Dominick and what an idiot I'd been. Not so much for kissing him (that part was pretty great), but for believing that our kiss actually *meant* something. I decided that from that point on, I would never let myself get so crazy over a guy. It certainly wasn't worth it. So when Friday rolled around and Dominick strolled over to our lunch table asking if I wanted to come and hear their band play in Mr. Ruffalo's room, I shrugged and said, "Oh, no thanks, maybe some other time." From the look on his face, I think it was the first time a girl had ever turned him down. "Besides," I added, "we SP girls have a whole new stack of naked men to look at, so I'm kind of busy."

He laughed. "Oh, okay, I get it. Well, have fun, but don't get too carried away. I guess I'll see you around?"

I flicked my hair and yawned a little. "Yeah, sure, see you around."

As he walked away, Brandi patted me on the back. "Congratulations, April. I knew you'd see the light. Eventually."

"Wow," Olympia said, watching him from behind, "he's really disappointed. In fact, I think you just broke his heart."

"Olympia, don't encourage her," Brandi warned. "He's bad news, and it's about time April realized it."

I sighed, popped a few carob-covered peanuts into my

129

mouth, and as Brandi and Olympia went back to their conversation about Julie Barone and how she really should be kicked off Boosters since she couldn't even do a cartwheel, I wondered what in the world I was trying to prove. If I was being honest with myself, I'd ditch the two SP goody-goodies, follow Dominick to the band room, listen to some cool music, and collect on my next kiss. I know that sounds pathetic, but I guess when you're in love, you don't exactly think straight. I mean, really, look at Matt.

The rest of the day dragged on, and when the last bell finally rang I picked up Larry from class and the two of us headed home. I was feeling pretty down since Brandi and Olympia had choir practice that afternoon and the only thing I had to look forward to over the weekend, beside worrying about Matt, was a tennis date with Bert and Walt. At the moment I didn't even have Larry to talk to since he was busy drumming on all the garbage lids that were still out from that morning.

As we walked along the avenue, I started thinking about what a jerk Dominick had been lately, but that got me even more depressed, so I tried to come up with an idea for the creative writing assignment Mr. Cornelius had given us. We had three weeks to complete a thousand-word short story. He hadn't given us a specific topic but said "write what you know," whatever that meant. My problem was, I didn't *know* much, and besides the fact that

I was in the pay of Soft Sal Luciano, my life was pretty boring.

.But just as I was considering a Dr. Jekyll and Mr. Hyde story with Matt as the protagonist, I heard someone call my name behind me. "April! Larry! Wait up!" I turned around and saw Dominick running toward us. His guitar case was strapped to his back, bouncing up and down with each step.

Larry stopped drumming, and a big smile spread across his face. "Hey, Dom! What's happening, man?" Since Larry had been initiated into the band he'd become fluent in rock star lingo. If I hadn't been in such a lousy mood I would have thought it was kind of funny.

When Dominick caught up to us, he put one arm around Larry and said, "Hey, not much, dude. Just wanted to say hi to my favorite drummer." Then he flashed me that amazingly cute smile. "So, April, what's going on?"

He said this like it was a perfectly normal question— like the two of us had been shooting the breeze all week. "Um, nothing," I said. "School's out and I'm walking Larry home."

He laughed. "Well, *yeah*, I can see that. What I'm trying to say is, maybe we can do something, you know, hang out, listen to music? You said we liked a lot of the same bands, right? And besides"—he leaned in a little closer— "we had a nice time in the playground that day, didn't we? I know *I* did."

Before I could answer, Larry said, "Yeah! Sure, Dom! You can hang out with us! Right, April?"

I rolled my eyes, said, "Whatever," and walked ahead of them.

"Hey, come on!" Dominick called. "What's with you? Why won't you talk to me?"

Because, I thought, kissing someone in the playground and then ignoring them for a week is not acceptable. Even if you are Mick Jagger.

I continued at a rapid pace, keeping my distance, but I couldn't help overhearing the two rock stars talk about how their band was really coming together and how awesome their first gig was going to be.

"Hey, Larry," Dominick said, "I really need to talk to April, okay?"

"Yeah, sure, Dom."

Larry went back to drumming the garbage cans while Dominick scooted up beside me. I tried to maintain my casual, blasé attitude, but it was getting more difficult with him standing so close. "Listen," he said, "I'm sorry we didn't get a chance to talk this week. I had some stuff I had to take care of, but now everything's cool, and I thought we could hang out."

I wondered if the "stuff" he had to take care of had anything to do with Roxanne DeBenedetto. "Oh?" I said. "What about *Bianca*?"

"Who?"

I could hardly believe those words had come out of my

mouth. I shook my head. "Nothing. I just . . . I don't *hang out*, okay? After school I have to take care of my little brother, Sammy. He's in kindergarten."

"That's cool," Dominick said. "I can help. I like little kids."

I looked at him. His wavy brown hair had grown even longer since the summer, and as he tucked a lock behind his ear, I noticed a gold hoop in his newly pierced lobe. On top of this, today he was wearing an especially evil-looking Black Sabbath T-shirt—the one that read SABBATH BLOODY SABBATH and featured a swarm of death demons hovering over their next mortal victim. It would have been enough to send my mother over the edge. "Um, I don't think so."

He leaned over, peering into my face. "Why not?" That was when I saw the silver marijuana-leaf charm dangling from a string of hemp around his neck. There was simply no way I could ever introduce him to my parents.

"Because my brother doesn't like strangers."

He flashed me that killer smile, and I felt something melt inside. "But . . . if I come to your house and meet him, we won't be strangers for long."

It was hard not to smile back. "No, I guess not."

"Please?" He nudged me a little. "Give me another chance? I promise not to bite." He turned around and pointed to Larry. "Besides, if you're worried, Larry can be our chaperone."

I looked at Larry tapping out a rhythm on the nearby

fire hydrant. Some chaperone. "Well . . ." I figured we'd have about an hour until Matt came home from basketball practice and my parents got home from work. The only problem was that I'd have to think of some way to bribe Sammy into keeping his mouth shut about our new house guest. "All right, I guess you can come over. For a little while."

"Great," Dominick said. He smiled and patted his guitar case. "And if you're a good girl I might even play you a song."

My mother had this system worked out where Sammy walked home from school accompanied by a third-grade boy, Johnny Falcone, who lived around the corner from us. The two of them were supposed to open the back door with a key hidden in the old milk box, wait in our kitchen, and have a "healthy snack" before I showed up about fifteen minutes later. It was kind of funny because my mother thought Johnny was a "mature and responsible boy," but what she didn't know was that by the time I arrived, he and Sammy were parked in front of our TV watching *Dark Shadows* and stuffing their faces with Yodels and Ring Dings from Johnny's lunch box. She would have died.

Today, however, was different. As Dominick, Larry, and I neared my house, Sammy poked his head out the front door, and when he saw me, he jumped onto the porch and started waving his arms around. "April! Guess who's here? It's the girl from the park!"

The girl from the park. This didn't sound good. Quickly, I scanned the street to see if Soft Sal, Gorgeous Vinny, or Frankie the Crunch was spying on our house, but except for a few kids playing jump rope, the block was empty. I raced up the steps; Dominick and Larry followed. "Sammy, what are you talking about?" I opened the door and peeked inside, but as far as I could see, no one was there.

"Wow!" Sammy said, ignoring my question and pointing to Dominick. "You're the guy! The one"—he started to laugh—"the one who mooned us on the baseball field!"

Immediately, Larry started laughing like a hyena. I didn't even think he knew what mooning was. "Hey, Dom, that's cool, man! Did you really do that? Moon them?"

I wasn't quite sure, but I think Dominick was blushing. He squatted down beside Sammy and said, "Actually, I was mooning that punk Frankie Ferraro. He thinks he's hot crap at baseball. Believe me, he deserved it."

"Ohhhh," Sammy said, nodding. Absently, he scratched his ear with the Chewbacca action figure he'd been holding in his hand.

When Dominick saw Chewy, he said, "Hey, you're a *Star Wars* fan? I am too!"

Sammy smiled wide. "I've got the whole collection. Wanna see?"

"Yeah. Definitely."

Sammy took Dominick by the hand and pulled him into the foyer while Larry and I trailed after them. "Sammy?" I said, looking around. "What girl are you talking about? I don't see anyone." But then I heard voices coming from the basement, and a moment later someone was calling my name.

It figured that the one time I brought Dominick to my house, the place became Grand Central Station.

"April? April, is that you?" Now I was *really* confused. The person calling me sounded like Matt, but (1) he was supposed to be at basketball practice, and (2) it was the first time in years he'd actually used my name and not some kind of monkey derivative.

The four of us padded downstairs and there, to my surprise, in the middle of the floor, stood Matt and Bettina in full Shakespearean costume. "Come on down, sis!" Matt said, waving us on. "Oh, and bring your friends. Hi, Larry!" When Matt's eyes landed on Dominick, I braced myself. But what came out of his mouth was about the last thing I'd ever have expected. "And I see we have a musician here! A guitar player!" He took Bettina's hand and twirled her around. "Maybe he can play a song for us."

I swear, either Matt was on drugs or he'd gone completely psycho.

Dominick leaned over to me. "Wow, your family is like totally crazy."

Tell me something I don't know.

Most of the furniture in the room had been pushed out of the way to create a miniature stage, except for the sofa, where Little Joe and his cousin Marcella sat sharing a bag of my mother's organic whole-wheat pretzels. Little Joe stopped chewing and stared at Dominick. It was not a friendly stare.

Meanwhile Bettina walked over to me. "Hi, April, it's nice to meet you. I'm Bettina." She gave me a quick hug, and I noticed that she smelled like Yardley's Old English Lavender. "Matt's told me a lot about you."

"He *has?*"

Sammy elbowed me. "See, I told you. It's the girl from the park. Only she's all dressed up."

Bettina laughed and tousled his hair. "That's right. Sammy showed me his four-leaf clover that day. Which was pretty awesome. I'd never seen one before."

Larry had been standing there with his mouth hanging open. Bettina smiled at him. "Hi, Larry. It's me. Bettina."

For a second I thought it was really weird that she knew Larry, but then I realized, Of course she does. Their fathers are in the same crime family.

"But . . . ," Larry said, "it doesn't sound like you. You talk funny."

She laughed, reached over, and gave him a hug. "Oh, we're just rehearsing for a play, so I have to talk with this English accent."

Larry nodded slowly. "Ohhh."

Suddenly a loud "A-*hem*" came from the sofa.

"Oh, sorry," Bettina said. "This is my friend Marcella. She and Joe have been kind enough to be our audience."

"Hi, April," Marcella said. "Actually, Joe and I were the only two suckers they could find. Right, Joe?"

But Little Joe didn't even seem to hear her. He kept his eyes glued on Dominick and grunted. "Yeah, whatever."

"Anyway," Bettina went on, "I hope you don't mind us taking over your house. Matt and I really need to rehearse."

"Oh . . . no, not at all."

"Thanks." She strolled back to Matt, smiling mischievously. "Matt's having a little trouble with the suicide scene. He needs to learn how to die less, shall we say, dramatically?"

Matt grinned. "Okay, Juliet. Remember, I've only been Romeo for a couple of weeks. Cut me a break."

They were doing this teasing-flirting thing and it embarrassed me. I mean, really, this was my brother—the guy with the pimples who hogged the bathroom and flexed in the mirror every morning.

"Hey, Sammy," Dominick said. "Can we see your *Star Wars* collection a little later? I love *Romeo and Juliet*."

Sammy shrugged. "Okay."

So the four of us took seats against the wall while Matt sprawled out in the middle of the floor. Held loosely between his hands was the same Fred Flintstone cup he'd used before, so apparently he'd already drunk the poison and died. He closed his eyes and Bettina knelt over him. She began to recite, *"What's here? a cup closed in my true love's hand? Poison, I see, hath been his timeless end. . . ."* Dominick scooted closer to me and put one hand on my knee. Little Joe's eye's narrowed into slits. *"I will kiss thy lips. Haply some poison yet doth hang on them. . . ."*

When Bettina finally kissed Matt, he grinned, opened one eye, and kissed her back. She gave him a quick slap. "Cut it out, Matt!" she said. "You're supposed to be dead!"

"All right, all right." This was seriously getting to be too much.

Bettina picked up Sammy's toy sword. *". . . O happy dagger! This is thy sheath; there rust, and let me die."* I had to admit she did a pretty good job of killing herself. It was certainly way better than Matt's sorry excuse the other night.

As the two of them lay there motionless, Dominick started to clap. Loudly. "Wow!" he said. "That was awesome! Bravo!"

Now Little Joe looked like he was about to burst. "Who the *hell* are you?" he blurted out.

"Joe!" Marcella said. "That's rude!"

Startled, Matt and Bettina sat up.

"Oh, sorry," Dominick said, looking around. "I guess I should have introduced myself. I'm Dominick DeMao. April, Larry, and I go to school together."

"Yeah," Larry chimed in. "Me and Dom are in a band."

"Oh, really?" Little Joe said.

Sammy piped up. "And Dom's a *Star Wars* fan. I'm gonna show him my collection."

Little Joe was obviously not impressed. I wasn't sure, but I thought his eyes had landed on Dominick's necklace.

Matt, however, was still in Shakespearean la-la land. He stroked Bettina's hair. "Hey, Joe, what's with you? Why are you giving this poor guy the third degree?"

This was definitely *not* my brother.

"Yeah," Bettina said. "What's your problem, Joe?"

Little Joe frowned. "Nothing. *I'm* not the one with the problem." Then he stood up, shot a few more daggers in Dominick's direction, and stormed up the stairs.

Dominick leaned over and whispered, "I think that guy Joe may have a thing for you. He sure as heck doesn't like me."

"Oh, no," I said. "He's my brother's friend, that's impossible."

Now Sammy was studying all the rock band stickers on Dominick's guitar case. "Hey, Dom?" he said. "Will you and Larry play us a song? Please?"

Matt jumped up. "Great idea, Sammy! Enough rehearsing! Let's have some music! Let's dance!" He helped Bettina to her feet and twirled her around again. She started to laugh.

This was going to be interesting. I'd lived with Matt my entire life and never once had I seen him shake his booty. Even to Jim Morrison.

"I've got bongos up in my room," Sammy said. "Larry can use those."

Instantly Larry whipped out his drumsticks and said, "Solid! Bongos! I can dig it!" Everyone laughed.

"What do you say, Dom?" Matt said.

Dominick shrugged. "Sounds good to me."

"Okay then, let's take this party upstairs. See if we can get Joe out of his funky mood."

When we reached the kitchen, Little Joe was sitting at the table, brooding over a cup of my mother's Red Zinger tea. "Come on, Joe," Matt said. "Larry and Dom are gonna play a few songs for us. We're gonna party!"

But Little Joe just sighed, sipped the tea, and gazed out the window. "Nah, no thanks. You guys go ahead. I'll stay here."

Matt shrugged. "All right, man, suit yourself."

The rest of us gathered in the living room while Dominick took a seat on the piano bench and began tuning his guitar. Sammy ran to his room for the bongos, and when he returned, he placed them in front of Larry.

"So, do you guys like Skynyrd?" Dominick asked, still plucking the strings.

Matt nodded enthusiastically. "Yeah. Love Skynyrd."

"All right then." Dominick strummed the guitar a few times and the sound filled the room. "We'll do a few of their tunes." He turned to Larry. "Ready, man?"

Larry did a drumroll. "Ready!"

They started out with "Sweet Home Alabama" and

after that went into "Gimme Three Steps." At first I wasn't going to dance, but soon Bettina took my hand and pulled me into the center of the room. Before I knew it, all of us were shaking our booties around the living room like a bunch of crazy people. Let me tell you, it sure beat doing the Hustle with Brandi. We went on like that for a while, and then Matt started doing this stripper routine, lifting his tunic and showing us even more of his disgusting hairy legs. It was pretty hilarious.

After that, Dominick and Larry started "Free Bird," which is really slow and pretty in the beginning, so Matt took Bettina in his arms, and Marcella began slow-dancing with Sammy. Just as I was about to sit down and take a rest, Little Joe came out of the kitchen and said, "April, may I have this dance?" I was totally floored.

"Um . . . okay." At first I didn't know where to put my hands, I mean I'd never danced with one of Matt's friends before, but Little Joe took the lead. He held me a lot closer than I expected, and as we swayed back and forth I kept thinking about the bikini incident and could barely look him in the eye.

"So, is he your boyfriend?" Little Joe didn't seem angry anymore, just sad.

"Oh . . . you mean Dominick? No, not . . . really."

He hung his head for a moment, and when he raised it again he pulled me even closer. "Listen, April, be careful, okay? I don't want you getting hurt."

His face was really close to mine now, and for a minute

I actually thought he was going to kiss me. But just as I was about to say, "Don't worry Joe, I'll be fine," Mr. Luciano walked through our front door.

"Would you look at that?" he said. "You're having a party! Now how come I wasn't invited?"

THIRTEEN

We all stood there gaping. All of us, that is, except Larry. "Dad! Hey, Dad! Look! I'm playing the bongos!"

Mr. Luciano smiled and shook his head. He walked over to Larry and put one hand on his shoulder. "That's great, son, really, I'm glad you're having a good time with your friends. But your mother and I have been very worried. You're supposed to come right home after school. You know that."

Sammy gave me one of his uh-oh-you're-in-trouble looks.

Larry's face crumpled. "I'm sorry, Dad. It's just . . ." He looked around the room. "Well, first Dom wanted to hang out, and April said it was okay, and then we watched Matt and Bettina practice, and Sammy asked if we could play a song, and—"

Mr. Luciano laughed. "Larry, Larry, it's okay. I figured you were over here."

"It's my fault, Mr. Luciano," I said. "I should have taken Larry home first. I wasn't thinking."

"Yeah," Sammy agreed. "It's April's fault."

Jeez. Some brother.

Thankfully, Mr. Luciano gave me a reassuring nod. "No harm done, sweetheart. You're a good girl. I know you'd never let anything happen to Larry." I shot Sammy a smug look while Mr. Luciano smoothed Larry's hair affectionately. I glanced around the room. Matt, I noticed, was looking rather nervous, but Bettina had placed both hands on her hips and was rolling her eyes to the ceiling. According to *Redbook*, this would be labeled a "combative stance."

"Why, hello there, Bettina," Mr. Luciano said. "Fancy meeting you here."

"Hello, Sal," she answered dryly.

"Just Sal?" he asked. "Not *Uncle* Sal?"

"You're not my uncle."

"Well, that depends on how you look at things. According to your father, we'll always be family. He's uh, away on a business trip now, isn't he?"

She blew a wisp of hair from her forehead. "Yes, Sal, you *know* he's on a business trip. And for your information, we're just rehearsing for the play."

From across the room, I saw Little Joe and Marcella

casting worried glances at each other while Dominick set down his guitar and gazed at Soft Sal like he was some kind of celebrity.

"Ah, yes, the play," Mr. Luciano said. "And it looks like someone has a new dress." At first I thought he was talking about Bettina, but then I realized he meant Matt.

Matt glanced at his tunic and laughed nervously. "Oh, yeah. It's a different costume. I've got the part of Romeo now."

Mr. Luciano nodded. "Interesting."

"Not that I . . . *asked* for it, or anything," Matt said. "You see, Brandon Ritchie—he was the original Romeo—well, he came down with chicken pox and I was the understudy. Anyway, Bettina's here because I needed some extra practice. I'm not very good at the suicide scene." Matt swallowed and his Adam's apple jiggled up and down.

"Hmmm." Mr. Luciano tapped his chin. "That's kind of ironic, don't you think? You and Bettina, playing two . . . what do they call them? Oh, yeah, star-crossed lovers?"

Matt's eyes shifted back and forth. "Um, well—"

"Leave him alone, Sal," Bettina said. "We're rehearsing. That's all. As you know, I don't go out with boys. But when I'm thirty-five and my father gives me permission, I'm sure it will be with some fat, bald, greasy friend of his with connections and lots of cash."

Larry started laughing, and then Sammy joined in,

even though I was sure neither of them had any idea what Bettina was talking about.

"Whoa, whoa," Mr. Luciano said, putting up both hands. "Let's not get into that, okay, sweetheart? Especially in mixed company. Besides, I was just joking around. Matt knows that. Right, Matt?"

"Oh . . . sure, Mr. Luciano."

"Well then," he said, addressing the entire room, "I'm glad you kids are having a good time, but Larry and I better get home before his mother faints from worry."

"Wait, Dad!" Larry said. "I want you to meet Dom!" He grabbed his father's hand and pulled him to the piano bench. Dominick stood up. "Remember? I told you? Me and Dom are in a band!"

Mr. Luciano chuckled. "Well, of course. Hello there, Dom. Larry never stops talking about you." He shook Dominick's hand and surprisingly didn't seem to mind the long hair, satanic T-shirt, and hoop earring.

"It's nice to meet you, sir," Dominick said. "Larry's a great drummer."

Mr. Luciano nodded humbly. "Yes, well, unfortunately I can't take any credit. Larry gets all his charm, talent, and good looks from his mother's side of the family." Dominick smiled politely at the joke, but now Mr. Luciano's eyes were zeroing in on his marijuana-leaf necklace. "Hey, uh, Dom, you don't smoke that stuff, do you?" His tone was still friendly, but you could tell he meant business.

Dominick's hand flew to his throat. "Oh, no, sir. No. I've never touched it. In fact, I really don't know where I got this thing." He tucked the charm into his shirt. I had to say, he was a pretty convincing liar.

"Mm-hmm," Mr. Luciano said. " 'Cause I'll tell you right now, I don't want Larry hanging around with anyone who smokes dope." I thought this was a bit hypocritical, since it was common knowledge that the Mafia was into drug dealing, but I was not about to bring that up.

"Oh, no," Dominick agreed. "Definitely wouldn't want Larry hanging around with anyone like that."

Mr. Luciano gave Dominick a firm pat on the shoulder. "Great. Looks like we're speaking the same language, Dom. I like that. Oh, and one other thing." There was an amused grin on his face. "Don't go stealing any more drums from that band teacher, Ruffalo, okay? If you need something, just come and ask me."

Dominick blinked a few times. "Oh . . . sure. Thank you, Mr. Luciano."

"No problem. Now, Larry, we really need to go. Get your books and say goodbye to your friends."

After Larry had gathered his things, we said goodbye, but before leaving, Mr. Luciano turned to Matt and said, "I'll see you around, Romeo. Stay out of trouble, okay? And good luck with that suicide scene." I wondered if there was any hidden meaning behind that.

When they were out of sight, Matt sank onto the sofa and let out a gust of air. "So that went well, don't you think?"

Bettina took a seat beside him and gently kissed his cheek. "Don't worry, Matt, it'll be okay."

Meanwhile, Little Joe was frowning and mumbling to himself, "See, I told them we shouldn't have come here, but does anyone listen to me? Noooo." Suddenly he seemed to remember that Dominick was still in the room, and he went back to giving him the death stare.

"Hey, uh, Sammy?" Dominick said, glancing worriedly at Little Joe. "Want to show me that *Star Wars* collection now?"

Sammy's whole face lit up. "Oh, yeah! I almost forgot. Come on, it's up in my room."

As the two of them raced upstairs, Little Joe and Marcella took a seat on the sofa across from Matt and Bettina. It looked like they were about to have a what-to-do-when-the-Mob-is-after-you brainstorming session. I figured if Matt wanted me to leave, he'd certainly let me know, but for the moment, I decided to take an inconspicuous seat in the corner of the room.

"Listen, guys," Bettina said. "Don't worry. I've known Sal all my life. He won't say anything to my father."

Matt stared at her in disbelief. "But . . . Bettina, how can you say that? I mean, did you hear him?"

"It's true, Matt," Marcella said. "Sal talks a lot, but he'd never rat on Bettina. Besides, why do you think they call him *Soft* Sal?"

"Well, that's reassuring," Little Joe said, throwing up his hands. "I mean it's nice to know we're dealing with a sentimental murderer."

"Hey, Bettina?" Matt said. "What's your father's . . . you know, code name?"

She didn't answer.

"Go on," Little Joe said, "tell him, Bettina. Tell him what they call your father."

She sighed. "Okay, fine, I'll tell you. My father is Roberto 'Bobby the Bull' Bocceli, known for strangling a man with his bare hands and lighting a cigarette while the poor sucker took his last breath. Nice, huh?"

The room fell silent. I was beginning to feel a bit woozy, so I put my head between my knees and breathed deeply. Hushed voices rose from across the room, and Little Joe said something about the party being over. Just as I was about to get up and leave, I heard Bettina's dress rustling as she crossed the floor. "April?" I looked up and saw her face looming above me. "I can't stay much longer, but I was wondering, can we talk? Privately?"

"Oh, sure." Matt, Marcella, and Little Joe had gone to the kitchen to clean up, so I quickly led Bettina to my room and closed the door. Sammy's bedroom was right next to mine, and you could hear Dominick doing a Darth Vader impersonation while Sammy made Wookiee noises.

"I really like your posters," Bettina said, looking around. "Cat Stevens is one of my favorites. He's a great songwriter."

"Oh, thanks. Yeah, he is." It was kind of embarrassing since my room was a total pigsty, but Bettina didn't seem to mind. She tossed aside the half-empty bag of Bar-B-Que chips (my own personal stash) and took a seat on my bed. Hanging over my chair was a lace bra sprouting broken elastic and a pair of dirty underwear. I crumpled them into a ball and sat down.

Now she was looking at my half-melted skull candle. "I especially like that song," she mused aloud, "The Boy with the Moon & Star on His Head," from *Catch Bull at Four*. "It's so . . . deep."

I nodded. "Yeah, it is." I really liked that song too, but the truth was I had no clue what the lyrics meant. I tossed my dirty underwear into a corner. "So, what did you want to talk about?"

"Actually," she said, "I wanted to give you something."

Uh-oh. She pulled an envelope from her dress pocket, and I held up both hands. "Oh, no, please, I don't need anything, really."

She gave me a puzzled look. "But it's a letter. For Matt. I wanted him to have it in case . . . well, in case anything happens."

I stared at the envelope. I was relieved to hear there was no cash inside, but the alternative didn't sound too good either. "What do you mean?" I asked. "What might happen?"

"Well." She paused for a moment. "It's no secret about my family. You know who my father is. And he's made it clear who I can see and who I *can't* see."

I nodded, figuring that a blond-haired, blue-eyed sixteen-year-old Scandinavian boy was in the category of Can't See.

"And," Bettina continued, "I know this sounds weird because Matt's your brother and everything, but I really love him. He's so different from other guys. I've never met anyone like him before."

There was definitely some truth in that last statement, but I didn't think Bettina meant it the same way I did.

Now her eyes were starting to well up. "It's complicated. I mean, I know this sounds crazy, but in my own way, I love my father, too. And if anything should happen, like, if it becomes too dangerous for me and Matt to see each other, I want him to have this letter. It'll explain everything."

Reluctantly, I took the envelope from her hand. "All right," I said, my voice barely a whisper. "If anything happens, I'll make sure he gets it."

"Thank you." Now a tear was rolling down her cheek, but she quickly wiped it away. "I'd better get going. My mom's expecting me for dinner."

I hid the letter in my sock drawer and the two of us went downstairs. Matt, Little Joe, and Marcella were waiting by the front door. "Come on, Bettina," Matt said, "we'll walk you girls home. Well, halfway, anyway."

From the porch I watched the four of them stroll down the street. When they reached the corner, Matt took one look behind his shoulder, and when he saw that the coast was clear, gently placed his arm around Bettina.

A moment later, a loud voice bellowed from inside the house. "Luke Skywalker! This is your master, Darth Vader! Put down your light saber and surrender to the dark side of the Force!"

"No! Never! I will never surrender to you, Darth Vader!"

I stepped inside and saw Sammy and Dominick charging down the stairs, action figures in hand. They jumped onto the sofa and started wrestling.

I stood there shaking my head at the two of them, and when Dominick saw me he yelled, "Wait! Hold on, Luke! Now we must set aside our differences, join forces, and capture the beautiful Princess Leia!" He ran, scooped me up in his arms—which I have to say was an amazing feat since I was more like Helga the Gargantuan Viking Princess—and dropped me onto the sofa. Together, they started tickling me mercilessly.

"Cut it out! Sammy! You know I hate getting tickled!" I kicked and flailed and at one point I think I whacked Dominick right in the head.

They tortured me for a while, but amid all my protests I was basically enjoying the attention from Dominick. His breath smelled like spearmint gum, and I liked the way his hair felt when it brushed against my cheek. When I was completely out of breath and about to give up, I heard someone calling my name. "April?" Through a tangle of arms and legs I saw my mother and father standing just a few feet away. They did not look amused.

"Oh, hi, Mom! Hi, Dad!" Sammy jumped off the sofa and gave them each a hug. "We're just playing *Star Wars*."

"Uh-oh," Dominick whispered under his breath. He stood up and fluffed a pillow back into place. "Um, hi, Mr. and Mrs. Lundquist. Sorry about that. Sammy and I were just goofing around. I guess we got carried away. I didn't mean to—"

"Who, *exactly*," my mother interrupted, "are you?"

Before Dominick could answer, Sammy said, "That's Dom! April's new boyfriend!"

"What?" My mother's eyes widened. She turned to my father, but he just shrugged.

"Sammy!" I blurted out. "That's not true! I've never even *had* a boyfriend." I could have shot myself for offering that last bit of information.

"But . . ." He looked at Dominick, confused. "That's what Dom told me."

My jaw fell open. I was horrified yet intrigued at the same time.

"Oh . . . well." Dominick laughed a little. "I think you got that mixed up, Sammy. You see, April and I are just friends."

Surreptitiously, he turned and winked at me. I still wasn't quite sure how to interpret this, but I decided to play along. "That's right," I chimed in. "Actually,

Dominick came here to see Larry. Not me. They're in a band."

My dad didn't seem to be buying this. He looked at Dominick. "You're in a band with Larry? The kid across the street?"

"Yeah," Dominick said. "Larry's a great drummer. We play together at school."

"It's true, Dad!" Sammy said. "Larry was here before you guys got home. You should have seen it! He was playing my bongos, and Dom was playing the guitar, and Matt was dancing with Bettina, and I was dancing with Marcella, and then . . . well, Mr. Luciano came over to get Larry, and Little Joe said the party was over." He shrugged. "It was fun, though."

As Sammy blabbed, my parents seemed to be only half listening. In fact, they didn't even catch on that Matt and Little Joe were here with two strange girls. Instead, they were busy studying Dominick. While my mother focused her attention on Sabbath Bloody Sabbath's death demons, my dad took in the long hair, earring, and questionable necklace. I swear, if their thoughts could have been broadcast on their foreheads, they'd both have read: DANGER. SPAWN OF SATAN.

"Well, I'd better get going," Dominick said. "My dad's probably wondering where I am right now. It was really nice to meet you."

My parents nodded silently. Neither of them mentioned that it had been nice to meet him too.

Dominick handed Sammy his Darth Vader action figure and picked up his guitar. "Well, goodbye, April. I'll see
you at school." He patted Sammy on the head. "Bye,
Sammy. I had fun."

"Me too! Bye, Dom!"

As Dominick disappeared out the front door, I inched
my way toward the staircase.

"April!" my mom called in that no-nonsense voice of
hers as I raced to my room. "You better get back here! We
need to talk!"

FOURTEEN

The rest of the weekend was one miserable lecture after another. Friday night's topic, over a bowl of broiled tofu and steaming bulgur wheat, was how teenagers need to choose friends wisely. On Saturday morning when I cranked up my favorite Grateful Dead tune, my mother stormed into my room, flipped off the stereo, and gave me an earful about "these rock groups who promote drugs, sex, and suicide." After arguing with her that the Grateful Dead was actually a peace-loving, melodic band, I was informed that all good music died with Elvis, and was then handed the Lundquists' New House Rules, number one being: No strange boys allowed over when parents are not home.

As you can imagine, it was very tempting to spill the beans about Matt, their fine upstanding young son, sneaking around with Roberto "Bobby the Bull" Bocceli's daughter, but a promise is a promise, and I was not about to break mine. Besides, I had to admit, I liked Bettina, and Matt was way less of a jerk when they were together.

Anyway, by Sunday afternoon I was actually looking forward to smacking around a tennis ball, even if it was with Bert and Walt. The only downside was that Poly Prep, the snooty high school where Walt insisted we play because his family owned a permit, had a dress code: standard, all-white tennis gear. Since I usually played tennis in a ratty old T-shirt and cutoffs, I had to borrow my mother's hideous white skirt—the kind with the bloomers underneath—along with her collared Izod shirt, with the little alligator on the breast pocket.

"You know," I said, glancing in Brandi's full-length mirror and cringing, "I still don't understand why we couldn't just have played tennis at the park like we always do. Then we wouldn't have to wear these pathetic clothes."

She was sitting at her vanity applying mascara and paused for a moment to roll her eyes to the ceiling. Unlike me, Brandi had gone against her principles and used some of the money Mr. Luciano had given her to buy a Chris Evert tennis outfit. She even had matching socks with pom-poms. "Look, April, will you stop being so negative? I already told you. The courts at Poly Prep are really nice. Besides, Walt did this as a special favor, just for us. Remember, we're his guests."

I wanted to remind Brandi that *I* was actually doing

this as a favor for *her,* but at this point I figured it would be an exercise in futility.

"Anyway," she said, applying a few more strokes of mascara, "before we go, I wanted to give you the heads-up about Bert."

I narrowed my eyes at her reflection. "Bert? What do you mean?"

"Well . . ." She spun around. "I was talking to Walt on the phone last night, and he told me that ever since the dance Bert's had this mad crush on you."

"Brandi! Oh my God! I don't believe this."

"Come on, April, you got to admit, Bert's a nice guy. I know he's kind of short, and okay, not really that cute, but he's got a great personality."

I flopped on her bed. "Brandi, that's not the point!"

"Well, what is the point? Jeez, April, I didn't think you were so superficial."

"Superficial? Brandi, I already told you, Dominick came to my house Friday when you were at choir. We're sort of . . . together now."

"Then why hasn't he called you?"

I'd actually been wondering the same thing, but I was not about to say this. "I didn't give him my phone number, okay?"

"But you're the only Lundquist in the book."

"Will you shut up? Look, I know you don't *approve* of Dominick, but I really, *really* like him. For your information, he's nice, funny, talented, sweet—"

"Hold on. Did you just say sweet?"

"Yes! Look at the way he treats Larry. I mean, how many people would even bother with a fourteen-year-old retarded boy? And you should have seen him and Sammy together. Sammy absolutely loved him."

"Mm-hmm. Sounds like your parents did too."

"I don't care what my parents think. I'm sick and tired of trying to please them. Besides, nothing I do is ever good enough."

Brandi didn't say anything for a while. Finally, she picked up a brush, sat beside me, and began running it through my hair. "April, look, I'm sorry for giving you such a hard time about . . ." I could tell she wanted to say "that creep," but she stopped herself, "Dominick. It's just, there's something about him I don't trust. I mean, you *know* he's gotten into a lot of trouble at school, and it's not just the drum set he took, it's all the other stuff too, like cutting class, getting into fights, smoking pot in the bathroom. And what about Roxanne?"

"What about her?" I said.

"It's just, well, she's been hanging around him a lot lately. I know they're not going out anymore but still, you're my best friend. I don't want you getting hurt."

I sighed while she swept my hair up into a ponytail. Roxanne was not a person I wanted to think about right now. "Don't worry, Brandi. I'm not going to get hurt."

* * *

Since Walt's brother wasn't available to chauffeur and Poly Prep was within walking distance, we told Bert and Walt we'd meet them at the courts at three o'clock. It was a beautiful October day—the air was cool and crisp, the sky blue, and the leaves on the trees different shades of red, orange, and yellow. In fact, everything would have been perfect except for the big Lincoln parked on the corner outside Frankie the Crunch's house. It was like an ink splotch on a beautifully painted sky.

As we passed by, the electric window slowly rolled down. "Hi, dolls, playing a little tennis today?" Brandi and I looked at each other, then peered inside the car. In the driver's seat sat Gorgeous Vinny, and next to him was Frankie the Crunch. I wondered if Vinny was delivering a freshly killed body from his restaurant.

Frankie tipped his hat. "Hi, babes."

Brandi was hiding behind me now, breathing down my neck. "Oh . . . hi, Mr. Persico," I said. "Hi, Mr. Consiglione. Um, yeah, we're playing tennis at Poly Prep today."

Gorgeous Vinny nodded and glanced toward the backseat. It could have been my imagination, or Brandi making noises behind me, but I thought I heard a muffled yelp. "Listen," he said, "I just wanted to tell you, I talked to John Travolta's agent the other day—turns out he's definitely coming to town. I'll see if I can get you girls tickets for the show."

"Oh . . . thank you, Mr. Persico. That would be nice."

"Yeah, right," Brandi whispered in my ear, "not only is he a creep, he's a pathological liar."

"Okay, well, have a good time. Win a few games for me, huh?" Gorgeous Vinny winked, and I noticed that today he wasn't wearing his toupee. In fact, he looked like he'd had a pretty rough night.

"Yeah," Frankie chimed in. "Enjoy. Oh, to be young again."

As the window rolled up, I could have sworn I heard thumping coming from the trunk. Then again, it could have been my own heart pounding inside my chest. "Let's get out of here," I said to Brandi.

"Yeah, no kidding."

As we walked along the avenue crunching piles of dead leaves beneath our feet, I thought of the Lincoln getting crunched in one of Frankie's machines. But I didn't have too much time to consider this because a minute later Tony and Fritz popped out of Tony's driveway. "Whoa-ho, look who it is!" Tony said. "The Apester and Brandi." He cupped one hand around his mouth and called, "Hey, Matt, your sister's here!"

Oh, well, I thought, at least Matt wasn't bound and gagged in the back of the Lincoln. It wasn't long before the rest of the imbeciles piled onto the sidewalk.

"Just keep going," I whispered to Brandi. "Ignore them."

"Whoa, wait a second," Fritz said. "Let's get a better look at you two. Nice outfits. What's the occasion?"

"No occasion, Fritz," Brandi said. "Now leave us alone."

Little Joe took a seat on the hood of a parked Chevy while Matt and Big Joe barricaded the sidewalk so we couldn't pass. "Where are you going, Monk?" Matt said. "And why are you dressed like that?"

"None of your freaking business," I answered. "Now move!"

Big Joe grinned. "Nice skirt, Ape. But be careful when you bend over."

Matt gave him a hard shove. "Shut up, Joe!" He looked at me. "Now, I asked you a question. Where are you going?"

When I didn't answer, Brandi twirled her racquet. "Take one guess, Matt."

He glared at both of us. "Last time I checked, the park was in the opposite direction."

"Maybe we're not going to the park," Brandi said. "Maybe we were invited to play tennis with some sophisticated people. Unlike yourselves." I could have clobbered her.

Matt crossed his arms over his chest. "Wait a minute," he said. "Does this have anything to do with those fairyland punks? The shrimp and the mama's boy you went to the dance with? Are you gonna play tennis with those two clowns?"

I motioned to Brandi to keep her mouth shut, but she didn't heed my advice. "For your information," she said,

"*Walt* has a permit at Poly Prep. We're going to play doubles with him and Bert. Now, if you jackasses would move out of the way—"

They all started cracking up. "Ooooo, Walt has a permit at Poly Prep!" Tony said. "How special!"

"Oh, I wanna play!" Fritz squealed. "Wait, let me run inside and get my little white skivvies."

I glanced toward the parked Chevy, but now Little Joe was nowhere to be seen. "Will you guys grow up?" I said. "I swear, you act like two-year-olds."

Finally Matt and Big Joe let us pass. "Tell the fairies we'll be checking up on 'em," Matt said.

"Yeah," Big Joe agreed. "Who knows, we might just pay a little visit to Poly Prep this afternoon." He flexed his bicep. "Put a little fear into those boys."

Fritz tossed the basketball to Matt, and the four of them went back to their game of H-O-R-S-E in the driveway. Brandi and I continued along, but just when we thought the coast was clear, Little Joe appeared from behind a tree.

We both jumped. "Joe!" Brandi said. "You scared the crap out of me. What are you doing?"

"Um, I need to talk to April. Alone."

She looked at me, then back at Joe. "Ohh-*kay*. Whatever. I guess I'll just walk ahead and let you guys chat. Privately."

Brandi strolled along, casting curious glances behind her. Meanwhile, Little Joe seemed more concerned about

Matt seeing the two of us together. His eyes kept darting in the direction of Fritz's house. "Listen, April," he said. "I've been thinking, you know, about things."

"Things?"

He cleared his throat. "Yeah. Like . . . the two of us. I mean, I know you're Matt's sister, and you're younger than me, but when you think about it, we're only two years apart, and . . ." He hesitated. "Aw shoot, how can I say this? I've just . . . I've been having a hard time seeing you with other guys. I mean, I know you're gonna date and everything, but—"

"Joe! What the hell are you doing?" Matt stood at the entrance of Fritz's driveway with his hands on hips. "We've been looking all over for you. It's your turn. H-O-R." He held up the ball.

"Listen, I better go," Little Joe said. "Just, think about what I said, okay? I'll see you around."

I stood there dazed, watching Little Joe sprint up the street. When he reached the driveway, Matt tossed him the ball. "Jeez, Joe, what's the matter with you lately?"

Brandi was waiting for me at the corner. "So what did he want?" she asked. "What was so *private* that he couldn't say it in front of me?"

"Oh . . ." I waved this away like it was nothing. "Just something about Bettina being over at our house the other day. Apparently his uncle knew about it." I didn't like lying to Brandi, but what could I say? That Little Joe might have the hots for me? It was unthinkable.

165

"Well, that's no secret." She frowned and shook her head. "Ever since that day at the beach Little Joe's been acting so weird. Have you noticed?"

I shrugged. "Um, maybe."

"I know," she said, grinning. "I bet he was traumatized after you flashed him your boob."

I gave her a shove. "I didn't flash him my boob. It fell out of my swimsuit, remember? All because *you* had to wear my yellow bikini."

She laughed. "Oh, yeah, that's right. I forgot."

It was amazing how Brandi always blew off the most important details.

"Oh, well," she said, "we better hurry up. Don't want to keep the boys waiting."

Bert and Walt were already on the courts warming up by the time we arrived. From a distance I could tell they weren't total spazzes, they obviously knew how to play, but I was certain that Brandi and I could kick their butts if we really wanted to. "There they are," Brandi said. "Hi, guys!" she called. "Sorry we're late."

"Oh, no problem," Bert said. Apparently he was still the spokesman for Walt, who remained hopelessly silent. "Come on over and we'll volley a little."

As we walked onto the court, the breeze blew, lifting my skirt, and as I quickly smoothed it down I caught Bert gawking at my long, gangly legs. "Hey, sorry about the dress code," he said. "It sucks, but the tennis Nazis in the office will kick us off the court if we don't comply."

I shrugged. "Whatever, no big deal." I could tell Bert was trying to be nice while also impressing me with his wry wit, but the last thing I wanted to do was encourage him. Not after what Brandi had told me.

He bounced the ball a few times. "So have you girls played much tennis?"

I looked at Brandi and shrugged. "Yeah, some." I didn't want to let on just how good we were. At least not yet.

"How about we hit the ball around for a while, then start up a game?" Bert suggested.

Walt and Brandi nodded while I squeezed the neck of my racquet, feeling a powerful surge of adrenaline. "All right, let's warm up." Now that we were here, I thought it might be fun to cream the two Xavierian boys. But just as I was about to scoop a ball from the ground, I saw Brandi heading over to Walt's side of the court. "Brandi, where are you going?" I said.

She turned around. "What do you mean? We're playing mixed doubles."

I blinked. "*Mixed* doubles?"

Meanwhile, Bert hopped the net onto my side of the court. Minus the platforms, his eyes were about level with my chest. "Wow," he said, "you even have an alligator on your pocket. Very preppy."

I was not in the mood for this. "Um, excuse me for a

minute," I said, marching over to Brandi. "Since when, may I ask, do we play on opposite sides?"

"April," she said, giving me the eye. "Come on. We're doing the boy-girl thing today. I thought you knew that."

Across the way Walt was looking a little confused. "Is everything all right, Brandi?"

She turned and gave him a reassuring smile. "Yes, everything's fine. We've never played on these courts before, and April was wondering if there were any new rules we needed to know about."

"Liar," I whispered.

"Oh." He scratched his head. "No, I don't think so."

She threw up her hands. "Great, then let's play."

While Brandi the Traitor joined Walt, I reluctantly took my place beside an eager-looking Bert. He handed me a couple of balls, which I quickly stuffed into my pockets. Now my skirt flared on either side, making me look like a giant seagull in flight. "Hey, uh, April?" he said.

"Yeah?" Across the net, Brandi was pretending she didn't know how to hold a racquet, so Walt had to lean over and show her.

Bert cleared his throat. "Well, this might come as a surprise to you, but because of my, shall we say, height disadvantage, you probably want to play the net. That is, if you'd like to win."

Now Brandi was giggling while Walt showed her the

proper way to stroke the racquet. "Oh, sure," I said, "no problem. I'll play net."

He breathed a sigh of relief. "Great. Didn't want Walt abusing me today, if you know what I mean."

It turned out that Bert was pretty good at lobs and low passing shots, and after the four of us volleyed for about twenty minutes I was able to detect Walt's major weaknesses. He couldn't return anything with heavy topspin, and his backhand was definitely his Achilles heel. As for Brandi, she was hitting the ball like a total patsy, and if she didn't step it up they were sure to lose. "Are you guys ready to play a game?" I said.

Walt shrugged. "Sure, we're ready."

"Okay, you guys serve first." I tossed them a couple of balls and turned to Bert. "Listen," I said, "here's our strategy. Any chance you get, hit to Brandi, otherwise use lots of topspin, and always, *always* make sure Walt swings backhand. I'll control the net and cover midcourt. You play deep."

Bert nodded. "Cool. I, uh, didn't realize you were such a serious player."

"I'm not," I said. "I just want to win."

After Bert and I killed Walt and Brandi 6–1 in the first set, I noticed a man who'd been giving a girl lessons leaning against the fence, watching us play. It was my turn to serve, and when Bert handed me a ball he whispered, "Looks like you've got a scout interested."

"Scout?" I said. "What are you talking about?"

He rolled his eyes in the direction of the man. "That's Frank Stapleton, head coach of the Lady Firebirds. I'm telling you, he likes what he sees."

"Really? You think so?"

He nodded. "I know so. Now go ahead. Serve the ball. Show him what you got."

Even though I was more interested in creaming Walt and Brandi, I kind of liked the idea that this coach was watching me. That I might be good enough to play for his team. I stepped to the line, stared long and hard at Walt, tossed up the ball, and fired it to his backhand. He swung and didn't even make contact.

"Whoo-hoo!" Bert said. "How do you like that, Walt? She aced you!"

I had to admit, Walt was a pretty good sport. He shrugged. "It's pretty humbling. Oh, well, great serve, April."

"Thanks." I almost felt sorry for the guy. Almost.

Brandi was obviously annoyed that I was showing up her new partner. But as we continued to play she didn't put on the pressure like I thought she would. Instead she acted all ladylike, allowing Walt to take most of the shots. I'd never seen her play a more pathetic game of tennis in my life.

Just as I was about to serve for the final set, Matt and his idiot friends came strolling toward the courts. On the immaculate grounds of Poly Prep, they resembled a pack of mangy sewer rats. "Hey, Ape, looking good!" Tony called. "Go on, slam that sucker into the ground!"

Tony, Fritz, and Big Joe jumped onto the fence and hung there like a bunch of chimpanzees while Matt bounced his basketball, staring fiercely at Bert. Little Joe had a ball too, only he was twirling it on his finger, watching me.

Bert waved. "Hey, hi, guys, how're you doing?" I glanced over at Walt and noticed that his eyes were darting in all directions. Obviously he didn't want to be associated with the riffraff.

"Not bad," Matt said. "Just checking up on my little sister." He peered over at Walt. "And Brandi, too. You girls doing okay?"

Brandi rolled her eyes. "Yes, Matt, we're fine. Now would you please leave? If you haven't noticed, we're trying to play a game of tennis."

"Hey, come on, now," Big Joe said. "Is that any way to treat us?" He jumped off the fence and rolled up both sleeves. "We just wanted to know if you needed any help."

I shook my head. "No, Joe, we don't need any help. Now, don't you guys have anything better to do? Or are you so bored you have to follow us around?"

All of a sudden I felt a hand on my shoulder. "Hey, April," Bert said, "don't look now, but the tennis Nazis just barged out of the office. There's even a police officer with them, so you might want to tell your brother to scram."

I crossed my arms over my chest. "No, I don't think so. Let the morons get in trouble. In fact, I hope they get arrested."

When Matt and his friends saw the cop approaching,

they froze. Slowly, Big Joe rolled down his sleeves. "Excuse me," the police officer said gruffly. "Do you boys have a permit to play here?"

Dumbfounded, the rest of them looked at Matt. "Um, no, actually, you see, Officer . . ." While Matt went on to explain how he and his friends were just checking on his sister without any idea they were trespassing on private property, Frank Stapleton, the supposed tennis scout, walked onto the court. He marched directly up to me and handed me a business card.

"I've been watching you play," he said. "Do you compete around here?"

I looked at the card. On top it read LADY FIREBIRDS and underneath, Mr. Stapleton's contact information was written within a miniature tennis racquet with flames rising from the center. "Oh, no, I don't compete. I usually just play at the park. For fun."

He raised both eyebrows. "Really? Well, today it looked like you were playing for blood."

I glanced at Bert, who had a big grin on his face. "Oh," I said, a little confused, "I didn't mean to—"

"No, no," Mr. Stapleton said, holding up one hand. "Don't apologize, that's a good thing. It's not often you find such a focused player. I'm glad I spotted you."

Bert elbowed me and whispered, "See? What did I tell you?"

Mr. Stapleton reached over and tapped the card. "That's my number if you're interested in trying out for my team. You've got a lot of raw talent, but there are certain things you need to learn. And I won't lie to you. I work my girls hard. Very hard. We've got a few more tournaments this fall, and after that we practice all winter in the bubble courts. If you make the team you'll be training for the spring season. Think about it and give me a call."

He nodded at me quickly, turned on one heel, and marched briskly off the court. I realized he'd never even asked my name. "So are you gonna do it?" Bert said.

I watched Mr. Stapleton get into his car, start the engine, and peel off down the street. It was strange. He'd been watching us play for a while, but now he seemed in a tremendous hurry. I shook my head. "No, I don't think so."

"Why not?" Bert said. "You'd make the team. He obviously *wants* you."

I shrugged. "I don't know, I'm kind of busy." But instead of tossing the card into the nearby trash can, I slipped it into the pocket of my skirt and ran my thumb along the embossed letters.

Meanwhile the police officer escorted Matt and his friends off the grounds of Poly Prep. "See you later, Matt!" I said, giving him a little wave. Then, with a sudden burst of energy, I tossed a ball into the air. "Come on, guys, let's finish this set! Five–two. Our advantage!"

FIFTEEN

I didn't call Mr. Stapleton, but I tucked his business card safely away in my drawer just in case. In the meantime, I decided to ignore the fact that my brother might be running around Brooklyn with a million-dollar price tag on his head and live my own life of danger and doom. So on Monday afternoon when the lunch bell rang, instead of joining Brandi and Olympia in the cafeteria, I headed straight for Mr. Ruffalo's band room. I was sure to catch grief from Brandi about this later, but I was on a mission and nothing was going to stop me.

However, when I exited the stairwell and turned the corner, I saw Roxanne standing alone outside the girls' bathroom. There was no way around it; I had to pass her. "Well, look who it is," she said. "Bet I know where you're going."

Now I had a decision to make. I could (a) chicken out

and make a beeline for the cafeteria, (b) walk by and let her abuse me, or (c) confront the enemy. Danger and doom, I repeated to myself, over and over, with every step I took, until the two of us came face to face.

"I'm going to Mr. Ruffalo's room to eat lunch with Dominick and his band," I said, hoping she didn't notice the shakiness in my voice. "Do you have a problem with that?"

She didn't seem the least bit daunted by what *Redbook* would call my "assertive chin-tilt." "Me?" She laughed. "Sorry, but I'm not the one with the problem."

"Oh, and you think I am?"

I expected a seething comment in response, but to my surprise Roxanne didn't argue. "Listen," she said with a sigh. "It's April, right?"

I relaxed my shoulders a little. "Um, yeah."

"Well, you may not realize this, but Dom and I went out for six months last year—"

Five and a half, I thought.

"And the thing is, I know him pretty well. Better than anyone, really. So I have to be honest. You're not his type. You're the kind of girl who gets straight As, joins the Boosters, has to be home before dark—"

"Wait a minute," I said. "I do *not* belong to the Booster Club."

She waved this away like it didn't matter. "Whatever, you get my point, right? You're like Polly Purebred. I mean, have you even *had* a boyfriend before?"

Of all the possible questions in the world, she had to ask me this one. "Um, not exactly, but—"

"There, see what I mean? Trust me, you and Dom are complete opposites."

I thought about this for moment. "Yeah, maybe. But opposites attract, right?"

She made a face. "Not always."

"Okay," I said, mustering all my courage. "Now it's my turn to ask you something. Why are you so against Dominick and me being together? Is it because you want to go out with him again?"

She shrugged and shook her head. "No, I'm seeing someone else right now. Besides, Dom and I are probably better off as friends."

I wasn't sure I believed her. I wanted to, but her eyes kind of shifted around as she spoke, like she was hiding something. Also, I wondered what new guy she was "seeing" but decided not to ask, since I didn't want to appear too curious. "Well, thanks for the advice," I said. "But I think I can handle things on my own."

A second later a toilet flushed and a member of Roxanne's posse walked out the bathroom door. "Suit yourself," Roxanne said, linking arms with the girl, "but don't say I didn't warn you."

I watched the two of them stroll down the hall, and when they disappeared around the corner, I made my way, shakily, to the band room.

"Hey, come on in!" Dominick said as I peered around the door. "You guys remember April, right?"

Cautiously, I stepped inside. Mr. Ruffalo was sitting at the piano, munching a sandwich and composing a tune. He looked up and smiled.

Ronnie, the bass player, set down his carton of milk. A white mustache stretched across his face. "Yeah, sure! It's Goldilocks, Keeper of the Sticks!"

Pee Wee stood up, grabbed his guitar, and bowed toward me. "Enter, O tall, brainy, blond one." In an instant he was strumming wildly and singing one of my favorite Emerson, Lake and Palmer songs. *"Welcome back, my friends, to the show that never ends, we're so glad you could attend, come inside, come inside!"*

Larry took a giant bite of his veal-and-pepper sub. With his mouth full he said, "Hey, April! You gonna listen to us play today?"

"Of course she is!" Pee Wee said. He continued singing.

I had to admit, it was quite the reception. I wasn't used to getting so much attention—especially from guys like Pee Wee and Ronnie. I started to laugh and before I knew it I'd forgotten all about my run-in with Roxanne. Well, almost.

Dominick motioned for me to take a seat next to him. "You'll have to excuse Pee Wee. He's on a high right now."

"Oh?" I glanced at Pee Wee, wondering what kind of high Dominick meant.

"Hey, don't worry," Dominick said with a chuckle. "A *natural* high. He's really excited about our first gig. We just got booked for a Halloween block party. And get this, they're even gonna pay us."

"Wow, that's great! Where will it be?"

"Right near you. Seventy-seventh between Twelfth and Thirteenth. You'll come, right?"

In the back of my mind I remembered promising not only to take Sammy trick-or-treating, but to St. Bernadette's Halloween Festival as well. Right now that didn't seem to matter. "Sure, I'll come."

But as Pee Wee belted out the next verse, I began to wonder if *Bianca* was invited to the gig as well.

"So I guess all your friends will be there, huh?" I said.

Dominick shrugged. "Yeah, I suppose. But I really don't care as long as you come."

Ha, ha, Bianca. You lose. "Thanks," I said, "that's really sweet." I glanced over at Larry, who was still stuffing his face with the sub. A slice of green pepper dangled from the corner of his mouth. "I bet Larry's in heaven."

"Yeah," Dominick said. "Actually, we all are."

That morning I'd thrown together a bag lunch, so while the guys went through their set for the block party, I nibbled on a thawed-out veggie burger, along with my mother's latest health snack—ants on a log. In other words, celery stalks filled with peanut butter and dotted with raisins and carob chips. She'd found the recipe in *Organic Living* and thought it was cute.

"Interesting food," Mr. Ruffalo said, taking a seat beside me while the guys paused for a short break. "Are you a vegetarian?"

Mr. Ruffalo had been my chorus teacher in seventh and eighth grade. He was one of those thirty-something-year-old former hippies who were always talking about Woodstock, Viet Nam, and the evils of capitalism. He was pretty cool for a teacher, but in my opinion, way too intense. "No, I still eat meat. My mother's just on this health kick. Right now it's all we have in the house."

"I see." He stroked his beard contemplatively. "So, tell me, April, what do you think?"

"Um, about what?" I picked a chickpea out of my veggie burger, popped it into my mouth, and hoped Mr. Ruffalo wasn't going to ask me about animal rights or communism or socialism, or one of those isms I didn't understand very well.

He laughed and motioned toward the guys. "About their music."

"Ohhhh." Dominick and his band had just finished working out the kinks to the Beatles' "Norwegian Wood" and were now gearing up to play Larry's new Who favorite, "Pinball Wizard." I said, "I think they're really good." I thought this would be a sufficient response, but from the look on Mr. Ruffalo's face I could tell he wanted me to elaborate. "They, uh, play an interesting variety of songs," I added. "I especially like their music from the sixties—the Beatles, the Stones, Dylan."

I could tell Mr. Ruffalo liked that answer. He nodded. "Yes, yes, I agree. I have to admit I'm not a fan of what they're playing on the radio these days—sell-out bands putting on shows with pyrotechnics, painted faces, lizard tongues." He shook his head sadly. "Then there's Bowie with his new alter ego, Ziggy Stardust. And don't even get me started on disco." He sighed. "Oh, well, things change."

"Hmmm, yeah, I guess they do." I took a big bite of the burger and chewed, hoping the conversation would end. No such luck.

"So, April, I assume you're still studying piano?"

That was the other thing about Mr. Ruffalo. He expected every living, breathing creature on the planet to play an instrument. I could hardly believe he remembered I'd been taking piano lessons in eighth grade. I swallowed and chased the burger with a sip of milk. "Not exactly. I quit a while back."

Immediately his eyebrows shot up. "Quit! Oh, no, please don't tell me that! You? With those long, graceful fingers?" He looked at my hands. "But why?"

I picked up a celery stalk and pushed a carob chip ant into its peanut butter log, wishing I could disappear that easily. "Well, it's just, the instructor I had . . ." I paused, realizing it might not be appropriate to say that Mrs. Higgenbottom had a bad case of cat-food halitosis, not to mention a dangerous behind that covered half the piano bench. Besides, to satisfy Mr. Ruffalo the excuse had to be meaningful. "She didn't allow me to express myself musically. Instead of teaching me songs, she focused on scales, finger exercises, sight-reading, stuff like that." I took a bite of celery and prayed the band would begin to play really loudly.

"Well," Mr. Ruffalo said, "I suppose I understand, although it's still no reason to quit. The piano is a wonderful instrument, but some instructors are set in their ways. As for me, I use a holistic, modern approach, allowing my students to choose their own style of music. It works quite well." He gazed longingly at my fingers. I noticed his were short and stubby. "I don't usually solicit, but if you're interested I'd be willing to teach you."

Now I was trapped. "Um, I don't know . . ." I couldn't imagine taking lessons from Mr. Ruffalo. Besides having to practice a lot, it would mean brushing up on events like Watergate and the Cuban Missile Crisis.

He laughed a little. "Don't worry, I'm not expecting an answer right now. Think about it. You know where to reach me."

I gave him a weak smile. "Okay. I will."

At that moment Dominick cranked up the volume on his amp and began to sing, *"Ever since I was a young boy I played the silver ball. . . ."* I'd never been so happy to hear "Pinball Wizard" in my whole life.

Afterward, while the band was packing up and I was about to slip out the door, Dominick said, "Hey, April, wait up, I'll walk you to class."

The first bell had already rung, and next period was English with Mr. Cornelius, aka Count Dracula. Presently there were two red "X"s beside my name in his little black book—both for being late to homeroom on account of Larry and his drumsticks. This put me in danger of Saturday detention, and now if I was late to English I'd be on the path to a failing grade. On top of that, because of my recent preoccupation with Dominick, along with the possible fate of my brother, I hadn't handed in a rough draft for my short story, which had been due three days ago.

"So," Dominick said, hoisting his guitar strap over his shoulder as we walked out the door. "I guess your parents weren't exactly thrilled to see me at your house on Friday, huh?"

The hallway was crowded and noisy. I had to dodge a girl who was laughing and running from a guy chasing her. "Oh, sorry about that," I said. "My parents are really strict. Don't take it personally."

With a wave of his hand he said, "Ah, don't worry. I'm used to it. Most girls' parents prefer the clean-cut all-American type. Which, of course, I'm not." He grinned. "But anyway, I wanted to tell you I had a great time that day. It was pretty wild with your brother and that Mafia chick doing Shakespeare in the basement, and then meeting Larry's dad, Soft Sal Luciano. And Sammy, man, he's such a great kid."

"Thanks, I had a good time too."

Suddenly, across the hall I saw Roxanne walking arm

182

in arm with Steve Rizzo. This was very strange for two reasons: one, I'd never seen Roxanne anywhere near my English class before, and two, although Steve Rizzo was one of the cutest guys in school, he boxed in the Junior Golden Gloves division and was practically brain-dead. Not that Roxanne was a genius, but still. So, I thought, this was the new guy she was seeing.

As the two of them strolled by, Roxanne glanced coolly at us; she pulled Steve closer, slipping her hand into the back pocket of his jeans. "Hey, Dom, hey, April," she said with a wave. I highly suspected that our crossing paths was not a coincidence.

When Dominick saw them he reached for my hand and held it tightly. "Hi, Roxanne," he said in a measured tone. He gave Steve a quick nod.

We continued along and when the coast was clear, I took a deep breath. "Um, Dom, I should probably tell you, Roxanne and I spoke today. Right before lunch, on my way to see you."

"You're kidding. What did she say?"

"Mmmm, basically that I wasn't your type. That we were opposites."

"Oh, really?" He closed his eyes for a moment and sighed. "That girl is such a head case. I mean, we're still friends and all, but she likes to play games."

The door to Mr. Cornelius's classroom was just a few feet away now. Dominick slowed down, leaned against the wall, and gently pulled me toward him. "Enough about

Roxanne," he said. "Thanks for coming today. Tell me, honestly, did you like our music?"

He was looking directly into my eyes. I ran my tongue over my braces, hoping a stray chickpea or raisin wasn't lodged between the metal bands. "Oh, yeah, definitely. You guys sound really good."

He nodded. "Thanks. And what about Ruffalo? He wasn't too intense?"

"Well, yeah, but that's okay."

He smiled, set down his guitar, and opened my hand. "Did you know that besides playing music, I also read palms?"

I looked at him warily. "No."

He began drawing circles. "Well, it's true. Hmmm, let's see, will Goldilocks with the beautiful blue eyes come again tomorrow?"

But before Dominick could reveal his answer, the late bell rang, and Mr. Cornelius stepped out of his room. His eyes darted up and down the hall, searching for stragglers. When he saw me and Dominick together he frowned.

"Hey, Mr. C.!" Dominick said. "How's it going?"

Unfortunately Mr. C. didn't find Dominick amusing. "It's going fine, Mr. DeMao. But Miss Lundquist needs to get to class now."

"Aw, that's too bad. We were just planning a rendezvous in the janitor's closet."

I stifled a laugh.

"Is that so? Well, maybe Miss Lundquist would prefer a

tardy, then. That can always be arranged." Mr. Cornelius pushed his horn-rimmed glasses farther up the bridge of his nose. His eyes looked huge and threatening.

"I better go," I said.

Dominick squeezed my hand. "But what about tomorrow, will you come?"

I shrugged. "Beats me. You're the palm reader."

The next day when Mr. Ruffalo caught me sneaking in the back door of the band room, he practically catapulted off the piano bench. "April! This is wonderful! You've decided to come back!" At first I got a little freaked out, thinking Dominick had told him about our palm-reading joke, but then I realized Mr. Ruffalo thought I was returning for a piano lesson.

"Oh, no, you see, that's not why—"

"I knew you'd reconsider. Now come, sit down." He led me to the piano, where I reluctantly took a seat on the bench. "I have a vast selection of sheet music you can choose from. Wait right here."

While Mr. Ruffalo shuffled through a stack of folders on his desk, Pee Wee pointed the neck of his guitar at me and said, "Ha, ha. Busted."

Meanwhile Dominick strolled up behind, threaded his arms around my waist, and began playing "Chopsticks." He whispered in my ear, "I knew you'd come."

"Mmmm, you must be psychic."

When Ronnie saw us together, he whistled. "Watch

out, Blondie. You might want to stay away from Dom. He's trouble waiting to happen."

"Hey!" Larry said. "Dom's not trouble! He's my friend!"

We all laughed, except for Mr. Ruffalo. When he returned, he shoved Dominick out of the way and handed me a folder labeled POPULAR SONGS FOR THE BEGINNER. "Okay, now here's the deal. I don't usually work for free, but in your case I'm willing to make an exception. For a short while, that is, in the hope of sparking some interest."

I flipped through the pages and spotted some pretty cool songs. There were even several by Cat Stevens.

"Choose one you'd like to learn," Mr. Ruffalo said. "We'll have a lesson while the guys are eating. When you've mastered it, oh, say in a couple of weeks, we'll talk again. Now, of course, you'll have to speak with your parents, but if they agree, we can set something up on a weekly basis after school. I charge fifteen dollars per hour. Does that sound reasonable?"

I looked up, wondering how I'd gotten myself into this. "Um, yes, I guess so."

"Great." He smiled. "Let me know when you've made your choice."

So while the guys ate lunch, Mr. Ruffalo taught me the intro to Cat Stevens's "Oh Very Young." Surprisingly, I caught on pretty quickly, so I guess my lessons with Mrs. Higgenbottom hadn't been a total waste of time. At least, that was what Mr. Ruffalo said.

I returned to the band room every day that week, and

even though I'd explained to Brandi and Olympia that I was indeed learning piano, Brandi claimed I was ditching them for Dominick. Which of course was true, but that was beside the point.

Anyway, each day I learned a few more stanzas of the song, and afterward, while the guys practiced for their gig, Mr. Ruffalo and I ate lunch and listened to them play. I even brought some ants on a log to share with him, as well as banana chips, soy nuts, and dried mango slices. He liked it all.

But the best part was when the bell rang and Dominick would walk me to English, pretend to read my palm, and ask if I'd come see him the next day. Which I always did. Then, like clockwork, Mr. Cornelius would show up, ask if I'd like a tardy, and remind me of the rough draft I still hadn't turned in.

The thing was, I had tried several times to write a rough draft, but for some reason I couldn't come up with a topic. And now with Dominick walking me to class every day it was becoming impossible to concentrate.

"Do you want to come to my house after school?" Dominick asked. It was Friday, and the two of us were standing outside Mr. Cornelius's room waiting for the bell to ring. "We could hang out, listen to records, maybe get some pizza?"

"Oh, that sounds great, it's just . . ."

"Just what?"

"Well, I have to watch Sammy after school. And

tonight I have to babysit. It's my parents' anniversary and they have reservations at some fancy restaurant in the city."

He thought for a moment. "Well, why don't you bring Sammy? We could hang out for a little while, anyway."

If my parents hadn't been so lame this would have been a possibility, but I knew if I brought big-mouth Sammy along, they'd eventually find out. And if strange boys were not allowed at our house, I could just imagine their reaction to my spending an afternoon with Spawn of Satan in the apartment over Moe's candy store. "Hmmm, I don't know. . . ." But just as I was about to say it probably wasn't a good idea, a thought popped into my head. I could ask Brandi to babysit. She was still pretty teed off about the lunch thing, but the way I figured it, I'd done so many favors for her and Walt, she owed me one. "Well, actually," I said, "maybe I can."

Dominick smiled. He hadn't kissed me since that day in the playground, but now his lips were very close to mine. I looked into his eyes and my knees got all wobbly. He leaned closer and, very softly, we kissed. Not just once, but a few times. I wondered if what we were doing could be classified as making out. Whatever it was, I didn't want to stop.

Suddenly I heard a familiar voice. "Miss Lundquist? What, may I ask, are you doing?"

I looked up and saw Mr. Cornelius. The combination of horn-rimmed glasses, widow's peak, and furrowed brows made him especially frightening today. "Maybe this time you'd like a referral. And as for you, Mr. DeMao, I suggest you get to class before I call the principal."

Dominick grinned. "Sure thing, Mr. C." Then he whispered in my ear, "Please come today. I'll be waiting."

"I'll try." Mr. Cornelius got distracted by some guys throwing erasers across the room. I waved goodbye to Dominick. Right before I stepped into class, I turned my head, and there, halfway down the hall, stood Brandi and Olympia. Olympia was grinning widely, but Brandi looked like she was about to keel over and die. "What are you guys doing?" I said, wondering just how much they'd seen.

"What do you mean, what are *we* doing?" Brandi said. "What are *you* doing?"

Olympia gave her a sharp elbow. "Quiet, Brandi." She held up a pink slip of paper, pointed toward the nurse's office, and rolled her eyes in Brandi's direction. Cupping one hand over her mouth, she said, "Someone needs a *pad*."

"Miss Lundquist!" Mr. Cornelius bellowed from inside the room.

"Listen, I gotta go. See you guys later."

Brandi was unusually quiet as she, Olympia, Larry, and I walked home from school. Normally Olympia didn't join us since she lived in the opposite direction, but Saturday morning the Booster Club was having its yearly bake sale, and she and Brandi were planning to whip up Betty Crocker recipes all afternoon. Originally I'd told them I'd help out, but now, hopefully, I had other plans.

"So, April," Olympia said. "Tell us, what's going on with you and the infamous rock star, Dominick DeMao? Now that you've made out in the hallway, has he popped the question?"

Behind us, Larry was oblivious, beating a trash can, while Brandi walked a few paces ahead and kicked a tree branch into the gutter. I shot Olympia a warning look. "First of all," I said, "we didn't *make out*—"

"Oh, come on, April, what would you call it, then?"

"We kissed, okay? And anyway, what do you mean, 'popped the question'?"

Olympia grinned. "You know, did he ask you out?"

I shrugged. "Sort of. I'm . . . not really sure."

"Well," she said, "from the looks of things today, I'd say yes. Anyway, how *was* it?"

At that moment, Brandi turned around. "Will the two of you *shut up*! God, Olympia, you act like April should be proud of what she did. Personally, I think it's disgusting!"

"Brandi, come on," I said. "You're making a big deal over nothing. It was a kiss, that's all."

"Yeah, Brandi," Olympia chimed in, "and maybe if you'd stop acting like such a prude, Walt might finally plant one on you."

Olympia raised an eyebrow at me, and I couldn't help it; the thought of dorky Walt kissing Brandi was just too funny. We started to laugh.

Brandi's eyes widened; she turned and ran up the street. "Brandi, wait!" I yelled. "We were just joking!"

Olympia and I chased after her, and when we finally caught up, Olympia grabbed her by the arm. "Leave me alone!" Brandi said, fighting back tears. "Go away!"

"Brandi, we're sorry," I said pleadingly. "We shouldn't have laughed."

"Yeah, Brandi," Olympia said, "and I shouldn't have said what I did. It's just . . . you *are* overreacting. April's right, it *was* just a kiss."

"It's not that!" Brandi exploded.

"Well, what is it, then?" I said.

"How do you think it feels when your two best friends have kissed a guy and you haven't? Let me tell you, it *sucks!*"

A tear trickled down her face. Olympia and I looked at each other, and together we wrapped our arms around Brandi. It was just like one of those group hugs my parents did with Sammy. A moment later, Larry came up from behind. He smashed the stop sign on the corner with his drumsticks and said, "What the heck are you girls doing?" Brandi was the first to start cracking up; Olympia and I joined in.

"Oh, Larry, we're just hugging," Olympia said.

I brushed a tear from Brandi's face. "Listen," I said, "don't worry about the kiss, okay? It'll happen soon."

"You think so?"

Olympia and I nodded in unison. "I *know* so," I said. "I mean, really, how could Walt resist?"

Everyone was in a happy mood now, so as we walked along, I thought it might be a good time to pop the real question. "Hey, uh, Brandi? Olympia? I know I was supposed to help you guys bake this afternoon, but something came up, and actually, I was wondering if you'd do me a favor."

"Oh?" Brandi said. "What is it?"

"Well." I chewed my lip. "You see, Dominick asked if I'd come to his apartment after school today. He said I could bring Sammy along, but if I do, I know he'll blab to my parents."

"Ooooo," Olympia said. "This sounds *interesting*." She elbowed Brandi. "Sure, we'll do it, April. Come on, Brandi, say yes."

Brandi frowned. "I don't know. Sounds deceitful to me."

"Exactly," Olympia said. "That's why it's called a *favor*."

As I stood there, waiting for Brandi to make her decision, a car whizzed by, beeping its horn. "Yo, Larry!"

The three of us turned around and saw Larry waving. "Hey, Nicky! Nicky *Jag*!" The car slowed down and I almost died. It was the young gangster in the black Jaguar convertible—the one who'd rescued Bettina from the clutches of my lovesick brother in the park. I watched as he pulled up to the curb.

"Oh my God," Brandi said. "It's *him*."

"Gimme five, Lar-*rey*." The two of them slapped hands, front and back. "You're still playing those drums, huh?"

Larry stood up tall. "I'm in a band now."

"A band! That's hard-core!" They slapped each other

five again. "I'll have to come hear you play sometime. But listen, I gotta go now—places to see, people to meet. I'll see you around, all right?"

"Okay, bye, Nicky Jag."

Before the young gangster pulled away, he looked directly at me. "Hey, Blondie, take good care of my buddy Larry, all right?" There was a strange, crooked smile on his face. A shiver passed through me as I remembered that awful dream—sitting on the hood of his car in Sammy's Underoos while this young guy planted kisses up and down my neck. I stood there frozen as he revved his engine and took off.

Suddenly I had a feeling, deep in my gut, that something was wrong. "Listen," I said to Brandi and Olympia. "You guys take Larry home, okay? I'll meet you at my house."

I took off running and didn't stop until I reached my front stoop. Breathless, I raced up the stairs two at a time. Inside, I heard *Dark Shadows* playing in the basement. Barnabas Collins was laughing sinisterly, and Johnny was yelling, "Hey, Sammy, cut it out, that's my Ring Ding!"

I searched for signs of Matt, but his shoes weren't in their normal place and his jacket wasn't hanging over the banister. Maybe he was at basketball practice after all. Maybe there was nothing to worry about. But then I saw a box of frozen veggie burgers sitting out on the dining room table. I knew I hadn't left them out that morning. Something was up.

I gripped the banister and slowly walked upstairs. The door of Matt's bedroom was closed. I knocked a few times, and when there was no answer I pushed it open.

There, on the floor, crumpled in a corner of the room, sat Matt. He was holding a veggie burger against one eye, and the rest of his face was red and puffy like he'd been crying. When he saw me, he grimaced and yelled, "Get the hell out of my room, Monk!"

SIXTEEN

I was not about to take orders from him now. "Matt! Oh my God! Are you okay? What happened?" I ran into his room and knelt beside him.

Slowly, he took the frozen patty off his eye. It was black and blue and the lid was swollen shut. A chickpea was stuck to his eyelash, and I wanted to brush it off, but from the look on his face I figured it wasn't a good idea. "I'm fine, Monk. Got hit with an elbow at basketball practice. Now get out of here and leave me alone."

"Are you kidding? Do you really expect me to believe that?"

He glared at me. "Why shouldn't you believe me? Stuff like this happens all the time. Just the other week, Gus Picini got his front tooth knocked out."

"But . . . I saw that guy on Twelfth Avenue. Bettina's

cousin—the one with the Jaguar convertible. Larry called him Nicky Jag."

"Oh, so you think *he* did this? Nicky *Jag?*" He laughed a little, then winced at the pain. "Sorry, Ape, I know you want to believe someone's out to kill me, but it's not happening." Gently, he placed the burger back on his eye. Only now the patty was beginning to crumble, and some lentils fell on his lap. "Listen, Monk, the only reason I'm sitting here, pissed off at the world, is because the first performance of *Romeo and Juliet* is next weekend." He pointed to his face. "And I look like freaking Quasimodo. I swear, they better not give my part to someone else."

The burger had completely disintegrated now, so I got a better look at the damage. Either Matt was a pretty convincing liar, or some giant on his basketball team had an elbow made of steel. Anyway, if he was telling the truth, I figured he'd gotten what he deserved, dancing around and rejoicing when he found out Brandon Ritchie had chicken pox.

"Well, Mom has some makeup you could use," I said. "That might cover it up."

"Yeah, that's all I need. A little help from Cover Girl." He tossed the remains of the burger into the trash can. "Look, Monk, if you want to help, why don't you go downstairs and get me another one of those stupid vegetable pieces of crap?" He let out a deep sigh. "Why can't we be like a normal family and have a few steaks in the freezer?"

I looked at his eye, thinking he did bear a resemblance

to the deformed hunchback from Victor Hugo's novel. Too bad they weren't putting on that play. "All right, hold on, I'll get you one."

When I got downstairs Brandi and Olympia were walking in the back door. "Is everything okay?" Brandi said. "Is Matt home?"

Olympia ran and gave me a hug. "Oh, April, Brandi told me what's been going on. I can't believe you guys are involved with the Mob! And your poor brother!"

I shot a few daggers at Brandi, wondering just how much she'd told Olympia. Meanwhile, from the basement I heard Johnny and Sammy fighting over the remaining Hostess cakes. "Give me that Yodel, Sammy, now!"

"All right, Johnny!" I yelled. "It's time to go home! And Sammy, turn off that stupid show before I tell Mom why you've been having nightmares!"

Immediately the TV went off, and as the two of them fought over the last Yodel, I grabbed the box of veggie burgers off the dining room table. By now they were mostly thawed, so I stuck them back in the freezer and pulled out a bag of tutti-frutti tofu pops. Leave it to my mother to find a frozen confection made from tofu.

"April?" Brandi said. "What are you doing?"

I pulled out one of the pops, and through the cellophane I could see that it had a bad case of freezer burn. "These are for Matt," I said. "He's got a black eye."

Olympia gasped. "Oh, no! Don't tell me he got beat up?"

"Was it him?" Brandi said. "The guy in the Jaguar?"

I held up one hand. "Okay, before you guys jump to conclusions, I don't think there was any foul play. Matt said he got elbowed at basketball practice."

"Do you believe him?" Brandi said.

I shrugged. "I don't know."

Sammy and Johnny were approaching the top of the stairs. "Listen, April," Brandi said, "Olympia and I were talking and, well, why don't you go ahead with your plans this afternoon? We'll watch Sammy."

I looked at her. "Really, you mean it?"

She motioned for me to move along. "Yes, I mean it. Now run upstairs and take care of Matt before Sammy starts asking a million questions. And have a good time later with you-know-who. But not *too* good, if you know what I mean."

"Thanks. I will."

As I ran up the stairs I heard Brandi say, "Come on, Sammy, let's go to my house. We're baking brownies."

"Ha, ha, you can have your stupid Yodel, Johnny! *I'm* baking with the girls!"

I walked into Matt's room, and when he saw the bag of pops he managed a small smile. "Hmmm, tutti-frutti tofu. Not a bad way to get rid of those things." He plucked one from the bag, pressed it to his eye, and reached in for another. "What do you think, Ape, should I eat one?"

I examined the bag and noticed the PAREVE label. "Well, they're kosher."

"Eh, what the heck." He ripped one open and took a bite. "Yeah, just what I thought. Tastes like crap. Oh, well." He finished chewing and took another bite.

"Hey, Matt," I said, plunking down next to him. "Seriously, are you telling me the truth? Did you really get elbowed at practice? Because, well, Bettina . . ." I was thinking about the sealed envelope sitting in my drawer, wondering if and when I should give it to Matt.

He stopped chewing and looked at me. "Bettina *what?*"

"Well, that day she was here, she told me if anything should ever happen, I mean, if the two of you weren't able to see each other again—"

"Listen, Monk, I already told you! I got hit in the eye at practice. And besides, even if I did get nailed by one of those creeps, I don't care. I'm not afraid of them. No one is gonna tell me I can't see Bettina." He took another bite of the pop and chewed.

I was startled to noticed a band of bruises on his upper arm. Five purple fingerprints. "Matt," I said, pointing. "What are those?"

He looked at the bruises like he was seeing them for the first time. "I don't know. After the moron elbowed me, he must have dragged me off the gym floor. I was seeing stars at the time, so I don't remember." He took the last bite of the pop and tossed the stick into the trash. "Look, Ape, I've got a dress rehearsal tonight, and I need to sleep this thing off." He handed me the bag of pops. "Get out of here now. And tell Sammy to be quiet."

"Sammy's not here," I said. "He's at Brandi's."

"Perfect." Matt stood up and flopped onto his bed. "Now shut off the light and go away."

The house was eerily quiet. I looked at the clock ticking in the hallway. My parents wouldn't be home for another hour and a half. I ran downstairs, grabbed my bike from the garage, and took off for Thirteenth Avenue.

It was a beautiful afternoon, and lots of kids were outside in sweaters playing hopscotch, jump rope, and stoop ball. When I reached Thirteenth Avenue, I saw that the vegetable stands were speckled with bright orange pumpkins and purplish red pomegranates. A group of high school kids waiting for the bus had swarmed around the counter of Tony's pizzeria for a quick slice or a bag of zeppole. As usual there was a funeral going on, but for some reason today it didn't seem so morbid. When I arrived at Moe's candy store, the bells of St. Bernadette's began to sound. I took it as a good sign.

I locked my bike to the parking meter just outside Moe's and stuck the key in my pocket. I could see Moe behind the glass, smoking and shooting the breeze with some guy at the counter drinking coffee and eating a slice of pie. We locked eyes for just a moment, but since I wasn't in the mood for his nosy questions I quickly ducked away. I took a deep breath and pressed Dominick's doorbell firmly. After a minute or so I expected to hear something— footsteps on the stairs, maybe a window sliding open above me—but there was nothing. Total silence.

Another minute went by, and Moe stuck his head out the candy store door. "Hey, I thought that was you."

I waved unenthusiastically. "Hi, Moe."

He pursed his lips. "If you're, uh, looking for the kid who lives upstairs, I don't think he's home yet."

Moe was such a busybody. Worse than the old ladies who read the gossip columns in the beauty parlor. It was amazing he was still in business. "Oh, okay, well, thanks."

"Probably has detention again. That's my guess, anyway. You can wait inside the store if you want. I've got pie."

I was not about to be interrogated by Moe. "Oh, no thank you. I think I'll just ride around for a while." Quickly, I unlocked my bike and hopped on.

"All right, but tell that cute little brother of yours we have a new flavor of Blow Pops. Raspberry."

"I will. Bye, Moe."

I rode up and down the avenue, hoping I might spot Dominick on his way home. When I passed the florist for the third time I heard someone call, "Hey, Goldilocks!" I turned and saw Pee Wee and Ronnie. They were talking to some girls outside the store.

I waved hello but didn't dare stop. Better to let them think I was riding around for exercise instead of stalking their buddy, who'd apparently stood me up. The only thing I could think to do now was park in front of St. Bernadette's, pass some time inside the church, and try Dominick's doorbell a little later.

It was pretty empty inside, but there was a priest at the

altar burning incense for Friday-night Mass. I took a seat in one of the back pews and looked around. I'd never been inside St. Bernadette's without Brandi, and for some reason it seemed spooky sitting there alone. An unseen organ from the balcony started to moan, which really gave me the creeps, so I got up and walked around.

As I strolled among the statues of martyred saints, I came to one I recognized—St. Christopher carrying the Christ child. Surrounding him were many candles. There was a box of matches sitting in a little brass cup, and a small collection box for change. I dug in my pocket, pulled out three quarters, dropped them into the slot, and lit three candles—one for Brandi's sister, who'd died at birth, one for Uncle Jimmy, who'd died in Viet Nam, and one for Matt. He wasn't dead yet, and I was hoping to keep it that way.

"Hi, babe." My stomach plummeted as a shadow loomed up beside me. An arm in a black trench coat reached out and lit a candle next to my three. I turned and saw Frankie the Crunch. "You know, it's kind of funny," he said, "most people think St. Christopher is my patron saint because he's supposed to help guys in the automobile industry. But actually, that's not the reason."

My heart thumped unsteadily. "Oh, no?"

He shook his head and pointed to the statue. "No. I'll tell you why. You see how he's carrying the Christ child on his shoulder?"

I nodded.

"Well, there's this story about St. Christopher. He was a strong guy, built, kind of like me, and he used to help all these people get across the river. Anyway, one day he's about to carry this little kid, thinking it'll be easy and all, but it's not. For some reason the kid weighs a ton and St. Christopher can't figure out why. But when he finally gets to the other side, completely exhausted, he finds out he's been carrying Christ. All the sins of the world have been on his shoulders." He paused and sighed deeply. "That's how I feel sometimes."

Slowly I turned and looked at Mr. Consiglione. His eyes were shut now and his mouth was moving silently like he was praying. Very carefully, without a sound, I slipped away, splashed myself with a few drops of holy water for good measure, and ran out the door.

Thankfully, Dominick was outside Moe's, digging in his pocket for his keys. In his arm was a stack of albums. I hopped on my bike and flew across the street, dodging a taxicab. "Hey, Dominick! Wait up, it's me!"

He pushed open his door and turned around. When he saw me riding toward him, a big smile spread across his face. "April! All right! I knew you'd come!"

I hoisted my bike onto the sidewalk and chained it to the parking meter for the second time. Meanwhile, Moe stuck his head out the door. He took a long drag on his cigarette and blew two streams of smoke from his nostrils. "So, you came back." He looked at Dominick. "It's not nice to keep a young lady waiting, you know."

Dominick's eyes widened. "Waiting? Oh, shoot, I'm sorry. Were you here before?"

"Oh, it's no big deal—"

"Yes, it is," Moe said. "A very big deal. Dominick, this lovely young girl rang your doorbell"—he glanced at his watch—"almost an *hour* ago. And you weren't home."

Dominick hung his head, and I thought it was strange that he didn't mouth off at Moe and tell him to mind his own business. I mean, Moe was just the guy who owned the candy store downstairs. "I'm really sorry." Dominick held out the albums. "I borrowed these from a friend, and I guess I stayed a little too long at his house. I didn't realize—"

"Well, next time, you better realize," Moe said. "The problem with you, young man, is you take things for granted. Don't even know when you've got something good." He shook his head. "Run along now, and behave yourself."

"Don't worry, Moe," Dominick said, "I always do." He held the door for me and led the way upstairs. It was dark and musty, and the walls leading to his apartment were covered with graffiti. I tried not to notice.

"So, what's with Moe?" I said. "He acts like he's your father or something."

Dominick laughed. "Yeah, well, he practically is. My mom split when I was five and my dad's not around too much. He works all day and plays at the jazz clubs in the Village at night. He's a saxophonist."

"Wow, that's cool. I mean, not that you don't see him, but that he's a musician, like you."

"Yep, we get along pretty well, and we've got a lot in common. Anyway, here we are." Dominick flicked on the lights and ushered me inside. The apartment wasn't exactly dirty, but it was cluttered, mostly with instrument cases, piles of sheet music, albums, eight-track tapes, and cassettes. Posters of Muddy Waters, B. B. King, and other musicians I didn't recognize decorated the walls. He set down the albums he'd been carrying, searched through the stack, and pulled one out. "Look at this," he said, brushing his fingers across the album cover like it was made of gold. "*Slowhand*. Eric Clapton's latest. Wanna hear it?"

"Sure, only . . ." I looked around for a clock on the wall but didn't see one. "I can't stay too long. It's getting late."

"Oh, okay, just have a seat and I'll put it on. It won't take long."

I pushed aside a pile of clothes strewn across the sofa and sat down while Dominick lifted the lid of the turntable. Behind me was the window overlooking the avenue, and I saw Frankie the Crunch walking out of St. Bernadette's. I guessed he'd made his peace with God and was off to work again. "You know, it's pretty awesome how you can see everything from this window," I said. "The church, the funeral parlor, the pizzeria, and look at that, you can even watch a guy getting his hair cut in the barbershop."

"Yeah," Dominick said. "I write a lot of songs sitting in

205

front of that window. Actually, I've got enough for a whole album. When I get it all together I'm gonna call it *Livin' Atop Moe's Candy Store.*"

"I like that. I didn't know you wrote your own songs."

He nodded. "Right now our band is only doing covers, but I'm hoping to teach the guys some of my own stuff."

He set down the needle, and the album began to play. It was kind of weird because the first song was a heavily guitar-driven tribute to cocaine, but if you listened closely to the lyrics you could tell it was actually an antidrug song. Kind of a satire. Something my parents would totally not understand.

Dominick sat next to me. "Do you like it?"

I moved my head around to the beat. "Yeah, I do."

"Clapton's one of the greatest guitar players ever. You know why they call him Slowhand?"

"No, why?"

"Well." He stood up, his face suddenly animated. "You see, in concert, he plays so fast and so intense that he always breaks a guitar string. And instead of taking another instrument, like most guys do, he puts on a new string, and while everyone's waiting they do a slow-hand clap. Like this." He clapped his hands a few times. "Get it? Clap-ton. Slow-hand-Clap-ton. And the irony is that he's so fast."

I smiled. "That's pretty cool, how'd you know that?"

"My dad told me. He's even met him. Next time Clapton's on tour he's gonna take me to one of his concerts."

When the song finished, Dominick opened the lid of

the turntable and flipped the album to the other side. "Now, you got to hear this one. It's amazing, and it reminds me of you."

"Of me?"

"Yeah, come here, I'll show you."

He set down the needle and held out his arms. The music was soft and the guitar played in this really beautiful way. I stood up and walked toward him; he put his hands on my waist while I placed both of mine around his neck. We swayed from side to side. After a while I leaned my head against his shoulder, closed my eyes, and listened to the words. It was a love song about a guy who had a girlfriend with long blond hair, and how wonderful she made him feel. After a while I raised my head.

"So, what do you think?" Dominick said.

"It's nice. I like it." He brought his lips to mine and we kissed until the song was over.

Outside an ambulance wailed, and when I looked out the window I realized it was getting dark. "Listen, I better go."

He nodded. "Okay, I'll walk you downstairs."

Dominick gave me one last kiss as I unlocked my bike. "Will you come back and see me this weekend?" he said.

"I'm . . . not sure if I can."

"Well, okay, but I'll definitely see you Monday, right?"

"Yeah, Monday for sure. Bye." I hopped on my bike and raced along the avenue. The vegetable stands were closing, and all the kids who had been playing in the street earlier had disappeared. When I reached my house I saw my mother's car in the garage.

Inside, Matt and Sammy sat at the kitchen table scarfing Gino's pizza. "Hi, April," Sammy said, holding up a slice. "Look what Mom brought home."

Matt took a swig of juice. "Where've you been, Chimp? Mom's freaking out." He was in his Romeo costume and apparently my mother had already done her magic with Cover Girl's Dunes of Sand. Still, he looked pretty bad.

I shrugged and took a seat. "Nowhere. Just around."

As I picked up a slice of pizza and took a bite, my mother walked in. She was dressed to the nines for her special anniversary dinner. "April, *finally* you're here. I've been so worried. Brandi brought Sammy home a while ago and said she wasn't sure where you'd gone."

I rolled my eyes. "Mom, it's no big deal. I was just riding my bike around the neighborhood."

"Riding your bike in the dark? Alone?"

Sammy put down his juice cup. "Oh, don't worry, Mom, April wasn't alone. She was with Dom."

My mother looked at me. "*Dom?* You mean the boy who was over here the other week? You were with *him?*"

I gave Sammy a dirty look. He covered his mouth. "Oops. I forgot. Brandi told me not to tell. Sorry, April."

Matt took a bite of his pizza. "You mean the kid with the guitar? Hey, Mom, don't have a heart attack, he's cool.

It's the shrimp in the platforms you've got to worry about. Now, *that* kid I don't trust."

My mother wasn't even listening. "I can't believe you did that. After everything we talked about."

"Mom," I said. "Come on. You don't even know him."

"And now you're lying to me."

"Mom, please—"

"No!" She threw up her hands. "That's it. This has gone too far. You're grounded until further notice. When your father gets home we'll decide the punishment."

Just then, the back door opened. "Hi, everyone," my dad said. "How's my lovely family tonight?"

SEVENTEEN

I sat in the living room while, in the kitchen, my mom filled my dad in on all the embarrassing details. I could tell he was pretty disappointed, but since he didn't want to ruin their anniversary dinner, he walked in, sighed, and in his best history teacher voice said, "April, your grounding begins tonight. Tomorrow we'll discuss the situation further and decide just how long the punishment will be."

Of course, I was still left to babysit Sammy the Snitch, so when my parents took off for the city and Matt left for rehearsal, I sent Sammy down to the basement with a box of his favorite action figures and picked up the phone to call Brandi. "I'm grounded," I said, "until further notice."

"What? Why?"

"Sammy opened his big fat mouth. He told my mother I was with Dominick."

"No way! I swear, April, I told him not to!"

"I know, it's not your fault. Anyway, she freaked out, and now here I am."

Brandi moaned. "That's too bad, but listen, how did it go with Dominick?"

"Um . . ." I decided not to mention my little run-in with Frankie the Crunch, my conversation with Moe, and the fact that Dominick had showed up an hour late. "It went okay, I guess. Thanks, you know, for helping me out."

"Yeah, sure. I'm just sorry you got in trouble."

"Same here."

"Oh, what about Matt? Did you find out anything after Olympia and I left? Was it the guy in the Jaguar who beat him up?"

I sighed. "Matt's still saying he got elbowed at practice, and my parents believe him. Of course."

"What do you think? Is he telling the truth?"

"Maybe. I'm just not sure."

We talked awhile longer, and before saying goodbye I promised Brandi I'd give her a call the next day when I found out the length of my incarceration.

Now, looking on the bright side, I figured being grounded over this particular weekend had its advantages. Especially since I had a thousand-word short story due Monday with no clue as to what I was going to write about and the evil Count Dracula breathing down my neck. So after taking a quick peek down the basement to make sure

Sammy was still alive, I went to my room, flopped onto the bed, and began racking my brain, trying to come up with an idea.

Just when I decided that Mikhail Baryshnikov would have been a *much* better muse than the Grateful Dead skull and crossbones, Sammy came barging into my room carrying a stack of board games. "Okay, I'm ready! What do you want to play first, April, Candy Land or Chutes and Ladders?"

I rolled over and sighed. "Sam, you've got to be kidding. Listen, why don't you go watch TV or something? In fact, I bet Mutual of Omaha is still running that special on Bigfoot."

He made a face. "No, I already checked, nothing's on. Besides, Mom said you would play with me."

I gazed over at the Candy Land board and thought Mr. Cornelius bore a strange resemblance not only to Count Dracula, but to Lord Licorice as well. "But, Sam, I've got stuff to do. Schoolwork."

"Uh-uh, it's Friday. Plus, you're grounded, the whole weekend at least, so you can do your work anytime you want."

That kid was definitely getting too smart for his own good. "Yeah, and whose fault is it that I'm grounded, Mr. Big Mouth?"

"Hey, I already said I was sorry."

"Yeah, whatever."

He leaned over the bed, peering at me. "April, can I ask you something?"

"I'd rather you didn't, but since you're going to anyway, shoot."

"Why doesn't Mom like Dom?"

I sighed. "I don't know, Sam. I guess it's the way he looks—his hair, his clothes, his earring. She's a mother, so she likes guys who are clean-cut."

"Well, that's stupid." He sat on the edge of my bed with his face all scrunched up, but after a while he began lining up the little gingerbread-man playing pieces on my rug. "Okay, I've got blue, so what color do you want—red, yellow, or green?"

That night Sammy and I not only played Candy Land and Chutes and Ladders, but Go Fish, Pick Up Sticks, Ants in the Pants, and Trouble. When it was finally his bedtime we read his favorite books for the millionth time. Just as I was about to turn off the light and kiss him goodnight, he moaned and said, "April, I'm hungry and thirsty."

"Oh, Sammy, come on—"

"Please, my throat's dry and my stomach is growling."

That kid was such a faker. "All right, fine, down to the kitchen with you, but let's make it quick." Since Sammy was not a big fan of rice cakes or raw sunflower seeds (the only snacks I could find in the cupboard), I wound up making him a grilled cheese sandwich and a milk shake. As I was sitting at the table watching him eat, realizing that if the little stinker had just kept his mouth shut earlier I wouldn't be in this mess, I came up with an idea for my short story.

I grabbed a pad and pencil and scribbled down some random thoughts. When Sammy took his last bite, I said, "Okay, mister, time for bed."

I tucked him in and quickly got the typewriter from Matt's room. Suddenly a whole story—characters, scenes, dialogue, even a title!—was forming in my brain. Mr. Cornelius had told us to write what we knew, and if there was one thing I knew it was babysitting. Who would have thought Sammy would be my muse? I typed away like a madwoman, and by the time Matt and my parents got home, I had a rough draft.

Since I didn't feel like talking to any of the annoying members of my family, I turned out my bedroom light, pretending to be asleep. The three of them talked in the kitchen for a while, mostly about Matt's black eye and how he needed to be more careful at basketball practice. When the whole house was quiet again, I gathered my papers together, took out my flashlight, and with a red pencil began to add, delete, and revise.

When I was finished I had a very dark comedy called "Babysitting Games." It was kind of a twist on Mark Twain's "The Ransom of Red Chief," but instead of the unruly boy torturing his kidnappers, it was about a babysitter playing "games" with a mischievous kid who seriously needed to learn a lesson. The climax came when the babysitter dressed up like an Indian—war paint and all—tied the kid to a stake in his own living room, doused the carpet with lighter fluid (actually water, but the kid didn't know that), and struck a match.

Of course, the whole thing was a total spoof, so I hoped Mr. Cornelius would get the humor. I figured if he didn't I'd probably be sent to the school counselor for a series of psychiatric tests. But, I didn't care. Writing the story turned out to be therapeutic, and when I woke up in the morning I didn't have the urge to string Sammy up on a clothesline or pack my bags for Grand Central Station.

Another good thing about being grounded is that you can catch up on some reading. So after breakfast I took a seat on the front porch and began *Brave New World*, by Aldous Huxley. Mr. Cornelius had told the class that it was one of his favorite books, and I could see why. After reading the first chapter, about a futuristic fertilizing room where genetically engineered people hatched human embryos, I was hooked. This guy Huxley was more bizarre than Poe, Conrad, and King put together.

Anyway, just as I was getting to the really good part where Lenina and Bernard meet a Savage (ironically, a guy born the old-fashioned way) I heard someone walking up the front steps. "Hi, April."

I looked up from page seventy-six and saw Bert standing in front of me. "Oh . . . hi." I glanced around. "Um, what are you doing here?"

He jabbed his thumb toward Brandi's house. "I came with Walt. Brandi just got home from a Booster bake sale, and the three of us were gonna go to the movies. I asked her if you'd want to come along, but she said you might be busy. Anyway, I saw you sitting here reading so I thought I'd come and ask."

I was grateful Brandi hadn't blabbed to Bert about my being grounded. It was kind of embarrassing. "Oh, I'd like to, it's just, well . . ."

Bert craned his neck, trying to get a glimpse of my book jacket. I turned it over so he could see. "Wow, that's crazy," he said. "I just read *Brave New World*. It's now officially my favorite book."

"I like it too. It's pretty weird."

He nodded. "Yeah, supposedly Huxley did a lot of acid when he was writing, you know, to expand his mind. Judging from the story, I'd say it worked."

I laughed. "Yeah, I guess so."

"Anyway, do you want to come with us? I voted for *The Exorcist Two*, but Walt insists on seeing *Star Wars* again. He's a little obsessive about the special effects."

I had already seen *Star Wars* three times that summer, but I would have loved to go again. Like Walt, I was obsessive, not about the special effects, but about Han Solo's killer smile. "I'd like to, but well . . . I'm grounded."

Bert thought this was funny. "Grounded? For what? Wait, let me guess. Drugs? Sex? Booze?"

"How about all three?" I picked up an acorn and tossed it at him.

"April, is someone here?" My mother stepped out the

door and smiled when she saw Bert. "Well, hello, Bert, it's nice to see you again." She looked at me. "Do you two have plans?"

My mother seemed to be having a brief bout of amnesia. As I recalled, she'd grounded me the night before, and my dad and she were going to discuss the details of my punishment today. She stood there waiting for an answer while Bert cleared his throat. "Well, I was hoping April could come to the movies with Brandi, Walt, and me, but it looks like—"

"Oh, how nice. What are you going to see?"

"Um." Bert glanced at me. "*Star Wars*. But if April can't go I understand—"

"What time does it start?"

"Mom?"

"Shhh." She made a face and waved me away.

"Actually"—Bert glanced at his watch—"the movie starts in half an hour, but it's playing at the Alpine, so if we leave now, we'd make it in time."

Mom raised both hands. "Well, what are you waiting for? Go ahead. Oh, but wait." She reached in her pocket and pulled out a few singles. "Here's some money for popcorn. Ask them to please salt it lightly."

I looked at the money. "Mom? Are you forgetting something? Like the fact that you grounded me until further notice?"

She sighed. "Yes, well, your father and I talked a few things over last night, and we'll discuss the situation later.

Right now, go ahead and have a good time with your friends."

I looked at Bert and shrugged. "Okay, whatever."

"I thought you were grounded," Brandi whispered to me when Bert and I showed up at her front door.

I shrugged. "Yep, me too. But here I am. Go figure."

As the four of us set off for the Alpine, Walt and Brandi fell behind, talking and laughing, which left Bert and me with about ten blocks' worth of conversation to make. "So," he said, "how's tennis going? Did you ever call that coach, Frank Stapleton?"

"Oh, no. I was thinking about it, but . . ." I shrugged.

"But what? Come on, you're an amazing player. In fact, you inspired me that day at Poly Prep. Now, don't laugh, but I'm planning to try out for Xavierian's team."

"Why would I laugh? I think that's great. You *should* go out for the team."

"Well, thanks, but if you recall, I'm not too swift at the net, and actually . . ." He smiled shyly. "I was wondering if you'd be willing to help me. Tryouts are next week and I could use a few pointers. It wouldn't be a date or anything—just a few friendly games." He put one hand over his heart. "Scouts' honor."

"Please don't tell me you're a Boy Scout."

"Yep, Walt and I are just one badge away from becoming top-ranking Eagle Scouts."

My jaw dropped. "You've got to be kidding!"

"Ha, ha. Gotcha."

"Eagle Scouts," I said, giving him a shove. "Very funny."

"Well, what do you say, will you help me improve my tennis game? Please, I'm desperate."

I sighed. "All right, but under one condition. We play on *my* turf—the park. I'm not wearing that stupid skirt again."

He nodded. "Deal."

After that we talked about *Brave New World* and whether there really was a possibility of genetic engineering. Bert thought there was, but I was holding to my theory that we'd all be zapped by a Russian nuclear bomb before anything like that could happen. Anyway, before I knew it, Bert and I were crossing Fort Hamilton Parkway, and up ahead stood the Brooklyn Performing Arts Center. In just one week, Matt and Bettina would debut as Romeo and Juliet, star-crossed lovers both on- and offstage. It was pretty unnerving. I noticed that the building was dark and empty, but as we passed by, voices drifted from the enclosed courtyard on the lower level. I stopped and listened. "Hey, Bert, will you wait here a minute? I need to check on something."

"Yeah, sure."

I took a quick look down the street and saw that Walt and Brandi were trailing pretty far behind. I had time. Quietly, I tiptoed down the stairs and peered over the marble banister. On a wooden bench, in front of a sparkling fountain, Matt and Bettina sat huddled together. Sammy's Kermit the Frog comforter was draped around their shoulders. They were speaking in hushed voices, and I watched as Matt reached over and tucked a lock of hair behind Bettina's ear. Before he could spot me, I hunkered down to listen.

"I'm really glad you came," Matt said. "I've missed you."

Bettina laughed a little. "Missed me? That's silly, Matt, we've been seeing each other at rehearsal almost every night."

"Yeah, but it's not the same. I like being here with you, alone, in our secret place."

"Mmmm, me too."

I didn't hear anything for a while, so I peeked over the banister and saw the two of them making out. It was strangely repulsive and fascinating at the same time. While they were going at it, a car out on the street honked its horn loudly. Bettina gasped, and they both looked around, startled. Luckily, I'd ducked my head just in time. "Bettina, it's all right, don't worry," Matt said. "It's just a car. No one knows we're here."

"I know, Matt, you're right. It's just sometimes I get scared, not so much for me but—"

"Shhh. Don't say anything."

It was quiet, so I figured they were kissing again. Meanwhile, I peered around checking for Nicky Jag or any other suspicious Mafioso-looking vehicles, but the street was empty. I realized that anyone driving by this building would have no idea that Matt and Bettina were busy making out in the courtyard below. Matt was right. It was the perfect hiding place.

I figured Walt and Brandi were about to catch up with us now, so I quickly padded up the stairs. When I reached the top, I saw Bert perched on a wooden crate next to a Dumpster. "So, did you have a good time down there? See anything *interesting?*"

"Look," I said, taking his arm and dragging him along. "When you're with me, don't ask any questions, all right? You're better off that way."

He shrugged. "Okay, whatever you say."

Inside the theater Walt bought Cokes for all of us, and with the money my mother had given me I ordered two large popcorns with extra salt *and* extra butter. As I handed a bag to Brandi, Bert piped up. "Wait a minute, April, didn't your mother say 'lightly salted'?"

I popped a few kernels into my mouth and chewed. After months of polyunsaturated fats, I was in heaven. I handed Bert the bag. "Hey, Bert, remember our agreement?"

He looked puzzled for a moment, and then the light-bulb came on. "Ohhhh, right. No questions allowed."

There were plenty of seats, so we filed into a row, four across. Bert sat to my right, and I made sure Brandi was on my left. As the previews began, I leaned over and whispered, "Brandi, you're not going to believe this. Matt and

Bettina were in the courtyard of the performing arts center—making out."

She gasped. "No way! Is he crazy? Doesn't he realize how risky that is?"

"I guess not."

She shook her head and handed Walt the popcorn. He smiled at her.

"You know what I think?" I whispered.

"What?"

"Today's the day."

"What do you mean?"

"Walt's going to kiss you, I can tell."

A few seconds later the lights dimmed, and as the movie began I saw Walt's arm creep across the back of Brandi's chair. Thankfully, Bert was smart enough to keep his hands to himself, and I enjoyed every kernel of my salty, buttery popcorn. About halfway through the movie, when R2D2 and C3P0 were getting ripped apart by aliens, Brandi nudged me. "April, did you see?"

"See what?"

"He did it. Walt kissed me."

She smiled, and even in the darkness of the theater I could tell she was blushing.

When I got home, my mother was in the kitchen cooking dinner. Surprisingly, it smelled pretty good. "Hi, April. Did you have a nice time with your friends?" She sounded overly cheerful, so I knew something was up.

I shrugged. "It was okay. Thanks, you know, for letting me go."

I kicked off my shoes, and as I was about to head upstairs, my mom turned off the stove and set down her spatula. "April, Dad and I would like to speak with you. Matt and Sammy aren't around, so maybe now's a good time." She pulled out a chair. "Here, have a seat." She walked into the living room and called my dad. "Honey, April's home! Can you come downstairs, please?"

I plopped into the chair, awaiting another lecture and the terms of my forthcoming punishment. When my father arrived, he gave my mom a little smile and patted her back a few times. I took this as a bad sign. They sat down on either side of me, and my mother cleared her throat. They both looked pretty uncomfortable. "Well, April," she began, "as I explained earlier, your father and I have discussed the situation, and well, we've come to the conclusion that you were right."

I looked at her, stunned. "Did you just say I was right?"

She glanced at my father, who nodded and motioned for her to continue. "Yes, you see, we've realized that we shouldn't have jumped to conclusions concerning this boy, Dominick, based on"—she paused for a moment, trying to find the right word—"well, based on appearances. So after talking it through, we've agreed that you can invite him over sometime. When we're home, of course."

"Oh." I glanced back and forth between them. I wasn't quite sure how I felt about this—a scheduled meeting with

Dominick and my parents. It wasn't exactly his style. "Um, all right. Thanks, I guess. Is that all?"

My mom looked at my dad. He nodded. "Yes," she said, "that's all."

"So can I go now? I've got to type up the final draft of my story for English. It's due Monday."

"Oh, of course, that's fine. Dinner will be ready by seven, and I'm making one of your favorites—baked ziti. Brandi's mother gave me some of her sauce and I even used whole-milk mozzarella in the recipe."

I smiled, leaned over, and kissed her cheek. As I did, my dad winked at me. "Thanks, Mom," I said. "Why don't you call me before dinner's ready and I'll set the table for you."

"Hey," my dad said. "Don't I get a kiss too?"

"Course you do."

On Monday morning, I walked to school with Brandi and Larry, carrying a crisp, clean typed copy of "Babysitting Games" tucked safely away in my loose-leaf binder. During lunch Mr. Ruffalo gave me another piano lesson, and while Dominick and his band practiced for their gig, I ate a huge Tupperware bowl full of cold ziti.

Later, as Dominick walked me to English, he said, "I missed you this weekend. I was hoping you'd stop by."

"I wanted to, but a lot of stuff came up." I paused, wondering if this was a good time to bring up my parents' offer. "Actually, my mom asked if you'd like to come over my house sometime. You know, when they're around."

"Really? Your mom wants me to come to your house?" He laughed. "Now, that's pretty wild. In fact, that's a first." He rubbed his chin and thought for a moment. "Well, sure, why not?"

The bell rang, and after Dominick kissed me goodbye, Mr. Cornelius stepped out of his room and cleared his throat. "I better go," I said to Dominick. "I'll see you tomorrow."

"Yeah, tomorrow."

As Dominick scurried down the hallway, Mr. Cornelius said, "So, Miss Lundquist, did you find any time over the weekend to write a story?"

I smiled, opened my binder, and handed Mr. Cornelius my beautifully typed pages. "Yes, actually, I did."

He gazed at the title page. "Well, what do you know? Wonders never cease."

At the end of the period, Mr. Cornelius decided to give us fifteen minutes of silent reading so he could begin grading our papers. When I opened *Brave New World*, nothing could have prepared me for what I saw. Staring up at me was President William McKinley. I'd never known his face was on the five-hundred-dollar bill.

EIGHTEEN

"Brandi! Brandi, wait up!" I called, plowing through the hallway, almost knocking down a seventh grader. English class had just let out, and sixth period was about to begin. I stopped, panting heavily. "Did you get one too?"

"April, calm down." Brandi glanced around and lowered her voice. "If you mean another hundred, no. We've already gotten four of those bills apiece. Why, did you?"

"Get a load of this." I opened my book and showed her the bill.

She gasped. "Oh my God!"

I snapped the book shut. "What are we going to do?"

"I don't know."

"We have to do something," I said. "This is getting ridiculous."

Brandi swallowed. "Um, listen, April, I know this might sound like I'm weaseling out, but Mr. Luciano gave *you* the bill, not me. And it's not that I don't want to help, but maybe it would be better if you talked to him alone. Maybe he'll even give you some advice on what to do about Matt."

"Alone?" I considered this for a moment, and even though I did think Brandi was hanging me out to dry, in a way I guessed she was right. Not only was I the sister of the guy stupid enough to date Bettina Bocelli, I was also the sucker holding the five-hundred-dollar bill. "Okay," I said. "I'll do it."

Brandi grinned. "And may the Force be with you."

"Very funny."

"Danger and doom," I repeated like a mantra on my way to class. *"Danger and doom."*

Bright and early the following morning, while Larry was getting ready for school and Mrs. Luciano was brewing a pot of espresso in the kitchen, I came face to face with Soft Sal. He sat on his papal throne and motioned for me to take a seat on the sofa. Hands shaking, I slid the money across the coffee table—four Ben Franklins plus the whopping William McKinley. "Mr. Luciano," I said. "I'm terribly sorry, but I can't accept this."

He glanced briefly at the cash, then paused to light a cigar. After a few puffs he picked up the five hundred and held it to the light. "Well, it's definitely legit. It's not a *fugazi*, if that's what you were thinking."

"Um, a what?"

"A *fugazi*. You know, a fake. Counterfeit."

"Oh, no, that's not what I meant."

"Coffee's ready!" The kitchen door swung open and Mrs. Luciano appeared, carrying a tray with two steaming cups of espresso and a plate of her famous cannolis. She set the dishes on the coffee table and didn't even seem to notice that almost a grand in cash was lying there. "*Mangia, mangia*—eat, eat. Now, I have some things to do, so you must excuse me."

"Thank you, Mrs. Luciano."

"Yes, thank you, Marianne." Soft Sal gazed lovingly at his wife, took a sip of espresso, and motioned for me to do the same. However, when I did, my hands were shaking so badly I spilled most of it on my jeans. "Well, sweetheart, now that we've established the fact that the bills are not *fugazis*, what's the problem?"

I looked at the five hundred. McKinley seemed to be saying *I wouldn't do this if I were you*. "I . . . I can't accept this money. You see, I *like* walking Larry back and forth to school, and, well, it's just way too much."

He pursed his lips, nodded a few times, and gazed at the ceiling. Finally, he said, "Sweetheart, I'm sorry, but I have no idea what you're talking about."

"But . . . it had to be you, putting money into my books. Brandi's, too. I mean, who else would do it?"

He shrugged. "Honestly, I have no idea."

This conversation was going nowhere fast. "Um, Mr. Luciano, can I ask you a question?"

"Of course, sweetheart." He took a puff on his cigar and blew a smoke ring. "Tell me, what would you like to know?"

"Well . . ." Actually, there were a lot of things I wanted to know, like how could he, Gorgeous Vinny, and Frankie the Crunch murder people and still sleep at night, but I figured it wouldn't be wise to ask. "You see, it's about Matt."

"Ah, yes, Sunshine Boy. Nice kid, your brother. What about him?"

I swallowed. "Well, you see, that's just the thing. Like, for instance, why do you call him Sunshine Boy? Is it a code name or something?"

"Code name?" He started to laugh. "Sweetheart, where do you come up with these things?" He pointed to his shiny bald skull. "It's the blond hair, of course. What else?"

This was not going to be easy—getting a hit man to break his vow of *Omerta*. "I guess what I'm really trying to say is, well, is Matt in trouble, you know, for seeing Bettina?"

"Ohhhh, Bettina. Yes, she's quite a girl, isn't she? Hmmm." He tapped his chin. "What kind of trouble do you mean?"

I felt like telling Mr. Luciano that *I* was the one who was supposed to be asking the questions, but I figured I was in enough hot water as it was. "Well, Matt came home with a black eye last week, and I was wondering if—"

"You know," he said, pointing his finger at me, "I'm

glad you mentioned that. I saw him looking a little, shall we say, under the weather. How's he doing now?"

"Um, he's okay, but I was wondering if you knew anything? Like, how it happened?"

"Me? No, I've got no clue."

I looked into his eyes. "Matt told me he got elbowed in basketball practice."

"I see. And you don't believe him?"

"I'm—not sure."

"Hmmm." He rubbed his chin. "In my opinion, sisters should always believe their brothers."

At this point I was slowly getting over my fear and beginning to get angry. "Mr. Luciano, look, I'm just going to say this plainly. There's a guy—Matt says he's Bettina's cousin—who drives a black Jaguar convertible. Larry calls him Nicky Jag. I'm wondering if he's following Matt."

"Nicky Jag, huh?" He rubbed his chin some more. "So, let me get this straight, you think he may have done the damage?"

"Yes, that's what I'm saying."

"Well, anything's possible. It could be, but I don't know."

I closed my eyes. "Mr. Luciano. Please understand. Matt is my brother and I love him. I don't want to see anything bad happen to him. Please, I'm afraid, and I'm asking if you can help."

Mr. Luciano didn't say anything for a long time. He took a bite of his cannoli and chewed thoughtfully.

Finally, he leaned over the table and looked me square in the eye. "Okay, sweetheart, now listen carefully, and what I say doesn't leave this room, is that clear?"

I nodded. "Yes, that's clear."

"Which means you cannot breathe a word of this to your friend Brandi, or to your brother, either. I have a fine reputation in this community, and I intend to keep it that way."

I nodded again. With the way Mr. Luciano was looking at me, you could be sure I'd keep my mouth zipped from here to eternity.

"All right," he went on. "Now, I don't usually do this, but the thing is, I like you. You've been good to my Larry and that means a lot. And, don't get me wrong, I like your brother, too, he's a nice boy. Actually, I like your whole family. And believe it or not, I've been in love before. I know what it's like to be crazy about a girl. Anyway, I'll talk to some people I know, see what I can do."

"Okay, but—does that mean Matt's protected? He won't get hurt?"

Mr. Luciano sighed. "I'm only one man, and there's only so much I can do. I can't promise anything. Some people are set in their ways. As for me, I have a beautiful son, and I thank God for him every day. If I had a daughter like Bettina I'd like to think that she could make some important decisions on her own. But that's just me. Not everyone I know is so open-minded. Anyway"—he picked up the stack of bills and handed them to me—"let's leave it at this: your brother would be much better off keeping to himself, but if he won't, well, then, maybe there's a reason why someone gave you this money. Nine hundred dollars could buy a lot of things, like a bus ticket, or even a plane ticket if you needed to disappear for a while."

"Disappear? Are you saying that Matt might need to disappear?"

"I'm not saying anything, sweetheart. All I know is that it never hurts to be prepared. So do yourself a favor, take the money."

Now that I had almost a grand of Soft Sal Luciano's illicitly earned cash, and had also sworn to keep the vow of *Omerta*, I began to feel a strange kinship with Frankie the Crunch. As Larry, Brandi, and I passed his house that morning on the way to school, I gazed at the statue of St. Christopher carrying the enormous burden of the Christ child, and figured that if I'd been Catholic he'd probably have been my patron saint too.

As promised, I didn't breathe a word of this to Brandi, and when she pressed me on how things had gone that morning, I said, "Oh, well, you know how Mr. Luciano is. He told me he knew nothing about the money. So, for now, I'm just going to keep it."

"Wow, really? That's a ton of cash. Almost a thousand, right?"

"Um, yeah. But, who knows, I might need it one day."

As it turned out I really didn't have to worry too much

about Matt—at least for the time being. His eye started to heal and over the next several days there were no more sightings of Nicky Jag. Also, Monday had marked the beginning of basketball season, so now Matt had longer practices after school, plus games twice a week. Add this to play rehearsal and there was very little time for him to see Bettina on the sly and endanger his life.

However, I had a new problem. Ever since my mother and I'd had our little heart-to-heart talk, she'd been hounding me to invite Dominick over for dinner. The thing was, every time I thought about him joining our family for spinach-lentil casserole I had a panic attack. I mean, what would we all talk about? Pink Floyd's latest psychedelic release? And with my luck Sammy would probably tell them the story of Dominick mooning Frankie Ferraro on the baseball field. That would go over big.

Anyway, it couldn't be avoided any longer, and on Friday afternoon I'd finally mustered the courage to ask him. But when I showed up for lunch in the band room, Pee Wee, Ronnie, and Larry were alone. "Hi, guys," I said, looking around. "What's going on? Where's Dominick?"

The three of them were sitting by their instruments, looking dejected. Larry lifted his drumstick and smashed a cymbal. "Dom's not here. He skipped town."

"What? Skipped town? What are you talking about?"

"It's true," Pee Wee said. "The bum bagged on us at the worst time possible. Our band's got a gig comin' up and we're nowhere near ready."

"But—where did he go?"

Pee Wee shrugged. "His dad had some shows lined up on Long Island, so I guess Dom decided to go with him. It pisses me off 'cause he left without saying a word, and we have no idea when he's coming back."

"Oh." I was about to say that Dominick's father probably wouldn't let him miss more than a day or two of school, but then I realized who I was talking to. Pee Wee and Ronnie weren't exactly the kind of guys who cared about attendance. "Well, I'm sure he'll be back in time for the gig. He wouldn't just leave you guys hanging."

Ronnie laughed. "Oh, yeah? Then I guess you don't really know Dom, do you?"

After my piano lesson with Mr. Ruffalo, I roamed the halls for a while and wound up outside Mr. Cornelius's class much earlier than usual. When the bell rang, he stepped out the door, and with a surprised look said, "Miss Lundquist, what good fortune, you're alone today."

I wasn't in the mood for any of his lame comments, so without answering I slipped inside and took a seat. To get my mind off my recent troubles I opened my latest library loan—*The Metamorphosis* by Franz Kafka—while the rest of the class filed in. The story was easy to relate to since it was about a guy who woke up one day, flat on his back, realizing he'd turned into a cockroach. But just when I was trying to decide whether Kafka had surpassed Huxley in weirdness, Mr. Cornelius's voice came booming across the room. "Today, class," he announced, "I will be handing back your short stories."

I looked up and saw that he was holding a stack of papers, staring right at me. Little hairs prickled up the back of my neck. After reading my dark comedy, I was certain Mr. Cornelius was going to send me to the school counselor for a psychiatric evaluation. Worse than that, he might even call my parents.

I closed my book and sat there with a feeling of impending doom. "I've read each story thoroughly," he went on, "and I must say, at times it was a trial. Nonetheless, I've given each of you a grade and have marked your papers with suggestions for revision. If you're unhappy with what you've received and would like to improve your grade, you may rewrite."

I shifted in my seat while several people in the class moaned.

"However, before I hand these back, I would like to read you a story written by one of your peers that stands out above the rest. Not only is it well written, but it shows creativity, wit, and an uncanny sense of humor." He pulled one from the stack. "I am not going to state the author's name, but I'm wondering if you'll be able to guess, after I'm finished, whose it is. The title is: 'Babysitting Games.' "

I almost fell off my chair.

"Is there a problem, Miss Lundquist?"

"Oh, no. No problem."

"Well, then I suggest you listen carefully and take notes. Maybe you'll learn something."

As Mr. Cornelius began to read my paper, I inconspicuously peered around the room. At first kids were yawning and whispering to each other, but about two paragraphs into the story, I noticed several who actually seemed interested. Halfway through, there were some grins and snickers, and when it came to the grand finale, where the babysitter ties the kid to the stake and douses the rug with make-believe lighter fluid, everyone was laughing.

When Mr. Cornelius finished, the whole class began to applaud. He looked up. "Can anyone guess whose story that was?"

"It's pretty obvious," John Gillespie said. "It's April's. Look how red her face is."

There was more laughter, and I wasn't sure whether I wanted to hide under my desk or stand up and take a bow.

Mr. Cornelius smiled and handed me the paper. There was a huge A+ at the top. Very quietly he said, "It's unfortunate that you didn't hand in a rough draft, Miss Lundquist. If you had, you would have received an A for this marking period instead of a C. But there's always room for improvement, isn't there?"

I ran my finger over the A+. Next to it were the words "Excellent Work" in bold letters. "Yes," I said. "I'm planning to bring up my grade."

He smiled again, and strangely didn't seem to resemble

Count Dracula or Lord Licorice. "That's good news, Miss Lundquist. And please see me after class. I'd like to speak with you about something."

When the bell rang I waited for everyone to leave, then walked slowly to Mr. Cornelius's desk. Without a word he opened a drawer, pulled out a sheet of paper, and handed it to me. "Every year there is a citywide high school short story competition. If you're interested, fill out this application and bring it back to me by next Friday. In order to qualify, the form must be signed by a parent or guardian and submitted by the student's teacher. In other words, me. I must say, Miss Lundquist, I've been teaching English for twenty-five years and this is some of the best work I've seen. I think your story has a good chance of winning."

I swallowed hard. On the bottom of the application were the words "Parent Signature," followed by a long black line. "Um, Mr. Cornelius?"

"Yes?"

"I was wondering, do my parents have to actually *read* the story? I mean is there some kind of rule?"

"Well, let's see." He put on his reading glasses and scanned the paper. "As far as I can tell, no. All they have to do is sign."

"Oh, okay, thanks. I—better get to class now."

"Miss Lundquist?"

"Yes?"

He lowered his glasses and gave me a meaningful look.

"You took a risk with your story—exposed a part of who you are. That takes courage, and best of all, makes for great writing. Please, don't let anyone discourage you."

I nodded, slipped the application into my binder, and scurried off to sixth-period class.

NINETEEN

When I picked up the phone, I heard heavy breathing on the other end. "Hello, this is Darth Vader calling April Lundquist. My tennis instructor, Obi-Wan Kenobi, is out of town, and I desperately need a lesson. If you deny me, I will be forced to inform your mother about heavily salted popcorn."

"Bert?"

"Yeah, it's me. Listen, my tryout's coming up soon, and I'm freaking out. Help, please!"

We agreed to meet at the park Wednesday after school. When Brandi caught wind of this, she asked if she and Walt could tag along, so of course I said yes. Sammy wasn't too keen on being the ball boy, so after we'd plopped him in the stroller I bribed him with a Raspberry Blow Pop from Moe's, and he soon quit whining.

The days were getting shorter now, so we hurried down

the block, bouncing Sammy along the cracks in the sidewalk. I hadn't seen Dominick in school for several days—Pee Wee and Ronnie still didn't know where he was—and as we approached the candy store, I saw that the blinds in the upstairs apartment were drawn and not a single light was on.

Inside, Moe greeted us at the counter, an unlit cigarette dangling from his lips. "Why, hello there, girls. Hello, Sammy. Long time no see."

"Hi, Moe!" Sammy jumped out of the stroller and ran to the candy section.

"So you heard about our new flavor, huh?" Moe winked at Brandi and me.

"Yep, raspberry!"

While Sammy searched among the pops and Brandi looked over the new potato chip display, I dug in my pocket for change. Moe took the cigarette out of his mouth, slid it behind his ear, and leaned on the counter. "In case you're wondering, your friend upstairs arrived home today. I had a word with his father about taking him out of school for no good reason. Sorry to say, it didn't go over too well."

I set two quarters on the counter. "Yeah, I heard something about that."

By now, Brandi had made her selection—a bag of Cheez Doodles—and Sammy was back in the stroller peeling the wrapper off the lollipop.

Moe swept the change off the counter and opened the cash register. "He's not home at the moment—took off with those two delinquent friends of his—but listen, next time you see him, maybe you could help him realize that playing guitar is not going to get him a high school diploma."

"No," I said. "I guess not."

Moe handed me a nickel in change and looked me in the eye. "Be careful, okay? Dom's got a pretty good heart, but he's not all that reliable, if you know what I mean. And I'm not sure if he's the right guy for you, either."

As usual, I felt like telling Moe to mind his own business, but instead I nodded and said, "Okay, Moe, I'll keep it in mind."

When we arrived at the park, Bert and Walt were already warming up on one of the courts. It was a relief to see that they hadn't worn their little white outfits.

"Hi, girls!" Bert said, waving us over. "Look, it's perfect, we've got two courts, side by side!"

As we walked toward them, I craned my neck, peering past the redbrick wall of the bathrooms. I noticed that the words DISCO SUCKS had been redone in silver spray paint. I thought maybe Dominick had come to the park with Pee Wee and Ronnie, but the spot where the musicians usually sat was empty. In the distance, however, Big Joe, Little Joe, Tony, and Fritz were playing a game of two-on-two.

Matt was the only one of their posse who'd made varsity basketball this year, and he was at practice. At least I hoped so.

Bert and I took one court, and while I gave him several pointers for scoring big at the net, Brandi and Walt played a game of singles on the other. But after a while, Brandi got tired of this and suggested we play some doubles. Only this time she wanted to be on my team.

"All right," I said skeptically. "But you better not play like a pansy."

"Oh, don't worry," she answered, flashing me a devious smile. "Today you and I are going to kick their butts."

"Now, that's more like it."

Brandi and I won the first two games, but as Bert got the hang of playing the net, he started making some pretty excellent drop shots and they wound up winning the third. In the middle of game four, Big Joe spied us on the courts, so the imbeciles left their game of two-on-two and came strolling over. "Well, well," Big Joe said, leaning against the fence. "Looks like Brandi and the Chimp are creaming the two Xa-fairy-land boys. Way to go, girls!"

Little Joe was trailing behind, staring into the sky and twirling his basketball on one finger. "Hey, Joe," Fritz said, waving him on. "Get a load of this. Brandi and Ape are killing the fairies."

I sighed deeply. "Just ignore them," I called over to Bert and Walt. "The Neanderthals are bored and don't know what to do with themselves."

But just as I was about to serve for the next point, Walt raised his racquet and said, "Hey, April, hold on a minute, okay?" He left us and headed toward the fence. "Hey, guys?"

Big Joe crossed his arms over his chest and smirked. "Yeah?"

Tony and Fritz elbowed each other. Little Joe stopped twirling.

"What do you say we play some ball?"

Fritz guffawed. "What kind of ball are you talking about, Walt?" He grabbed the basketball from Little Joe, and as he bounced it, he swung his leg around and sang, "*A, my name is Alice, and my husband's name is Al . . .*"

Tony thought this was hilarious, but Little Joe didn't think it was funny at all. He grabbed his ball back from Fritz and told Tony to shut the hell up.

"Actually, I'm talking about *basketball*," Walt said. "A little two-on-two. Me and Bert versus Fritz and Tony. The two Joes sit out."

While the imbeciles thought this one over, Bert crept up behind Walt and tapped him on the shoulder. "Walt, are you crazy, man? They're gonna slaughter us."

Meanwhile, Tony stepped forward. "All right, yeah, you got it, let's play some two-on-two. In fact, we'll even be generous and spot you guys ten points."

Bert nodded eagerly at this suggestion, but Walt was already shaking his head. "Uh-uh, we don't want any points—just one game, fair and square. Take it or leave it."

Fritz nodded. "All right, we'll take it. Let's go."

*　　*　　*

While the guys left for the basketball courts, Brandi, Sammy, and I picked up stray tennis balls. "Wow," Brandi said. "I am so proud of Walt. He finally stood up to them."

"Yeah," I said, glancing nervously ahead. "I just hope he and Bert don't get their butts handed to them. If they do, we'll never hear the end of it."

After packing up our tennis gear, Sammy climbed into the stroller and we headed for the courts. They were about to start their game, and apparently Big Joe had declared himself referee. As we passed by the bathrooms, Little Joe stepped out from behind the redbrick wall. "April, can I talk to you for a minute?"

Brandi gasped. "Jeez, Joe! What's with you lately? Do you enjoy scaring us, or what?"

"Oh, sorry. I just need to talk to April. It's important."

She looked at me and rolled her eyes. "All right, fine, whatever, have your *talk*." She took the stroller from my hands. Come on, Sammy, let's go. They obviously don't want us here."

When Brandi and Sammy were safely out of earshot I said, "What's going on, Joe? Is everything okay? Is Matt all right?"

"Oh, yeah, I mean no, I mean . . . Matt's fine. That's not what I wanted to talk to you about." He shoved his hands in his pockets and glanced around nervously. His eyes landed on the nearby picnic tables. "Can we sit down together for a few minutes?"

244

"Um, yeah, sure."

We walked a little way, and I took a seat on one of the hard stone benches. As the coldness seeped into my jeans, Little Joe gently eased himself beside me. We were so close, our knees were touching, and I could even smell the clean sweat drying off his forehead and jersey. Without speaking, the two of us looked at the sky. The sun was just beginning to set, and through the bare branches of the tall oaks you could see a mixture of pink and purple clouds. "Wow, it's a pretty night," I said.

"Yeah." He tapped his fingers against the stone.

"Joe? What did you want to talk about?"

"Well"—he cleared his throat—"I was wondering if you had time to think about . . . things."

"Things?"

"Yeah. Like you and me."

"Oh—that." I glanced over at him; he seemed to be holding his breath. "Well, you see . . . I . . . sort of have a boyfriend now." A missing boyfriend, I wanted to add, but that was too complicated to explain at the moment.

He swallowed and lifted his eyes toward the basketball courts. Big Joe had just called a foul on Walt, and Fritz was taking his free throw. "You mean that guy—*Bert?*"

He said Bert's name the way I used to say *Walter*—like he was a total dork. I shook my head. "No, not him."

"So, the other one, huh? Dom?"

"Yeah."

"I see."

"But, Joe, I—"

"No, no, it's all right. You don't have to explain anything, I was just wondering, that's all. Besides, it probably wouldn't work out anyway. Matt would kill me." He patted my knee. "Come on, we better head over to the courts before the guys start talking." He stood up and rubbed his hands together.

"Joe?"

"Yeah?"

"I really don't care if they talk."

He shrugged and smiled. "Yeah, me neither."

We walked together in silence, watching the big orange sun sink behind a row of houses across the street, and for a moment I wondered what it would be like to walk along the path holding Little Joe's hand, talking, maybe even stopping for a moment to share a kiss. Things used to be so easy between us—before that day at the beach, before he started acting so strange.

But soon, Sammy was calling us. "April, Joe! Come and see! Bert and Walt are winning!"

We rushed over to watch the rest of the game, but in the end Fritz and Tony won by four points. However, Bert and Walt won something more important than a basketball game—respect from my brother's pathetic friends. "I gotta say, you guys put up a good fight," Big Joe said, clapping the two of them on the back. "Xavierian High School is officially two fairies below their normal quota. Keep up the good work, men."

It was starting to get dark now, so Brandi and I said goodbye to Bert and Walt, plopped Sammy in the stroller, and raced home. Brandi made it back just in time for dinner, and as I wheeled Sammy up the driveway I heard voices coming from the kitchen.

Inside, Dominick was sitting at the table, my parents flanking him. There was a plate in front of him, and on it was a half-eaten turkey burger on whole wheat, a mound of brown rice, and several asparagus stalks. "Dom!" Sammy ran and flung his arms around Dominick.

Dominick had a mouthful of food. He chewed quickly, swallowed, and hugged Sammy back. "Hey, buddy, how ya doin'?"

"I'm great!"

When Dominick saw me standing in the doorway, he flashed that cute smile. "Hi, April, sorry I didn't tell you I was coming. Actually, I just stopped by to say hello—the guys and I were practicing over at Larry's—but your mom insisted I have something to eat."

"Oh, okay."

He turned to my mom. "And by the way, Mrs. Lundquist, this food is delicious. I wish my dad cooked half this good." He picked up his cup and took a huge gulp. "And this tea is awesome. What do you call it again?"

My mother was beaming. "Red Zinger."

"You were practicing at Larry's?" I said.

"Yeah, I just got back in town this afternoon, and the guys wanted to catch up. Larry's got drums in his basement, and his dad let us play down there. Afterward, I was in the neighborhood and, well, I knew your mom mentioned I could stop by sometime—"

"Oh, yes," my mother said. "That's fine." She turned to me. "We even met the other members of Dominick's band."

I looked at her and then at my dad. "You guys met Pee Wee and Ronnie?"

"Yes," my dad said, nodding. "They're . . . interesting boys."

"Here," my mom said, patting her chair, "come and have a seat, April. You too, Sammy. I'll get you some dinner."

As Sammy and I took our places at the table, my dad said, "Well, before you came in, Dominick was just about to tell us what kind of music his band plays."

"Oh, right," Dominick said, setting down his fork. "Let's see, my tastes are pretty diverse. Pee Wee, Ronnie, and Larry mostly like mainstream rock, but I've been getting into some older stuff like CCR, the Yardbirds, Arlo Guthrie, Buddy Holly, some of the early Beatles—I'm writing some of my own songs, too."

My dad was obviously impressed. "Really? That's quite a list." Unlike my mother, who considered Neil Diamond and Barry Manilow cutting edge, he had pretty good taste in music. "So," he said, sighing deeply, "big tragedy this summer, huh?"

I had no idea what my father was talking about, but

apparently Dominick did. He frowned and shook his head. "Oh, man, when I heard the King died, I shut myself in my room and didn't come out for three whole days."

My mom set our plates in front of us and nodded sadly. That was when I realized they were talking about Elvis. I guess he was a big sensation in the fifties, but when I saw him perform on TV last year wearing dark glasses, fuzzy sideburns, and a jewel-encrusted white suit, I thought he should have put his legend to rest long ago.

Thinking about Elvis, my mother must have gotten all sentimental and nostalgic, because she placed one hand on Dominick's shoulder and said, "You know, Dominick, I think it's wonderful that you've taken Larry under your wing. What a kind thing to do."

"Oh, no," Dominick said. "You see, you've got it all wrong. Larry's a great drummer. We're lucky to have him."

"Is that so?" She smiled and began fiddling with my hair. "I'm not sure if you know this, Dominick, but April used to play piano. It's a shame she quit because she had talent."

"Mom," I said, waving her off. "You're talking about me like I'm not even in the room."

"You mean . . ." Dominick looked at me, confused. "You didn't tell your mom about Ruffalo?"

Up until this point I'd only been picking at my food, but now I shoveled some brown rice into my mouth. It had a gluelike consistency and a similar flavor. "No," I mumbled, "I guess not."

My mother scratched her head. "Do you mean—Mr. Ruffalo, the music teacher at your school?"

"Yeah," Dominick said. "He's been giving April piano lessons during lunch for the past couple of weeks."

She looked at me, stunned. "April, why didn't you tell us? That's—well, that's wonderful!" It was amazing how Dominick was racking up points with my parents—especially my mom. Not only was he an Elvis fan, but he'd shown benevolence to a poor retarded boy, and now he'd gotten me interested in piano. "Oh, my," she said, with a worried look, "we must owe him some money!"

I was about to explain that Mr. Ruffalo was teaching me on a trial basis for free, when the back door swung open and Matt and Little Joe walked in.

"Good news, everyone!" Matt announced. "The first three performances of *Romeo and Juliet* have sold out. However . . ." He fished in his pocket, then held up his hand. "Here are some prize tickets for the final show!" He slapped them down on the table and suddenly noticed Dominick was sitting there. "Hey, what do you know, it's the guitar player." He turned around. "Look, Joe, Dom's here."

Matt gave Dom a high five while Little Joe stood frozen in the doorway. Meanwhile, my mother picked up the tickets and flipped through them. "Matt?" she said, "there are ten tickets here. Who are the extra six for?"

"Well, let's see, Ape wanted a ticket for Brandi, that's one, and then there's one for Big Joe, Little Joe, Tony,

Fritz . . ." He paused, realizing there was still one extra, and smiled. "I guess the last ticket's for Dom."

Dominick had just taken a bite of his turkey burger, and when he heard the news he practically started choking. "Wow, are you serious? Thanks, man!"

Matt nodded. "Sure, no problem. Hey, Joe, what do you say? Looks like Dom's going to the show with you guys."

We all turned to see Little Joe's reaction, but he'd already disappeared out the back door.

TWENTY

By the first performance of *Romeo and Juliet*, Matt's black eye required just a light dusting from Cover Girl, and the purple bruises on his arm had faded to pale yellow dots. Since there were no further injuries and I hadn't seen Nicky Jag for quite a while, I figured that either (1) Matt had told the truth about getting clobbered in basketball practice, or (2) Soft Sal had worked his Mafioso magic and Bobby the Bull Bocceli had chosen to back off.

Now it was the evening of the final show. Matt had already left for the performing arts center, and Brandi and I were sitting on the living room sofa watching his friends stroll through the front door, each of their outfits more hilarious than the last. Big Joe was the first to arrive, in a mint green leisure suit he'd borrowed from his cousin. Next, Tony came in wearing an assembly uniform (navy high-waters, wrinkly white shirt, and red tie) that must have dated to seventh grade. But the one who took the prize was Fritz, sporting a silver-studded black leather jacket with matching pants. When Brandi saw him she said, "Hey, Fritz, where'd you hitch up your Harley?"

Last was Little Joe. He was the only one who looked classy and (I must admit) handsome in a nicely fitted charcoal suit, pale pink shirt, and black tie. He even had a white handkerchief tucked neatly into his breast pocket. For some reason, he seemed more at ease tonight, laughing and joking with his friends, and thankfully he didn't ask for any private chats. "Hey, April, Brandi," he said, pointing his thumb at the Three Stooges lined up against the wall. "You think they're gonna let these clowns into the theater tonight?"

Brandi shook her head. "From the looks of things, I doubt it."

"You know," Little Joe went on, "I heard the Village People are looking for a few backup singers. You guys might be perfect."

"Funny, Joe," Fritz said, flipping him the bird. "You're a regular riot."

By 7:15 everyone had arrived except Dominick, and since the play began at eight, my mom was pacing the floor and generally freaking out. "April, are you sure Dominick knew it was tonight?"

"Yes, Mom. I talked to him at school yesterday. He knows it's tonight."

"Well, maybe you should call him again. It's getting

late. If he hasn't left yet, we could always pick him up at his house."

I sighed. "All right, I'll try one more time." I got up, walked into the kitchen, and dialed Dominick's number. As it rang for the fifth time, I glanced into the living room and caught Little Joe's eye, but he quickly looked away and went back to ribbing his friends. "Oh, wait, I know, maybe Wild Cherry could use you in their opening act." He strutted around and sang, *"Play that funky music, white boy . . ."*

After ten rings there was still no answer. I hung up and walked back out.

"Well?" my mom said.

"He's not there."

She glanced at her watch. "We'll wait five more minutes, then we have to leave."

I watched the clock on the wall as the minutes slowly ticked by. To be honest, I wasn't surprised Dominick hadn't shown up. Ever since he'd eaten that turkey burger at my house he'd been acting kind of strange—more like his old Mick Jagger self—and on Friday when the bell had rung after lunch he'd told me he had someplace to go, and I wound up walking to Mr. Cornelius's class alone.

At exactly 7:27, my mother announced it was time to leave. Since there were nine of us, we had to take two cars, so Matt's friends drove with my dad, while Sammy, Brandi, and I piled into my mom's Volkswagen. I sat up front with her, silently staring out the window, and as we drove along the streets of Bay Ridge she leaned over and whispered, "You never know, sweetie, there's still a chance he might meet us at the theater."

I shrugged. "Yeah, maybe." Even though I figured the odds were about a million to one.

She squeezed my hand. "Either way, we'll have a good time. We always have a good time when we're together. And Matt is so excited for you to see him in this play."

The Brooklyn Performing Arts Center was ablaze with lights and swarming with people, inside and out. We parked and walked briskly through the courtyard where I'd seen Matt and Bettina making out just two weeks before. I was amazed at how different the place looked at night—the marble banisters gleamed in the moonlight, and the fountain reminded me of an exploding Roman candle on the Fourth of July. Inside, the lobby was thick with women's perfume, woolen suits, and hints of cigarette smoke.

We had the best seats in the house—sixth row center— and as the lights dimmed I glanced around at the people filling the auditorium. The Lucianos were just two rows behind us. I waved to them, noticing several more gangster types nearby, but with the lights low and everyone dressed to the nines it was hard to tell the criminals from the working class.

Then, just as the orchestra began to play, a guy in a black suit swaggered in, followed by an entourage of shady-looking characters. One wore dark glasses, and I was surprised he didn't trip over his own feet. I glanced at

Little Joe, who was sitting a few seats away from me. He'd been watching the guy too, and when he saw me leaning over, trying to catch his eye, he nodded gravely. There was no question about it. The guy was Bobby the Bull Bocceli.

Soon the curtain opened, and before I knew it I'd completely forgotten that half the mobsters from Dyker Heights were packed into the theater. In fact, after a while I didn't even care that Dominick had stood me up and the seat beside me was empty. I'd been transported to the ancient city of Verona, and my whole focus was on two hopelessly-in-love teenagers.

The entire production of *Romeo and Juliet* was awesome—the costumes, the scenery, the acting—but most of all, Matt and Bettina were brilliant together. When they looked into each other's eyes, you could practically feel the electricity between them, and when Juliet kissed the mouth of her already dead lover you could hear a pin drop, and I don't think there was a dry eye in the entire place.

"Wow," my mother said, dabbing her eyes with a tissue as the curtain closed. "Stephen, was that really our son?"

My dad sat there shaking his head. "I'm not sure. He did bear a strange resemblance."

By the time we got home it was pretty late. Sammy had fallen asleep in the car, and my mom had to carry him upstairs to bed. My dad had dropped off Big Joe, Tony, and Fritz at their houses, but Little Joe had gone with Matt to a cast party at Jahn's—a local teenage hangout that served cheeseburgers and banana splits till about one in the morning.

I was pretty restless, and since I hadn't gotten a chance to congratulate Matt after the performance, I decided to wait up for him. Also, the image of Bobby the Bull was still fresh in my mind, and I wanted to make sure Matt came home in one piece. I decided to pass the time reading, and because I was determined to raise my grade in English, I grabbed a blanket, snuggled up on the sofa, and cracked open our assigned text—*Hamlet*.

It wasn't too bad—there were some scenes with ghosts and crazy people that were sort of interesting—but soon I began to drift off, and the next thing I knew, the book was lying against my chest and someone was tapping on the back door. The clock on the wall read 1:30. I'd been asleep for nearly an hour.

Heart pounding, I tiptoed into the kitchen and peered through the peephole. "Joe?" I said, opening the door. A blast of cold air hit me. "What's going on? Where's Matt?"

"Oh, sorry, April, I hope I didn't wake you. I thought Matt would be here already. I guess he's on his way home."

"Oh, okay, well—come on in."

Little Joe was shivering, and since my mother didn't believe in heating the house past 10 p.m., I turned on the stove and made us each a cup of hot cocoa. As the milk steamed in the pot, Little Joe explained that Matt had driven home with Bettina and her friends, and since there hadn't been enough room for him in the car, they'd planned to meet at our house. He was going to spend the night.

We carried our cups into the living room where it wasn't so drafty and took a seat together on the sofa. "Thanks," he said, taking a sip. "This is really good."

I tossed him the other end of my goose-down blanket. "Here, this'll warm you up too."

He drew it over his lap and smiled appreciatively. Little Joe was still in his charcoal suit, but he'd loosened his tie and unbuttoned his collar. While we sat there sipping our cocoa, he made a face, reached behind him, and pulled my copy of *Hamlet* from the sofa cushion. "Yours, I presume?"

"Oh, sorry, I was reading that before you came in. Actually, it put me to sleep."

"Really? I'm surprised, it's a great play." He set down his cup and began flipping through the pages, smiling like he was remembering something. "I read this freshman year too. Since then we've done a lot of Shakespeare, but I think *Hamlet* will always be my favorite—probably because of the teacher we had. He made the story come alive."

As Little Joe spoke, I watched him with interest. I'd had no idea he even liked Shakespeare. Actually, there were a lot of things about Little Joe I didn't know. "So who was your freshman English teacher?"

"Mr. Cornelius."

"You're kidding, that's who I have."

"He's pretty awesome, don't you think?"

"Well . . ." I took a sip of my cocoa and eyed Little Joe skeptically. "Let's just say we've had our ups and downs."

"Is that so? Hmmm, then maybe you'll appreciate this." Little Joe gathered a shock of hair on his forehead and with a little spit made a huge widow's peak. Standing up, he draped an invisible cape over his shoulder and pulled back his lips to make vampire teeth. He opened *Hamlet* and began to do an amazing impersonation of Mr. Cornelius. *"To be or not to be: that is the question. Whether 'tis nobler in the mind to suffer the slings and arrows . . ."*

By the time Little Joe was finished, my ribs ached from laughing so hard. "You know," I said, "that bum was almost going to fail me this marking period, but then I wrote a story he really liked. Now I'm getting a C."

"Wait a minute," Little Joe said, sitting down and brushing back his hair. "You—Miss Brainiac Book Lover— are getting a C in English?"

"Yep. Late to class twice, plus I didn't hand in my rough draft when it was due."

"Oh, that'll do it. But he liked your story, huh?"

"Yeah." My cocoa was starting to get cold, so I downed the rest in two gulps. Little Joe did the same. "Actually, he wants me to enter it in the citywide competition."

Little Joe almost started choking. "Wow, then it must be, like, *fabulous.* Do you have it here? Can I read it?"

"Um . . ." I wasn't sure how I felt about Little Joe reading my story, but he looked so eager, I figured what the heck. "Yeah, it's in my room. I'll get it."

I tiptoed upstairs and retrieved "Babysitting Games" from the bottom of my desk drawer. I hadn't shown the story to my parents, and the application was still blank and unsigned. Downstairs, as Little Joe read, I held my breath, watching his face closely. By page two he was nodding and grinning, and when he got to the end he laughed out loud. "This is *really* good, April. I'm impressed."

My cheeks flushed. "Thank you. I'm glad you like it."

He fingered the pages and grinned. "So now I have a question to ask. Was Sammy your inspiration? Did you ever tie him to the stake? Tell me the truth, now."

I grabbed the pages and smacked Little Joe over the head with them. "No, of course not. It's a story, silly."

"Whew, that's a relief." He wiped one hand across his forehead, then looked me in the eye. "Now let me ask you another question. Have you shown it to your parents?"

"What do you think?"

"I think *not.*"

"Good guess, Einstein."

Little Joe watched me with an amused expression. "Well, whatever they say, I think it's a funny, original piece of writing. You should be very proud."

Neither of us said anything for a long time. Finally, Little Joe scooted closer and took a deep breath. "April, I've been meaning to tell you something for a while now. I'm sorry about that day at the beach. When you got hit by that wave and well . . . you know. I didn't mean to stare."

"Oh." I shook my head. "It's all right, Joe. No big deal."

"I didn't want you to think I was a pervert or anything. And if it makes you feel any better, Matt almost killed me that day."

I laughed a little. "Yeah, I remember."

He rolled his eyes. "You don't know the half of it. But listen, I'm sorry for acting like such an idiot lately. It was stupid to think that you and I could ever be together. I mean, you're my best friend's sister. It just wouldn't work."

"No, I guess not."

"Plus, you have a boyfriend now."

"Yeah, that too."

Little Joe sat there nodding, and I was grateful he didn't mention the fact that Dominick hadn't shown up for the play. "April?"

"Yeah?"

We stared at each other without saying a word for what seemed like an eternity. Then, just when I thought Little Joe was going to lean over and kiss me, the back door opened and a gust of cold air blew into the living room.

We turned our heads. Standing in the doorway was Mr. Luciano, and leaning on his shoulder was someone I didn't recognize. But as I looked closer, I realized it was a bruised, bloodied, busted-up version of my brother, Matt.

TWENTY-ONE

I gasped and was about to scream, but Little Joe clapped his hand over my mouth just in time. "Shhh, April, you'll wake your parents."

"Oh, God," I whispered through his fingers.

We ran to Matt, assessing the damage. Now his other eye was black and blue, his cheek was raw and busted up, and his nose was oozing blood. He was limping, too, and holding his right arm to his chest. Little Joe didn't say anything to Mr. Luciano. He didn't even look at him. He just wrapped Matt's good arm around his shoulder and led him to the bathroom.

Just as Soft Sal was about to slip out the back door, I said, "Wait a minute." We were on my turf now, and I had a few things to say to him.

"Yes, sweetheart?"

I felt this incredible rage building inside me. My chest

began to heave in and out like I was going to explode. "I thought you were supposed to help! I thought you were going to protect him! What kind of a person are you, anyway? Letting a sixteen-year-old boy get beat up like that? You and all your stupid friends are just a bunch of cowards." I was so worked up I didn't even realize what I was saying.

Very calmly, Mr. Luciano put up a hand to stop me. In the light I could see he was completely exhausted. There were bags under his eyes and his head was full of gray stubble. "Sweetheart," he said sadly. "I understand that you're upset, but I told you before, I'm only one man. When I heard they were gonna bust up your brother after the final show, I followed along and made sure they didn't put him in the hospital. Nothing's broken, I checked. His shoulder was dislocated, but now it's back in place. He's gonna hurt for a few days, but believe me, this is nothing."

"*Nothing?*" I motioned toward the bathroom, where Little Joe was tending to Matt. "How can you say this is *nothing*? And now what? Are they going to kill him next time?"

"If your brother's smart," Mr. Luciano said gravely, "there won't be a next time. I'm telling you right now, he can never see Bettina again. *Never.*" He opened the back door, and as the cold air filled the room, he disappeared into the dark.

Matt needed my help. I grabbed a stack of Sammy's old cloth diapers from the linen closet and soaked them in warm water, and then Little Joe and I cleaned up Matt the best we could. We used the rest of the tofu pops to take down the swelling on his eye, and I gave him some aspirin. After that, Little Joe helped him up the stairs and put him to bed, promising he'd wake up every hour or so to check on him.

That night I slept fitfully—dreaming we were back in the theater watching the last scene of *Romeo and Juliet*. Only, this time, Matt didn't rise up after his suicide scene to take a bow. Instead he was dead on the floor—shot right through the heart, blood spattered over his tunic and tights—and all the mobsters in the audience were standing and cheering. Bobby the Bull raised his gun and shouted, "Hey, Sunshine Boy, that's what you get for messing around with my daughter! Ha ha ha!"

I awoke with a start and realized my mother was in Matt's room, screaming at the top of her lungs. "Matt! Who did this to you? Tell us, please! Stephen, we have to call the police! Joe! Why won't he talk?"

At that moment, I realized what I had to do. I pulled on some clothes, slipped past Matt's room, and ran over to Brandi's. It was pretty early, and her mother answered the door with a look of surprise. "Sorry, Mrs. Rinaldi, but I need to talk to Brandi. It's an emergency." I raced past her and up the stairs. Brandi was still in bed. "Brandi! Brandi, wake up!"

"Huh?" She rolled over and opened one eye. "April, what's going on? What are you doing here?"

"Listen, I don't have time to explain, but I need your money. Now. Matt's in serious trouble."

She blinked a few times. "Okay. Hold on, I'll get it."

Brandi had hidden her money at the bottom of her hope chest. She gave me everything she had—three hundred and seventy-five dollars, no questions asked—and as I raced back home I realized that when you added it to my stash, the total was just shy of thirteen hundred. A very unlucky number.

Back at my house Little Joe was sitting at the kitchen table tying his shoes. "Joe, you're not leaving now, are you?" I said.

He nodded. "Your mom asked me to go. She's really upset." He glanced around to make sure no one was listening. "Matt's not telling them the truth. They think he got mugged last night. I don't know, April, something's got to give."

Upstairs, my parents were in their bedroom talking in hushed voices while Sammy sat outside Matt's room, crying. I knelt down next to Sammy and pulled him close. "Hey, it's all right, kiddo. Matt's gonna be okay."

He shook his head. "Uh-uh, he's really hurt. And he won't talk to me. He keeps saying he wants to be alone."

I dried Sammy's tears with my shirt and kissed the top of his head. "Give him a little time, bud, he'll come around, you'll see."

In my bedroom I dug out the nine hundred dollars, added it to the money Brandi had forked over, and, last but not least, grabbed the letter Bettina had given me the day she was at our house. After stuffing everything into my pockets, I tiptoed into the hallway and opened Matt's door. He was lying in bed, eyes open and staring at the ceiling. "Matt?"

"Go away."

"No, I need to talk to you." Gently, I closed the door behind me and knelt by his side. He looked even worse than the night before. The torn flesh on his cheek was covered with a loose bandage, my mother's handiwork. I reached into my pocket and pulled out the letter. "Bettina asked me to give this to you."

At the mention of Bettina's name, he turned his head, wincing from the pain. "What do you mean?" he said, eyeing the envelope. "What is that?"

"A letter. Bettina gave it to me the day she was here. I don't know if you remember, but we came up to my room alone. She told me if anything happened—if the two of you couldn't see each other anymore—I should give this to you. She said it would explain everything."

The room was deathly quiet, and I could hear Matt's ragged breathing. "Throw it out."

"Matt, no, I can't do that, I promised her—"

"Throw it out! And get out of my room, Monk! Now!"

In the distance I heard my mom's voice. "April, Matt, what's going on?"

I didn't have much time. "Matt, you know you can't see her anymore!"

He looked at me. "No one is going to tell me what to do."

"Matt! Don't be stupid! You can't!"

Now there were footsteps in the hallway. "All right, fine, if you won't take the letter, then at least take *this*." I pulled out the wad of bills and shoved them into his hand. Matt stared at the money. "Where did you . . ."

"It doesn't matter *where*. Just take it."

As my mother opened the door, Matt shoved the money into his pocket and rolled over. There must have been guilt written all over my face because when she saw me kneeling beside his bed, she wagged her finger and mouthed, *"Come here, now."*

I told my parents everything—well, almost everything. I didn't tell them about the money. There was simply no way to explain how I'd accumulated such a large amount of cash without mentioning Soft Sal, and there was no way I was going to drag him into this. Besides, if all else failed and Matt insisted on seeing Bettina again, twelve hundred and seventy-five dollars might be his only form of protection.

After I spilled the beans, my parents had a meeting of the minds and together marched upstairs to confront Matt. Since I wanted to be as far away from my brother when the bomb dropped as possible, I hightailed it to the garage and hopped on my bike.

Outside it was business as usual—Larry was blasting

"Pinball Wizard" from his front window, Frankie the Crunch was watering mums around his St. Christopher shrine, and Gorgeous Vinny was waxing his Coupe, adjusting his toupee, and no doubt dreaming about the day John Travolta would walk through the doors of his discothèque.

I rode around the streets of Dyker Heights, up and down the steep hills, to blow off steam, but before long my empty stomach led me to Thirteenth Avenue. I hadn't eaten breakfast, and it was approaching lunchtime, so I parked my bike beside Tony's Pizzeria and ordered a slice at the counter. Across the street, Pee Wee and Ronnie were talking to a group of girls—some of them, I noticed, were part of Roxanne's posse. None of them noticed me. I folded my slice in half, downed it in less than two minutes, then hopped on my bike for St. Bernadette's.

Inside the church there was a Mass going on, so I sat in the back pew and waited until it was over. As the people filed out I walked slowly to St. Christopher, dropped a few coins in the box, and lit a candle for Matt. Even though I knew I had to tell my parents about him and Bettina, I still felt guilty for breaking my promise. Quietly I said a prayer, hoping Matt would understand, but for some reason I knew I was asking the impossible.

I headed out into the blinding sunlight. When my eyes adjusted, I saw that the curtains in the apartment above Moe's candy store were open. Someone was home. Mostly, I'd been angry that Dominick had stood me up the night before, but now, after getting all these good vibes from St. Bernadette's, I decided maybe there was an explanation—a legitimate reason why he couldn't make it. I took a deep breath, hopped on my bike, and rode over.

As I pressed the doorbell, Moe popped his head out of the candy store. "I, uh, don't think Dominick's home right now. Maybe you better try him some other time."

"Oh, okay, it's just . . ." I pointed upstairs. "The curtains were open and I thought—"

"Nah, he ain't there."

Just then the buzzer went off. I gave Moe a puzzled look and pushed the door open. "Well, it looks like some-one's home," I said.

I stepped inside and heard Dominick's voice from the top of the stairs. "Hey, Pee Wee, what's the deal, man? I thought you and Ronnie were gone for good."

When he saw me standing there, his face went slack. "Oh, April, it's . . . you."

Two hands slipped around his waist, and a moment later Roxanne was peering over his shoulder. In the si-lence of the hallway, the three of us stood there staring at each other. Blood rushed to my face. "I'm . . . sorry. I shouldn't have come."

As I turned to leave, Dominick called, "April, wait! Let me explain!" I heard him racing down the stairs, but I hopped on my bike and took off.

I pedaled hard and fast. Behind me I heard Moe yelling, "You never learn, do you, Dom? Think you can go around doing whatever you please? Well, it doesn't work that way!"

Tears streamed down my cheeks as I pedaled home, and what the wind didn't dry, I quickly wiped away. In the garage, I leaned my bike against the wall and braced myself for what awaited me inside.

In the kitchen, my mom and dad sat quietly at the table drinking cups of Postum. "So," I said, looking back and forth between the two of them. "What happened? What did Matt say?"

"He's not going to see the girl—Bettina—anymore," my mom said.

"You mean . . . he's agreed?"

My dad nodded. "Yes."

I breathed a sigh of relief. "That's good news."

"And," my dad said, "considering who we're dealing with, we're not going to call the police. Matt seems to be all right—Mom gave him something for the pain—and he's sleeping now. We'll have to keep an eye on him for a while, but hopefully things will blow over."

Suddenly, the events of the day started caving in on me, and I began to feel very tired. "Mom, Dad, I'm going to lie down for a while. I didn't sleep very well last night."

"Okay, honey," my mom said. She stood up, walked over, and wrapped her arms around me. It felt good to be held. "Listen, April, I understand how you wanted to be loyal to your brother, but he was in danger, and you should have told us right away."

"I know, Mom. I'm sorry."

She ran her fingers through my hair. "I'm not saying it was your fault, honey. It's just, well, Dad and I want you to know that you can always come to us. We love you, and we're here to help."

I guess it was pretty selfish of me considering Matt was lying in the next room, beat up and brokenhearted, but as I curled into a ball on my bed, all I could think about was Roxanne and Dominick at the top of the stairs—her arms circling his waist, her chin resting against his shoulder. I wondered if he'd played her the Eric Clapton album too—if they'd danced to the slow, pretty love song, and if he'd kissed her the same way he'd kissed me. I felt like such a fool, but worse than that, I felt raw, like someone had scraped out my insides with a paring knife. I closed my eyes, and after a while I must have drifted off to sleep because the next thing I knew, it was 2 p.m. and someone was knocking on my door. "April, can I come in?"

It was Brandi. I'd never been happier to hear her voice. She snuggled up next to me on the bed, and I told her everything—first about Matt and then about Dominick. When I was finished, I expected a lecture, which would have been okay considering how stupid I'd been, but instead she opened a fresh box of tissues, and said, "Don't worry, April, everything's gonna be all right, you'll see. And no matter what, we always have each other."

For the rest of the afternoon Brandi and I played gin

rummy, and when we got sick of that we flipped through my old *Tiger Beat* magazines, laughing at pictures of Donny Osmond and David Cassidy. Matt slept most of the day, and occasionally my mom went in to check on him. She brought him stuff like soup, yogurt, and Jell-O, since his jaw was too sore for chewing. But when she carried the trays out I noticed he'd barely touched his food.

Finally, Brandi went home for dinner, and when my parents and Sammy retreated downstairs to watch TV, I picked up Bettina's letter, tiptoed into the hall, and knocked on Matt's door.

"Matt? Are you awake? Can I come in?" No answer. I tried again. "Matt, can I talk to you, please?" Nothing. Finally I turned the knob and pushed the door open.

Matt wasn't asleep; he was sitting in the dark, on the edge of his bed, bent over and staring at the floor. "Matt, what's going on? Why didn't you answer me?"

He didn't move.

"Matt?"

And then I realized he was beyond angry. He was pretending that I didn't exist.

"Matt," I pleaded, "I had to tell them, what else could I do?" I held out the letter. "Please, take this. Bettina said it would explain everything."

He raised his head slightly and stared at the envelope. Finally he took it from me, and in one swift motion tore it in half and then in half again. He flung the pieces across the room.

"Fine!" I screamed. "Go ahead! Let them kill you, what do I care?" I gathered the torn pieces, stormed out of the room, and threw them back into my drawer.

Later that evening Little Joe came over. I waited in the hallway while he spent about an hour with Matt in his room. They talked in hushed voices, and even with my mother's stethoscope pressed to the door, I couldn't hear what they were saying. "Any luck?" I asked when he finally came out.

He sighed. "It's hard to say. Matt knows he can't see her, but . . ." He trailed off. "Well, anyway"—he patted the back pocket of his jeans—"he gave me a note for her—I'm going to give it to Marcella, and she'll pass it on to Bettina. He swears it's a breakup letter, saying it's too dangerous for them to be together."

By midnight I was exhausted, so when I saw that Matt had turned out his lights, I did the same. Again I slept fitfully, dreaming that we were back in the theater watching the final scene of *Romeo and Juliet*. Only this time Dominick was sitting next to me, and Matt wasn't dead yet. As Bettina leaned over to kiss him, Bobby the Bull stood up, holding a gun. Just as I was about to scream, "Matt, watch out!" Dominick clapped his hand over my mouth, and as the shot fired, I woke up with a start.

Breathless, I looked at the clock on the wall. It was 5 a.m. The house was dark and quiet. I got up, tiptoed into the hallway, and opened Matt's door. He was gone.

TWENTY-TWO

The streets outside were cold and eerie, dimly lit by an occasional lamppost, and the wind blew in great gusts. As I walked steadily toward the performing arts center, I fingered the jagged edges of Bettina's letter in my coat pocket. It was only a hunch that Matt would be waiting for her in their secret hideaway, but I figured it was worth a try. I couldn't imagine my mother's face when she woke up in the morning and found him gone.

When I arrived, the building looked dark and haunted, nothing like the previous night. The wind howled against my ears. I grabbed the handrail and padded slowly down the steps into the marble courtyard. It was like entering a cave.

"Bettina? Bettina, is that you?" I followed the voice, and in the moonlight saw Matt sitting on the edge of the wooden bench wrapped in Sammy's Kermit the Frog comforter.

"No, Matt," I said. "It's me, April."

"April? What are you doing here? How did you know . . . ?" His voice trailed off, and now we were face to face.

I sat next to him, thankful that he was at least speaking to me—that he'd said my name. At this point I wouldn't have cared if he'd called me Magilla Gorilla. "It was a guess," I said. "I woke up and saw that you'd left. I thought you might be here."

He stared at me in disbelief. I could tell he was wondering how I'd known about their secret place, but maybe part of him didn't want to ask. There was a suitcase beside the bench; I motioned toward it. "Are you and Bettina planning to go somewhere?"

He turned away. "That's none of your business. You should leave now."

"No, Matt," I said. "I'm not going to leave."

The wind blew fiercely, and he wrapped the comforter tightly around himself. "You're not dressed warm enough," he said. "You're going to freeze."

"I don't care. I'm staying right here. With you."

We passed about an hour in silence, and by then my teeth were clattering inside my head. It was the kind of cold that seeped right through you, into your bones. The hard bench didn't help matters either—my butt was numb, my feet and hands like blocks of ice, and my ears were throbbing. I pulled my coat up over my head and leaned back, and I must have drifted off into some kind of frostbitten unconsciousness because when I came to, the early-morning sun was peeking through the bare trees. Matt was crying softly. "I thought she'd come," he said over and over, like I wasn't even there.

"Matt?"

He turned to me, and it was not a pretty sight. Besides his face being all busted up, his lips were blue, his eyes red, and the bandage on his face stained with tears. I must have looked pretty bad too, because when he saw me, he moaned sympathetically and lifted a corner of his blanket. "Here, Ape. Slide over."

I scooted next to him, grateful for his body heat, and he wrapped the blanket tightly around the two of us. It was strange being so close to my brother; in fact, I couldn't even remember the last time we'd hugged. It might have been years. The sun was rising higher every minute, and I figured it must have been getting toward seven o'clock. There wouldn't be much time before people nearby would be starting their day, traveling to school and work.

"Matt, I'm really sorry I told Mom and Dad. I didn't know what else to do."

He stared straight ahead and said nothing.

I fingered the pieces of the torn envelope in my pocket. "That day Bettina was at our house," I said, "she told me how much she loved you." It felt weird saying this to my brother. I wanted to tell him that I loved him too, but I couldn't seem to find the right words. Instead, I took his hand. "Please, Matt, take this. She wanted you to have it."

Matt sighed deeply and hung his head. Finally, he grasped the torn letter. After placing the pieces safely in his coat pocket, he reached into the back pocket of his jeans and pulled out the wad of bills I'd given him the day before. "I don't know where you got this money, Ape, but I don't want it."

As he handed me the money, a strong gust of wind blew. I could have grabbed at the bills if I'd really wanted to, but instead I let them go. They fluttered away, rising and swirling, and for a split second they looked beautiful, like a flock of birds taking off. As they blew around the courtyard, up the steps, and onto the sidewalk above, a sparrow swooped down from a tree. It snatched one bill in its beak and flew off with its prize. Matt and I watched in awe.

"Thanks for coming to get me, Ape," he said.

"Yeah, sure." I snuggled closer to Matt, and as we watched the rest of the bills scatter, I imagined all the people smiling as they picked them up, thinking Wow, this is my lucky day. I wanted to shout out, let them know they were not *fugazis* but the real thing. Legit.

As Matt and I walked home together, taking turns carrying his suitcase, I lifted my face to the sun. It had been a long time since I'd felt so free.

*   *   *

Things weren't perfect after that. Matt was moody and miserable—moping around the house, sleeping a lot—and when his friends came to call, he sent them away, even Little Joe. My parents hovered over him nervously, watching his every move, which irritated him no end.

He didn't talk much to me, either, and the only one he allowed in his room was Sammy. In fact, Matt became quite the babysitter, teaching Sammy to play chess and poker, and showing him how to bet on the football games in the newspaper (which, of course, they didn't mention to my mom). But one morning, when I got out of the shower, I heard Jethro Tull's *Aqualung* blasting from Matt's room. "Hey, Chimp!" he yelled above the music. "Stop hogging the bathroom! You're not the only person in this house!" I knew then that things were definitely looking up.

During this time I had my own demons to face. In school, I avoided Dominick as much as possible, but on a Friday, after my piano lesson with Mr. Ruffalo (happily paid for in full by my parents), he came to the band room to pick up his guitar. We hadn't spoken since the afternoon I'd seen him with Roxanne. Rumor had it they'd gotten together briefly, but split up after Chris Capelli, the guy with the beach cabana on the Jersey Shore, lured her back with a diamond-studded ankle bracelet.

"Can I talk to you for a minute?" he said.

"Um, yeah, sure." I said goodbye to Mr. Ruffalo, told him I'd be back next Friday with the second half of "Peace Train" committed to memory, and walked into the hallway with Dominick.

"Listen," he said. "I'm really sorry, and I need to explain what happened. You see, the night of your brother's play, Roxanne stopped by my place. She had two tickets to this sold-out Rolling Stones concert at Radio City, and, well—"

"I understand," I said. "Totally. I mean the Rolling Stones? Who wouldn't go?" What irony, I thought. Bianca scoring tickets to a Stones concert.

"I did call you," he said. "I swear. But by that time I guess you'd already left."

There was a moment of awkward silence. "So," I said, "I heard the two of you got back together."

"Oh . . . yeah." He looked a little embarrassed. "That night, after the concert, Roxanne and I started talking, and it's just . . . we'd been together for a while last year, and I guess we hadn't gotten over each other. I was pretty mixed up. Anyway, it didn't work out. She's with Chris Capelli again."

I wanted to say, *What goes around comes around*, but instead I just nodded.

He looked at me with pleading eyes, and for a moment I actually felt sorry for him. "Our, uh, Halloween gig is tomorrow night. I was wondering if you'd come."

I felt my throat closing up. "No. I promised Sammy I'd take him trick-or-treating. And after that we're going to the St. Bernadette's festival."

"Oh, okay, maybe you can stop by afterward?"

I shook my head. "I'll be busy—you know, carving pumpkins, bobbing for apples, riding my broomstick, stuff like that."

He smiled a little. "Okay, I understand."

"But if you *do* see me there," I said, looking him square in the eye, "it'll be for Larry. I'd like to see Larry play his drums that night."

Another demon I needed to face was Mr. Luciano. Since the night he'd brought Matt home and I'd given him a piece of my mind, he'd made himself scarce when Brandi and I picked up Larry for school in the mornings. But on Saturday I spotted his car parked in the driveway. I walked up the steps and rang the bell.

"Why, hello, sweetheart."

"Hi, Mr. Luciano. Do you have a minute?"

"For you? Of course. Come in."

We sat together in the living room—me on the plastic-covered sofa and him on his papal throne. "So what can I do for you?" he asked, striking a match and lighting a cigar.

"Well, first," I said, "I want to thank you for helping Matt. I understand now what happened that night, and I'm sorry I spoke to you that way."

He blew a ring of smoke. "No problem, sweetheart. No harm done."

"I want you to know he's not going to see Bettina anymore."

He nodded. "I figured as much."

"And now," I said, "I have another favor to ask you."

"*Another* favor, is that so?" He seemed vaguely amused.

"Yes. It's about the money. If you happen to know who's been placing those rather large bills in my books—Brandi's, too—I'd like it if you would please ask them to stop."

"Stop?" He tapped the ashes from his cigar into the ashtray. "And why would you want this person to stop?"

"Because," I said, giving him a measured look, "there are things more important than money. Like friendship, for example—caring for someone who might need a little extra help, wanting to do something without expecting anything in return."

He pondered this a moment. "Friendship, huh? But what if this person doesn't want to cooperate?"

I shrugged. "Well, I suppose you could twist his arm a little."

He smiled. "Hmmm, interesting thought. I'll see what I can do."

Since I had promised there'd be no more secrets in my family, and because the deadline for the short story competition was drawing near, I decided to give my parents the pleasure of reading "Babysitting Games." The three of us sat at the kitchen table, and I watched as my mother read first. She didn't smile, she didn't laugh. Mostly she frowned, and when she was finished, she stared at the floor and passed it to my dad. As my dad read, he scratched his head, winced, and cleared his throat a few times.

Afterward he handed me the paper. "Well, April, that was . . . interesting. Your, uh, teacher, Mr. Cornelius, gave you an A-plus. Must mean he liked it?"

"Yes. He says it has a really good chance of winning." I looked at the two of them. "Mom, Dad, it's a comedy. A *dark* comedy. *Fiction.*"

"Well, that's good to know," my mother said. She managed a small smile.

"Yes," my dad agreed. After another minute of awkward silence, he picked up a pen and scribbled his signature on the application. "We may not always understand you, April, but we want you to know we're very proud of you."

"Yes," my mom said, signing her name next to my dad's even though she didn't need to. Enthusiastically, she dotted the "i" in "Lundquist." "We are. Very proud."

On Sunday afternoon, Bert called to tell me he'd made Xavierian's tennis team, and we decided to celebrate by playing a few games of mixed doubles with Walt and Brandi. But before leaving for the park, I dug out Frank Stapleton's card from my sock drawer and dialed his number.

"Hello, Mr. Stapleton?"

"Yes."

"I'm not sure if you remember, but last month you saw me playing tennis at Poly Prep with some of my friends. You gave me your card and asked me to call. Anyway, I was wondering if you were still having tryouts for the Lady Firebirds."

There was silence on the other end, and just when I'd decided that it was a stupid idea to have called and I should just hang up, he cleared his throat and said, "You're a little late. We finished tryouts two weeks ago."

"Oh, okay, I was just wondering, sorry to bother—"

"But," he said, "there is one more spot on the team. I think I remember you—the tall blond girl with the killer backhand?" He seemed to be smiling on the other end.

"Well, I am tall and blond, but—"

"Tuesday," he said firmly. "Four-thirty at the indoor bubble courts. Do you know where they are?"

"Yes, I—"

"Great. Meet me there. We'll have a look at you again."

"Oh, okay, thank you. And Mr. Stapleton?"

"Yes?"

"My name is April. April Lundquist."

"Well, April Lundquist. I'm glad you called. See you Tuesday."

"Yes," I said, "Tuesday."

Now that Sammy was an official chess player, poker player, and gambler, he decided he was too big for a stroller and would walk to the park with Brandi and me. It was a beautiful day—warm enough for just a light jacket. Out front, Larry was blasting the Who's "Teenage Wasteland," and even though it wasn't trash day, he'd dragged one metal can and one plastic can to the front of his house and was doing his thing.

"Larry!" I called. "Great show last night!" After taking Sammy trick-or-treating, Brandi and I had gone to hear their band play.

"Yeah, Larry!" Brandi said. "You were awesome!"

He smiled, waved, and smashed the lids together proudly.

As we were about to leave, Little Joe came strolling up the block, basketball in hand. "Hey, April, is Matt around?"

"Uh-huh." I pointed to the front door, which was ajar. "He just got the script for *Julius Caesar*. He's rehearsing in front of the mirror."

"Is that so?" Little Joe grinned. "Hey, Julius!" he called. "Come on, the guys are waiting for us! We're gonna play some ball!"

The three of us walked along, and on the corner, parked in front of Gorgeous Vinny's house, was a late-model Mercedes I'd never seen before. As we approached, the electric window slowly rolled down. "Oh, no," Brandi said, "not again."

From the corner of my eye, I saw Frankie the Crunch in the driver's seat, and Gorgeous Vinny beside him, wagging his finger. "Hey, dolls, come here, I've got something for you."

"Oh, Lord," Brandi mumbled. "Must we?"

"Hi, Mr. Persico, hi, Mr. Consiglione," Sammy said, spreading out his arms. "Notice anything different about me?"

They looked puzzled for a moment; then Frankie the Crunch said, "Oh, yeah, yeah, you're walkin'? Got rid of that stroller, huh?"

"Yep!"

Meanwhile Gorgeous Vinny dug in his pocket and pulled something out. "Here you go," he said. "Just like I promised. Tickets to see John perform at my club. Actually, the whole cast from *Saturday Night Fever* will be there. I'm telling you, this is gonna bring the disco scene to a whole new level."

Brandi and I looked at each other.

"There's four total," he said, "so you each get to bring a guest."

I walked over and took the tickets from his hand. "Thank you, Mr. Persico. We'll definitely be there."

Brandi offered him a quick smile. "Yes, thank you."

As the window rolled up, I heard a basketball bouncing behind us. Matt and Little Joe were already halfway down the block. "Brandi," I said, "wait here a second. I need to talk to Little Joe."

Nervously, she eyed the trunk of the Mercedes. "All right, but make it quick. I don't feel like being eyewitness to a murder, okay?"

"Okay." I clutched the tickets in my hand and ran up the street, calling, "Joe, hey, Joe!"

Author's Note

If you've come this far (or if you've flipped to the back of the book for a sneak peek), you're probably wondering why our narrator, April Lundquist, shares my first name. It really happened by accident.

When I began writing *Brothers, Boyfriends & Other Criminal Minds*, which is in part autobiographical, I decided to use the name April as an experiment in an attempt to get in touch with my inner fourteen-year-old. All along I had plannd to rename my heroine, but when April's brother Matt began calling her Ape, Chimp, and Monkey, her name became an integral part of the story, so I kept it. Simple as that.

Now, to separate fact from fiction, here's what's true: I was a teenager in the mid-to-late seventies (best decade ever!), and lucky enough to live in the colorful neighborhood of Dyker Heights, Brooklyn. My two brothers, Mark and Adam, were similar in a lot of ways to April's brothers, Matt and Sammy, and although Mark seems to have amnesia on this point, I was teased mercilessly by him and his friends. Like April, I was a bit of an oddball—tall, blond, Scandinavian, and very shy—among a majority of warm, friendly, robust Italians. Like Soft Sal, Frankie the Crunch, and Gorgeous Vinny, several big-name mobsters lived on my street, and Joe Colombo's house was just a few blocks away. Occasionally, one of these men would "disappear," and a few days later we'd see his mug shot in the *Daily News* or the *New York Times,* saying he'd been arrested, or even worse, was missing, which meant *La Cosa Nostra* had given orders for one of its members to be "whacked."

And now, to set the record straight: My brother never dated a mobster's daughter, I never took money from a hit man, and unfortunately, I never dated anyone as exciting or mysterious as Dominick. Hope this doesn't disappoint anyone too much!

As for the Mafia, they still exist today, but thanks to the FBI, the members have much less power than they did in earlier years. In 1975, unknown to me at the time, FBI agent Joe Pistone went undercover in Brooklyn, posed as a jewel thief named Donnie Brasco (check out the movie *Donnie Brasco* starring Al Pacino and Johnny Depp), and was able to infiltrate the Bonanno crime family. In fact, when he left his post six years later, he was about to get "made." And if you've read this book carefully, you know what that means! Agent Pistone's bravery and hard work led to more than a hundred federal convictions, and in the end every Mafia boss was indicted, imprisoned, or dead. *La Cosa Nostra* had changed forever.

Still the legacy goes on, and as for me, fuhgeddaboudit! I will always be fascinated by the Mob.

Acknowledgments

A big hearty thank-you to my agent, Laura Rennert, for her much-needed support, and to my lovely editor, Françoise Bui, who always knows how to make a story better. And, of course, many thanks to my husband, Ed, who not only reads all my crummy first drafts but encourages me to do what I love: write.

About the Author

April Lurie is a native New Yorker and the author of *Dancing in the Streets of Brooklyn*. She now lives near Austin, Texas, with her family and is working on a third novel for teens. Visit her at www.aprillurie.com.

7/31/07

$15.99

LONGWOOD PUBLIC LIBRARY
Middle Country Road
Middle Island, NY 11953
(631) 924-6400
LIBRARY HOURS

Monday-Friday	9:30 a.m. - 9:00 p.m.
Saturday	9:30 a.m. - 5:00 p.m.
Sunday (Sept-June)	1:00 p.m. - 5:00 p.m.